BLUE FIRE

By Richard Willis

BLUE FIRE

ISBN: 978-0-98936061-0-2

RICHARD WILLIS

To Paula

Page is intentionally blank

Prologue

Blood covered the Ranger's buckskin shirt, not his blood but Thunder's. The big roan stallion had taken the Comanche arrows in the throat and gone down in a heap.

Buck McDougal jumped clear as they skidded up to a little gully at the end of the meadow. He flopped belly down in the shallow arroyo. A quick look confirmed that only his front needed to be defended. Behind him stood a seven-foot wall of dense, thorny south Texas brush that not even a coyote could penetrate. To the left and right, brush and old flood debris choked the arroyo. Thunder lay gasping his final breaths just in front of him.

Buck reached up and snatched his Henry rifle out of the scabbard tied to the saddle. A rain of arrows and bullets thudded into Thunder's now lifeless body. The three Comanches had the advantage of higher ground but couldn't see Buck behind the dead horse. As long as Buck stayed hunkered down, he was safe, at least for now.

Buck could hear the buzz of bees working the mesquite flowers and the rhythmic ratcheting of grasshoppers. A pair of Inca Doves called back and forth. The southeast breeze brought the fragrance of huisache and mesquite blossoms mixed with the smell of dust and horse and leather and Thunder's blood. The relentless Texas sun beat down on his back from a cloudless deep blue sky.

Buck said out loud to no in particular, "How in the heck did I wind up in this ditch?"

PART I

Hardin County, Tennessee – Spring 1862

I

Caleb McDougal stepped down off the front porch where his mother sat shelling hickory nuts for a pie. She was a small woman with skin the color of saddle leather. She hummed a sad tune as she worked. *Maw always sings instead of cryin' when she's sad,* thought Caleb.

Caleb was big boned like his father. Though two years younger, he could easily pass for sixteen. Lanky now, he already had the beginnings of broad shoulders with the promise of some size when he grew to manhood. His raven-black, almost blue in the sun, hair came his mother's side of the family. But, what got your full attention when you looked at him were his deep blue eyes, just like Paw's. He considered himself the "man of the house" now. A neighbor, Mr. Mortimer, stopped by yesterday with word that the Yankees had killed Caleb's paw and two older brothers. They had all gone off to join the big battle just up river at Pittsburg Landing near Shiloh Church. Mr. Mortimer had taken a mini ball through the upper arm but the wound was not serious. He had been given two days leave to bring his son, Lem's, body home for burial before returning to the army.

Caleb and his mother had done their crying yesterday. The beauty of the spring day and the list of chores to be done had brightened them both a bit. Caleb picked up an ax from the tool shed and ambled over to the woodpile next to the old clapboard smokehouse.

Splitting wood was a simple task. Place a two-foot pine log on end atop the big hickory 'splittin' stump', aim for the middle, and swing the ax down as hard as he could. Repeat until each log was quartered into 'sticks' for the kitchen stove. The ax had been honed sharp enough to shave a dog's back so he had to pay a reasonable amount of attention to his work. But, he had split thousands of logs and could let his mind drift somewhat. He liked to think about what it would be like to leave the farm and set out on some sort of grand adventure like the ones he had heard the old men tell down at Pott's Store. Maybe he'd captain a steamboat, the paddle wheelers sure were exciting as they chuffed past the backside of their red-dirt farm on the Tennessee River. Or, even better, maybe he would go off west to be a Mountain Man. That's what the men said Paul Ledbetter had done. Caleb wasn't quite sure what a Mountain Man was but it sounded exciting.

He hadn't been splitting wood and daydreaming for ten minutes when he heard the dogs barking and then a man's scream followed by a half-dozen pistol shots. Caleb peeked around the corner of the smokehouse to see what all the ruckus was about. A fat Yankee soldier stood over Maw with a big butcher knife sticking out of his belly. The bowl of hickory nuts was spilled in the dirt. Maw's lifeless body sprawled across the front steps and both of the family dogs lay dead in the dust.

One of the soldiers set the house afire as two others headed for the barn. Two more soldiers walked toward the smokehouse. They would be coming for the bacon and hams.

Caleb flattened against the rough gray wood. Time slowed to a crawl. He could smell the hickory smoke creeping out of a crack in the wall next to him. It almost made him sneeze. He could feel his heart hammering in his chest. The clomping of the two soldiers' boots got closer and closer. Caleb was so filled with hatred and fright that he shook.

When the soldiers stepped around the corner, Caleb buried his ax into one man's midsection. The soldier fell back with a scream. The second made a grab for Caleb but missed. Caleb ran for the woods. He had three hundred yards of open ground to cross before he could reach the trees. The young cotton plants had not yet spouted in the rows of red dirt that he zigzagged across. He heard the bullet whine and felt its sting on his cheek before he heard the shot.

Then, he ran into the woods so fast that he thought he couldn't keep up with his feet. The men ran after him but Caleb had the advantage of knowing his ground. He lost them by easing down the gravel creek bed and then climbing up a tree. After an hour, the shouts of the men moved back toward the house. He heard shooting up that way off and on for much of the afternoon. *What in the world could they be shooting at?* thought Caleb.

Caleb spent all night hiding in the big hollow hickory tree. He was heart broken. In only two days, he had lost his entire family. He wanted to cry but didn't. He had always been tough even though he was the 'baby' of the family. Life was hard, with work from "can see to can't see" every day. This war with the Yankees was a mystery to him. Nobody he knew had slaves. Maybe some of the rich folks in Savannah, upriver twelve miles, but the families around here were as poor as his family.

His Paw and brothers had gone off to fight only to try to earn a few dollars and have a bit of an adventure. They all thought the whole thing would be over in a few days or a week at most. But the Battle of Shiloh, as it was later known, was the first great battle of the Civil War. Total casualties on both sides were larger than the total American casualties for all three of America's previous wars. Of the 100,000 men in the battle, nearly twenty-four percent were killed, wounded or captured. The battle changed both sides' perceptions of the nature of the war and convinced leaders on both sides that it would not end quickly. Now Paw, Nate and Zeke were killed, and Maw too. Though he knew he couldn't, he wanted to kill every Yankee soldier he could find.

He awoke just before dawn to the smell of wet wood smoke. A misty drizzle during the night made everything sopping and now a thick fog blanketed the farm. Caleb crawled out of his hiding spot and eased back toward the farmhouse. The soldiers were gone and so was the farm. Everything had been taken, burned or killed. The soldiers had even shot the mules, pigs, and most of the chickens. Poor Ol' Bess, the milk cow, lay dead and swollen with her right legs sticking up. *How mean would you have to be to shoot a milk cow, pigs and chickens*, he thought.

The house, barn and smokehouse were smoldering heaps of ashes. Only the red brick chimney of the house and the iron kitchen stove were left standing. He had never felt so alone. He knew that at least one Yankee soldier had gotten a real good look at him. They would kill him for sure if he were caught.

Caleb buried his mother's partially burned body under the big oak tree where she liked to sit and sing in her native Choctaw. As he dug the grave, he could not keep the tears from flowing down his cheeks. He cried out of anger toward the Yankees and with sorrow for his mother, and for himself. It took four hours and a bucket of tears to get the grave dug. By the time that he had placed her body in the bottom of the hole and covered her up, he was sobbing out loud. He fashioned a little wooden cross out of two scraps of burnt lumber from the barn and pounded the cross into the ground at the head of the grave with the shovel. He blew his running nose and wiped his eyes on his shirtsleeves. On the cross, he hung the string of beads that his mother had been wearing when she was killed. He could hear his dead father's voice saying, 'Stand strong and be a man, you're a McDougal by God. Don't let adversity beat you down.' Caleb straightened up and took a deep, ragged breath. *I'm on my own now,* he thought. *I best git hid somewhere before the Yankees come back and catch me.* That thought sent a chill up his spine. He knelt down one last time and kissed the mound of red dirt under which his mother lay. "Best be goin', I love you, Mama," he said.

He gathered up a knife he found in front of what had been the house. It was maw's butcher's knife, the same knife he had last seen sticking out of the Yankee's fat belly. He wrung the necks of two chickens he found scratching around in the pile of fresh dug dirt over his mother's grave and put them in a burlap tow sack he found hanging on the fence next to where the barn had been. There was nothing left for him here. Smoke rose from the neighboring farms on both sides and across the road, so he decided to head back through the woods the mile or so to the river.

The McDougal farm, like all of the others along this stretch of the Tennessee River, was long and narrow. It was a quarter mile wide by a mile long, more or less. This allowed the maximum number of farmers to have river access while still within the one hundred sixty acres or so of the typical farm. Also, since each farm had land along the river, each one had rich river 'bottom' land. Like the neighboring farms, theirs was a series of fields for crops interspersed by strips of dense hardwoods. The farmers matched up their strips of woods so that wild game could move back and forth and also so that the fields were side by side to allow them to help one another with planting and harvesting.

Caleb took his time walking to the river. He didn't want to stumble onto any Yankee soldiers and he was still dazed by the events of the previous day. When he got to the river, he sat down next to a big sweet gum tree and started plucking the chickens he had in his sack. He made a little fire and cooked them on a spit he made from a hickory stick. He ate one of the chickens and wrapped the other one in some of the big leaves from the sweet gum tree and placed it in his tow sack.

He fooled along the riverbank for most of the afternoon trying to decide what to do next. He missed his parents and his brothers. Zeke and Nate were six and eight years older than Caleb. In secret, he worshiped them both though they merely tolerated their baby brother. They acknowledged that Caleb was a better hunter and rifle shot than they were. He just seemed to have the knack for it. They had also learned that though he was slow to anger, once riled, Caleb was to be left alone. Once, Zeke had to pull Caleb off of Frankie Ledbetter for fear than Caleb would choke him to death. And, Frankie was a head taller and twenty pounds heavier than Caleb. Thinking about Zeke and Nate was like a knife in Caleb's heart. He sat down next to a tree and cried again. In his head, he could hear Paw saying, *Cryin' over it don't git the job done.* He wiped his eyes and vowed that he would not cry again, ever. But Lordy, he was lonely.

Exhausted from the events of the last two days, he made a little bed of Johnson grass and settled in for the night. It took a while to drift off to sleep. His thoughts raced back and forth across the events that had taken his family. He had roamed the woods and spent enough nights out hunting alone that he was not afraid except of being caught by the Yankee soldiers. Eventually, exhaustion overcame him and he slept.

He awoke with a start at the sound of hammering. A quick look around revealed that a big redheaded woodpecker was pounding away on a dead pine. As the bird chiseled away, chips of bark rained down through the light of the rising sun. Caleb sat up, stretched and yawned. He picked up his tow sack and discovered that the second chicken he had saved from yesterday was covered with ants. He knew better than to leave his food where critters could get at it! He would have to remember to keep his vittles tied up in a tree. He dumped the ruined chicken into the river and washed out his tow sack.

Up on the riverbank, tied to a white oak tree, he found the log raft his brothers had built last summer. He decided that he could just float away downriver if he could manage to drag it down the yellow clay bank to the water line. It was god-awful heavy and took half the morning to move it the thirty feet or so. The muddy yellow current ran strong with the recent spring rains. He cut a long pole, boarded the raft and shoved off into the flow. He had gone less than a mile when it suddenly struck him that the stream would take him north across Tennessee into Kentucky and on to the Ohio. *Bound to be too many Yankee soldiers that way. I'd best head up river towards Mississippi,* he thought. He poled across for the eastern shore. He wanted to be on the east bank and across from Pittsburg Landing when he got that far south. The big battle was likely over but there should be lots of Yankee soldiers still there. He abandoned the raft and headed back upstream. He concluded that he could do well enough as long as he stayed clear of bluecoats. *Half a day wasted!* He had to get away from here.

The old red brick store with a rusty tin roof at Cerro Gordo sat a half-mile upstream and across the river from his home place. The store would be a good place to find help. Caleb knew that the family who ran the store would take him in because they knew his folks. His paw often bartered for flour, lead, powder and such. And he, himself, had been to the store on several occasions. It was a wondrous place filled with all sorts of goods and teeming with delicious smells – new leather, corn meal and cinnamon candy. *Now that wouldn't be such a bad place for a boy to live!* thought Caleb.

But, he had to get there first. The woods were thick along the shore and the muddy bank was steep right down to the water. It was much hillier on this side of the river as compared to the side on which he lived. He found a game trail in the dense woods a few hundred yards back from the water's edge and followed it south. Silent movement was easy since the misting rain kept all the leaves and twigs on the ground wet. After a half hour or so, he heard voices and knew that he must be near the store.

"You killed yourself any Rebs?" said a deep voice.

"No, darn it!" said a young voice. "I was detailed to Grant's mess tent an' missed the whole battle."

"Well, we killed a slew of 'em and they killed a bunch of us. It was one heck of a fight," said the older man as he swatted a mosquito on the side of his face.

"If I'd been there, I would have killed me a few, for dang sure," said the young soldier. He spit a stream of thick brown tobacco juice onto the muddy ground to accent his statement.

The older man said, "You better watch yourself, pup. I heard that a Reb farm boy kilt Corporal Watkins with an ax day before yestiddy right over the river from here. Lad like that might skin out a pup like you."

Caleb edged back into the dense woods. His elation at the thought of living at the store was dashed. It had been taken over by the Yankees. He fought back the urge to cry. *Paw said to be a man and a man ain't supposed to cry,* he thought. He had never seen his paw cry nor any of the other grown men he knew. *Surely they must git sad,* he thought. *Maybe a man cries inside but not outside. That's what I'll try to do.* He could feel some of his sadness turning to rage at his circumstances and towards the Yankees soldiers. *By gol', I'll get even some day, somehow.*

The store backed right up to the bluff over the river and the front gallery faced the muddy road. No way to get past it on this side of the road. He would have to work his way across the road and into the dense woods on the other side. Caleb eased back up the game trail to the north a few hundred yards and slipped through the dense undergrowth toward the road. *How could the Yankees over here already know about the soldier I killed?* he thought. *I'd best be extra careful not to let 'em catch me.*

He waited in the brush until a group of wagons rumbled past and then darted to the far side of the road. The nearest town was Savannah at least ten or twelve miles upriver but it would be swarming with Yankees. He would have to swing wide of it. He needed to find a place to hide for the night and plan what to do. He kept moving south for another hour and then turned west so he could get back to the river.

As he walked through the dense green woods along the riverbank, Caleb found the dead Yankee cavalry officer more with his nose than with his eyes. The body had apparently floated downriver from the battle and snagged in some low brush at the water's edge. Caleb gritted his teeth and dragged what was left of the body part way onto a gravel sandbar. He took off the soldier's belt with the pistol and ammunition pouch. The revolver was heavy, a .44 caliber Colt's cap-and-ball. What a prize! The dull brass powder flask was full of wet powder. He rinsed the ruined powder out of the flask in the river. *No sense in carrying useless weight,* he thought. The officer's saber was gone and nothing else of use was to be found. Caleb pushed the body back into the current and swept his tracks out of the sand with a leafy willow branch. Now, at least he had a weapon, lead balls and percussion caps. He would have to find some powder but that might not be too difficult with all the soldiers around. He slung the belt over his left shoulder and let the holster and pistol hang down his right side. The long barrel of the gun reached almost to his knee.

A mile or two further on, where a small creek tumbled into the river, he gigged a couple of bullfrogs with a sharpened stick, skinned the legs and had them for his supper. Not much and they were raw since he was afraid to risk a fire. But, they filled his belly. At dark, he crawled into a canebrake for the night and stretched out to sleep.

When he awoke, it was still dark. Through a break in the clouds, he could see a sliver of moon hanging low over the western bank of the river. He could hear frogs croaking, crickets and katydids chirping, and the distant sound of a steamboat chuffing, probably at Savannah. A low fog hung over the river. He whiffed the sweet smell of a hickory wood fire on the gentle south breeze. The smoke reminded him of maw's home cooked breakfasts and how hungry he was. He gathered up his belongings and eased through the woods.

In twenty minutes, he could see the faint glow of a dying fire through the trees. He had the knack of stealth when needed. His paw had said it was "because you're half injun, son." Caleb crept up to the edge of the clearing. The half dozen men were sleeping in their blankets, including the sentry who was slumped against a big oak. In the dark, he couldn't tell whether they were Blues or Grays but either way, they would likely do harm to a boy alone or at least take his revolver. He looked in the back of their wagon and found a slab of bacon hanging on a hook and wrapped in a rag. He grabbed it along with a pound sack of what he took to be salt and eased back to the woods. The salt sack stunk like sulfur. Not salt but black powder! He put it and the bacon in his tow sack and tucked the top of the knotted tow sack under his belt. He silently worked his way through the woods around the soldiers and set off south toward Savannah.

By daylight, he had wolfed down several thick slices of the bacon and felt mighty pleased with himself. The cured bacon was raw but it tasted great. A little on the salty and greasy side but good enough for a hungry boy. He sat and thought about what to do next. His paw had been an orphan so there were no relatives on that side. The neighbors had been burned out and probably killed the day maw was killed. He decided that he would try to work his way south into Mississippi and see if he could find his maternal grandfather. He had never met him but knew from his maw's stories that his grandfather lived somewhere down there. The old man's name was Red Dog, or *Ofi Humma* in Choctaw. In fact, Caleb was named for the old man, in a way. His maw had wanted to name him Dog out of respect for her father and because he howled constantly as a newborn. His paw had said, "No McDougal's gonna be named Dog!" So his folks settled on Caleb. The preacher said that Caleb was Hebrew for 'dog'. And so, it was done: Caleb McDougal.

After his greasy breakfast and decision to find his grandfather, Caleb filled the powder flask from the sack. He carefully loaded five of the six chambers of the revolver using the measuring spout. Then, he rammed balls down with the loading lever, and pressed percussion caps on the nipples. He laid the hammer down on the empty chamber and holstered the pistol. Paw would have been pleased that he remembered just how to do it.

By mid morning, he had made it past Savannah without detection. From the amount of smoke in the air, the soldiers must have burned most of the town. Just past noon, he found a little abandoned shack perched on the riverbank. Good timing too, since the morning drizzle had turned into a downpour. The roof leaked here and there but most of the dirt floor was dry. He built a little fire in the cabin's hearth and fried up the rest of the bacon in an iron skillet that he had found in a corner of the room. The rain would cover the smoke and he was far enough upstream from his family farm that the Yankees would not be searching for him here.

He unraveled about ten feet of the twine from which the tow sack was made and fashioned a couple of fishhooks from the big thorns that he had collected from a 'Crown-o-Thorns' bush growing outside. Not the best but they would do. The pouring rain had backed off into a steady drizzle. He caught a few crickets for bait and cut a limb for a pole. It took less than an hour to catch two big bream and a two-pound catfish. He would eat well tonight! He would fry the fish in the bacon drippings he had saved in the skillet.

Tomorrow he would clear Pittsburg Landing and then look for a place to get back across river to head for Mississippi. He thought about what little he knew of the neighboring state. He had never been there, so other than to keep going south, how in the world would he ever find his grandfather? He didn't even know how big Mississippi was or in which part his grandfather lived. *I'll just have to worry about that after I git to Mississippi,* he thought. *I reckon I can ask somebody when I come to the first town. They must know where the Choctaws live.*

Getting past Pittsburg Landing proved to be a lot of worry for nothing. The battle had been over for more than a week and the bulk of the two armies had moved off toward Corinth, Mississippi. The river ran straight up from the south at this point but Caleb knew enough local geography to be aware that it would soon start bending toward the east. He wanted to get across to the west side before the stream turned. At mid-morning, he found a small, water-filled boat tied to a tree. He felt bad about taking the boat but he would leave it as near to straight across as possible and the owners should find it on the other side. He dumped out the water and paddled hard but the current was swift. Although it was less than one-half mile across, he was a long way downstream before he made the far shore. He walked along the shore pulling the boat back upstream. It was tiring wading through the sticky yellow mud and the boat kept fouling on snags and rocks. After a half-hour, he gave it up and tied the boat to a fallen willow hanging down the bank into the water. *Owner will find it, if he's supposed to,* he thought.

At noon, the river took a sharp bend to the east. He decided to keep to the woods and head due south. It rained hard all afternoon. He thought he could hear thunder off to the west but the solid overcast of dark gray clouds wasn't right for thunder and he had seen no lightning flashes. *Must be artillery,* he thought. He fashioned a bow from a Bois D'Arc limb and a bit of twine from his tow sack and made a few arrows from sharpened Bois D'Arc sticks. His mother had taught all of her sons to make bows and arrows from the hard wood of Bois D'Arc trees. His brother, Zeke, made the best arrows and Nate was the best bowshot but Caleb could shoot well enough if he had time to aim and the quarry wasn't over fifty feet away. The little bow was not much of a weapon, but useful for rabbits and such. He couldn't quite hold the revolver steady enough to aim with one hand. It was too big and heavy. For now, he would have to shoot it with both hands, if necessary, but he feared the noise would attract attention. He sure did want to be further from the home place before mixing in with folks.

He was soaked from the continual rain and exhausted from slogging through the sticky yellow mud. That night he made a meal of a 'possum he had shot with his bow. He didn't know it, but he had crossed into Mississippi an hour before sundown. He found a stand of dense piney woods and made a bit of a shelter from a few pine boughs. He was asleep before he got his eyes closed.

II

Caleb peered out from between the branches of the dense woods. An old woman who looked like she might be an Indian was splitting stove wood behind a white, two-story clapboard farmhouse. It was late in the day and he was hungry. He decided to chance it and see if she knew his grandpaw or maybe he could trade some wood-splitting for a hot meal.

"Hello, ma'am," he said as he stepped into the clearing.

She jumped like she had been shot.

"Lordy, boy! Don't sneak up on a person like that," said the woman.

"Sorry, ma'am."

"You lost? Laws, but you're a sight, and you smell a bit strong, too!" she said. "And, you look loaded for bear. What's with that bow and the big Yankee horse pistol you're totin'?"

"No ma'am. I ain't lost. Yankees killed my family and I'm huntin' my grandpaw. He's a Choctaw and runs a store somewhere down in Mississippi." That was more than he had said in a week.

"Well, you got a long ways to go yet," she said. "The Choctaws that're left in Mississippi live mostly a hundred miles south of here."

A hundred miles! His heart sank. He couldn't be more than thirty or forty miles from home and it had taken days. He wanted to cry but was too proud to let the woman see him do that.

"My name is Miz Johnson. Why don't you stay with us? My husband's out checkin' to see if'n all this rain's warshed out his cotton crop. He'll be home directly."

Caleb thought that maybe the man might know of his grandpaw since Caleb's maw had said he was a famous storyteller. The woman seemed nice enough. And, *she sure wasn't no Yankee! At least, I'll stay for supper,* he thought.

Caleb said, "I'll take over splittin' that stove wood to pay for my supper and stay the night, if that pleases you."

"Alright, fill up the wood box on the back porch and mind that ax. It's sharp," said Miz Johnson. "I'll take this little dab I've already split and get the stove goin'." She climbed the steps and entered the back door.

Caleb set his bow, handful of arrows, tow sack and revolver aside and started in on the woodpile. He went at the work with a vengeance. The thought of a real home-cooked meal lit up a big grin across his face. As he stacked the last armload to finish filling the wood box, Miz Johnson reappeared with clean clothes and said, "My oldest boy has outgrowed these. He and his brother're off yonder to the west fightin' with Gen. Beauregard's boys. Get out of them smelly duds and warsh yourself up over yonder by the crick. Then put this stuff on. I reckon we'll have to burn your things!"

Caleb did as he was told. As he walked back to the house, he heard a horse blow and a rider approaching. It turned out to be a mule and rider. Mr. Johnson was returning from his fields. "Hello, young feller! Who're you?" he said as he dismounted.

"My name's Caleb McDougal and I'm from up in Tennessee near Saltillo." He stuck his hand out to shake. "My family got killed by the Yankees and I'm off to find my grandpaw."

"What's your grandpaw's name and where's he live?" said Mr. Johnson.

"His name's Red Dog and he's a Choctaw. I don't know where he lives except it's in Mississippi and he runs a store," said Caleb.

"Well, there's a whole heap of Mississippi for him to store keep in. I ain't never heard of nobody named Red Dog around here. The Mizzus is half Chickasaw and I take it you've met her since you're wearing Nathan's britches. There ain't no Choctaws in this country," said Mr. Johnson.

"Yessir, I met Miz Johnson but we didn't get 'round to no particulars on my grandpaw, yet," said Caleb.

"Come with me. I need to put this mule up for the night and hang the tack up in the barn," said Mr. Johnson. "You old enough to work a mule?"

"Yessir, I help my paw and brothers with the plowin'." Then he added, "Well, I did but they're all killed now."

"Stay here for a while and we can ask about for the whereabouts of your grandpaw. You can help me with the plowin'. I got a thirty acre field that needs to be redone down in the crick bottom," said Mr. Johnson.

Caleb fell asleep in his chair at the dinner table. He awoke in a bed upstairs while it was still dark outside. He could hear the Johnsons stirring around in the kitchen downstairs. His own clothes were gone and none of his possessions were in the room.

"Mornin' Caleb," Miz Johnson said as he walked into the kitchen. "I put your things out on the back porch, except for your clothes. I burnt 'em. They weren't worth warshin'. Set down at the table and I'll fix you a plate of grits and eggs."

As they finished their breakfast, Mr. Johnson said, " I've got some business in town. Why don't you come with me and we'll ask around about your grandpaw? It's still too wet to plow today. The rain stopped last night and the sky looks clear to the west. Should be able to get at that field tomorrow or the next day. Eat your breakfast and then hitch up the mules to the wagon. You can connect up a team, can't you?"

"Oh, yessir, I'll get right at it," said Caleb.

Caleb sat on the wagon seat next to Mr. Johnson as they rattled through the town of Iuka about ten that morning. Mr. Johnson reined up in front of the cotton gin on the far side of town. "I need to get more seed to replant that bottom land. Just wait here in the wagon."

The warm sun felt good as Caleb sat on the wooden seat. It was good to hear the sounds of the little town. He could hear the ring of a blacksmith's hammer on an anvil, women chatting outside the General Store, and the rhythmic rasp of someone sawing lumber. A couple of dogs barked somewhere and a hen was cackling in the shed next to the cotton gin. A baby cried in the arms of her mother at the window above the general store and two boys argued and wrestled in the dirt out front of the blacksmith shop. Caleb had always enjoyed the sounds of a town.

The springs creaked as Mr. Johnson plopped the heavy sack of seed in the back. "Hop down off of there and come with me. Jake'll make sure no one wanders off with our buckboard and team. Let's go see if we can find anyone who knows anythin' about your grandpaw."

They had no luck at the saloon or the barbershop, but they got a lead at the general store. An old-timer said he that had once hunted black bear with some Choctaws down near the big hill they called 'Nanih Waya'. "That was before they moved off to the

Nations. Still some of 'em down in that country. I'd head down there. If'n he didn't go off with the rest of 'em to the Nations, I expect he'd be known in that area," said old Bill.

Caleb said, "I know he didn't go to the Nations because my maw got a letter from him last Christmas and he still ran his store in Mississippi. Of course, the letter burnt up with ever'thin' else when the Yankees burnt our house. So, I didn't have no way of findin' a town or anythin' else on the letter."

"Thanks, Bill," said Mr. Johnson. "If'n the lad decides to keep up his search, he's got a startin' point now down south at Nanih Waya."

"Gee, mule!" Caleb shouted. The mule obediently turned right. The plowing wasn't that bad since he was making rows in the red dirt of the rained out field that had been worked just a few weeks ago. The traces cut into his shoulder a bit but the mule was a good one and obviously knew more about this work than Caleb did. As the moldboard turned over the rich soil, Caleb pondered his future. He had concluded that he would work two weeks for the Johnsons to pay for their hospitality and the clothes he now wore. He had spent the first week helping Mr. Johnson clear brush from along the creek and the last two days redoing this field. Three more days and he would be on his way.

He finished just before dark. He put the plow and harness in the shed, watered and fed the mule, and put him in the barn for the night. After washing up, he headed for the kitchen door and supper.

"You did real good, Caleb," Mr. Johnson said. "I sure am goin' to be sad to see you go. You're a good hard worker."

"Well, I'm bound to find my Grandpaw and I want to get moving soon as I can," said Caleb.

Miz Johnson said, "Caleb, the Mister an' me've talked it out and think you should just stay with us. My boys're growed up and are off makin' war on the Yankees. Lord knows when they'll be home, or if. I kinda like havin' a boy around the place."

"I appreciate all you've done for me but I just gotta find my grandpaw. He needs to know about my mama and where maw's buried," said Caleb.

"Son, you've done a fair amount of work for a old shirt and a pair of britches," said Mr. Johnson. "If'n you got to go, I expect you should leave in the mornin' before the mizzus gets anymore attached to you."

Caleb said, "Yessir, I'm itchin' to go but I felt obliged to work off my debt. If you think we're even, then I'll be off in the mornin'."

At dawn, he packed his belongings into his tow sack and stood up as Mr. Johnson came into the room. "I'm sorry I can't give you some money but I don't have any," said Mr. Johnson. "But, here's some real fish hooks and fish line and an extra shirt. Come on down to breakfast when you're finished here."

"I'm finished now," said Caleb.

No one's eyes were free of tears as Caleb set off down the red dirt road. He had his revolver and other belongings in his tow sack. His bow hung over his shoulder along with a little quiver of arrows on his back. Mr. Johnson had fashioned the quiver from a piece of an old worn out buckskin shirt. Caleb decided that he would skirt around Corinth and then head west and pick up the Natchez Trace until he got far enough south to cut back east to where the Choctaws lived. Mr. Johnson had more or less mapped out a route for Caleb to take.

As Caleb walked down the road at mid-afternoon whistling to himself, he came upon a dozen Reb soldiers sitting around a wagon at the side of the road.

"Where you headin', Jaybird?" said a tall, skinny, freckled-faced, redheaded boy about nineteen years old. "You playin' Injun, or what?"

An older man wearing a Gray Coat with gold Corporal's insignia on the sleeves said, "Leave him alone, W.C, he ain't botherin' you." He said to Caleb, "Come here, son."

Caleb stopped and faced the older man. He didn't trust the Reb soldiers much more than he did the Yankees. He tightened his grip on his tow sack and didn't move. The older man stepped out into the road and stuck out his hand to shake.

As Caleb stepped forward to shake his hand, the Corporal made a grab for the tow sack. Caleb jumped to the side and swung the sack up between the man's legs. The heavy pistol in the sack found its mark with a thud. The soldier let out his breath in a loud "Oof" and then bent over double. The rest of the Rebs started laughing and hooting. Caleb sprinted down the road zigzagging like a rabbit.

Caleb ran until he had to stop and gasp for air. He was certain they would be after him but they didn't follow. He could still hear them hooting when he went around a bend and out of sight. *Can't trust any of 'em,* he thought. *This war's made 'em all mean and crazy.* Caleb's hatred for the Yankees had now spread to include soldiers from both sides.

The Natchez Trace runs south-southwest from Nashville to Natchez. Caleb took the Trace when the road he was on finally intersected with it. Just before dark, he made camp off to the side of the trail safely back in the woods. He had a cold dinner of the biscuits and bacon Miz Johnson had packed for him. The rain had stopped and the sky was filled with stars. Crickets and katydids sang and tree frogs were peeped from every tree. The drone of cicadas was so loud that it seemed they were everywhere. He heard an owl hooting off in the distance. Next thing he knew, a sliver sun edged over the horizon. Dew covered in him and each leaf around him dripped in the gold light of dawn.

Caleb pushed through the brush and re-entered the Trace just as a heavy wagon pulled by four mules rumbled up. "Hey boy, whar you headed," said the old man driving the team. He stopped the wagon next to Caleb.

"I'm off down south a ways to find my grandpaw," said Caleb.

"Well, jump in the back and I'll give you a ride as for as you're goin'," said the man. "My name's Henderson and I'm haulin' this here freight on down to Natchez. Ordinarily, we'd be floatin' it down by river or usin' the railroad but the Yankees got control of the Mississippi and Ohio Rivers and General Lee's Army is usin' the railroads, so it's overland or nothin'."

The man looked safe enough and Caleb decided that he would be able to jump out of the back if need be. Riding sure would beat walking!

Wooden kegs and crates filled the big wagon. Caleb put his tow sack between two crates and scrambled over the pile to the front of the wagon.

"Join me on the seat up here, I ain't gonna bite you," said Mr.

Henderson. "I don't mind a little company."

Caleb climbed over the seat back and sat down.

"Whar's this grandpaw of yours live and what your name?" asked Mr. Henderson.

"I'm Caleb McDougal and my grandpaw lives somewheres near a place called *Nanih Waya*," said Caleb.

Mr. Henderson rubbed his whiskered chin and said, "Well, we ain't goin' through that country, son. This here Trace heads southwest to Natchez and you're wantin' to go due south. Nanih Waya's the name of an Injun hill along the Noxapater Crick. We'll pass a good twenty miles west of it. Still that's a sight closer'n you are now. Tell you what; you can ride as far as French Camp. That's about as close as we'll pass and you can split off from there."

"How far's that from here?" asked Caleb.

"Let's see, we'll get to Tupelo day after tomorrow. So's, I expect we'll make French Camp in about a week. What you doin' headin' so far by yourself anyways?" asked Mr. Henderson.

Caleb told him the story of his paw and brothers dying at Shiloh and the Yankees killing his maw and burning the farm. He left out the part about killing the soldier. It didn't seem wise to tell that to a stranger. He told of the kindness of the Johnsons and the help they had given him.

"Yep, I think most folks is good at heart and want to help each other. The bad ones kinda stand out but they's few in number. Bad folks come to a bad end my pappy always said. I expect it's true."

"You say you come all the way from above Savannah," said Mr. Henderson. "You're a travellin' little chigger, ain't you? I'm travellin' now but mostly I'm a homebody. I got me a wife and four youngin's waitin' at my farm down near Natchez. I expect to make enough on this load to pay off a loan I had to make to keep our farm. I had a run of bad luck. A hayrack fell on my mule and killed him. I had to borry money to buy another one lest I couldn't plow and get my crop in. I heard that they was havin' trouble gittin' teamsters for this run down from Nashville because folks was skeered of the Yankees. I figgered I was more worried about starvin' than of any dang Yankees, so I signed on to drive this here wagon. Besides, this one run, if'n I make it through, will pay my debt and give us a little money to boot. So far, I only run into three Yankees and they was too drunk to even stand up, much less give me any trouble."

Mr. Henderson turned out to be quite a talker. He rambled on incessantly about growing up in the Mississippi River bottoms and his life on the farm with his wife and children. Caleb listened and dozed as the mules plodded along to the jingle of the trace chains and the creak and rumble of the heavy wagon. Every now and then, he and Mr. Henderson would dismount and walk along either side of the straining mules as they pulled up a hill. It felt good to walk and give his ears a break from the non-stop chatter. At night, they would pull off the road, hobble the stock and make camp for dinner. They took turns sitting up guarding but it seemed unnecessary. They rarely encountered anyone outside the few towns they passed.

The week passed quickly enough. Mr. Henderson had taught Caleb how to aim and shoot the heavy revolver with one hand. He had fallen square on his backside from the recoil of the first shot. The pistol threw a big orange flame, a huge cloud of smelly sulfur smoke and boomed like a cannon. With a little practice, he could hit something the size of a dinner plate at thirty feet. Mr. Henderson said that was good enough to discourage most anybody or any critter he would likely come up against. Tomorrow they would reach French Camp!

III

French Camp wasn't much of a town. Caleb said his goodbye to Mr. Henderson and, at the livery, found a man there who had been to his grandpaw's store!

"How do I get there from here and how far is it?" asked Caleb.

"Well, it's pritnear twenty miles down that there road headin' east," said the man as he pointed in the direction of a dusty road.

"Thanks," said Caleb. "I reckon I'll head on out."

He felt as light as a bird and fairly safe now that he was so far from the home place and the dead Yankee. *By gol, I'm finally almost to Grandpaw's place,* he thought.

At midnight, Caleb found the store. It sat by itself on the north side of the road on a little hill above a creek, right where the man from French Camp had said it would be. There was enough moonlight to see the sign over the front door that simply stated 'STORE'. Like every other store he had ever seen, the living quarters were at the back. He heard a dog growl when he approached the front. *I'd best wait 'til mornin',* thought Caleb. *No sense wakin' ever'body up this late at night and maybe get chewed up by the dog, too.* He edged back into the woods across the road and sat down with his back to a big sweet gum tree.

Cardinals, the early risers in the bird world, started chirping and singing as it was just getting light. Caleb sat up, yawned and stretched. He gathered up his possessions and walked across the road. He walked up the steps and across the gallery to the front door. He heard the growl again but it didn't sound like a dog after all. It sounded more like an old door hinge rubbing. There wasn't another sound coming from the store. Come to think of it, he hadn't heard a rooster crow or any livestock sounds. That was mighty peculiar.

He set his possessions down and walked around to the side. He saw nothing. He went around to the back and saw the growling door swinging back and forth on the breeze. "Hello," he said in a loud voice. Nothing. He looked in though the back door. Empty! He walked through the living quarters and out through the store. The shelves were all empty but not dusty enough to have been empty long. He walked out onto the front gallery and sat down on a bench. *Oh no*, he thought. *Now what!*

He hadn't been sitting more than fifteen minutes when he heard the creak and jingle of a team coming up the road from the east. A man and small boy walked along side of the mules. A woman with a baby in her arms sat on the seat. The wagon was piled high with household belongings and a crate of chickens. A milk cow plodded along tethered to the back. These people were obviously Indians.

"Hello!" shouted Caleb from the shadows of the store gallery.

"Mornin'," said the man as he stopped the team.

Caleb came down the steps and stuck out his hand. "I'm Caleb McDougal and I've come down to this store huntin' for my grandpaw. Do you know why the store is abandoned?"

"Yes, the old man who ran the store sold out and left two weeks ago. He took three wagons of stuff and a couple of young men off to the Nations to join the rest of our people there. We're doin' the same," said the man. "The war between the whites is moving this way and most of us have decided to join the rest of the Choctaws in the Nations lest we get caught up in their war. Is Ofi Humma your grandfather?"

"Yes," said Caleb. "He was my maw's paw. All of my folks got killed by the Yankees up in Tennessee and I came lookin' for my grandpaw to tell him. I never met him but I knew he lived down here somewheres. But now, you say he's gone off to the Nations."

"Do you wish to go with us? I'm sure we'll find him when we get there," said the man.

"I don't know what to do. I think I'll just stay here for a while to think it out. If I decide to join you, I'll catch up along the way. Thanks for the offer, though," said Caleb.

As the wagon rattled off down the road, Caleb sat back down on the bench. The way he figured it, he could move much faster alone instead of joining up with the Choctaw family. His grandfather had a two-week head start but would be slowed by the freight. The man with his family had laid out the route to Vicksburg for Caleb. From there, he had said most folks went by water down the Mississippi to the Red River and then up the Red to the Nations. *Best get movin'*, he thought.

It took Caleb five days of hard traveling to reach Vicksburg. It was the largest town he had ever seen. Folks rushed about in preparation for the coming attack by the Union Navy. Caleb wandered through the muddy streets until he found his way to the riverfront. He was amazed at the size of the Mississippi. The huge river was high and running fast. The brown muddy water swirled and churned as it rushed past. A hodgepodge of boats was tied up along the docks. He asked for information about his grandfather and one of the boatmen suggested that he talk to Mr. Adams who ran the ferryboats.

Mr. Adams was a short fat man with a fringe of bright red hair surrounding his bald head. He had wooly red mutton-chop side burns and a voice that would strip bark off a pine tree. He stood on a dock next to a steam-powered ferry. The ferry had two huge side wheels and hinged ramps at either end. It wallowed slightly in the current and strained against the thick ropes that tethered it to the dock. The near ramp was lowered so that wagons could drive straight down the riverbank, across the dock, and on board. "What'n the heck you want, boy?" roared Mr. Adams.

"Hello sir, I'm Caleb McDougal and I'm trying to catch up with my Grandpaw. He should have been through here in the last week or so. He's a Choctaw and probably headed down river to take the Red up to the Nations."

"Tain't likely," said Mr. Adams. "Farragut and the Yankee Navy's taken New Orleans and Baton Rouge. Word is that he's on his way now to Vicksburg. We'll teach him a lesson or two, by dang! We got the high ground of these here bluffs and our artillery'll blow him to bits. Anyhow, nobody's headed down toward the Red in the last couple of weeks. We did haul an old Injun and some bucks acrost about five or six days ago. Of course, that was before the river came up so high. They had three wagons loaded down with goods and said they were gunna cut over and pick up the Red River at Shreveport. One of th' pups called the old man Offy or some such."

"That's him!" shouted Caleb. "His name's *Ofi, Ofi Humma*, and he was in three wagons with the stuff from his store. How do I get across?"

"Well, it's a dollar to cross on the ferry. You got a dollar?"

"Nope," said Caleb.

"Waal, you could fly or swim but I doubt you can fly and the las' fool what tried to swim it, drowned!" laughed Mr. Adams. "Come back when you got a dollar."

Caleb had never seen a whole dollar in his life. He concluded that he might need to work a month to earn that much. He was hungry and he obviously couldn't hunt for his food here in town. He knew he could sell the pistol but he couldn't bear to part with it. He couldn't swim across the Mississippi weighted down with the pistol and sack. He would have to find another way. But first, he needed to find a safe place to stay the night.

He headed upriver out of town a half mile and found a dense stand of woods a few yards east of the riverbank where he dug a shallow hole near a big hickory tree. Caleb put his pistol and other valuables in his sack, buried them in the hole, and then covered the spot with leaves until he was satisfied that this spot didn't look any different from any other spot around. Using his knife, he marked an "X" in the bark of another hickory tree twenty feet to the left of the one where his things were buried. It would be easy for him to spot the "X" from the dirt trail along the top of the riverbank.

Back in town, he looked in the back door of a saloon and saw a huge pile of dirty dishes in a washtub. He went around to the front door and walked in. The big man behind the bar had shiny black hair that was greased down and plastered to his head. His long mustache was heavily waxed and pulled out to points two inches out from either side of his upper lip. Caleb walked up to the bar directly in front of the bartender.

"Sir," he said to the bartender. "I'll warsh them dishes out back for my supper."

"Well, Pup, you got yourself a deal," said the man. "My dish warsher done run off yesterday with one of the whores and I ain't got nobody to help me. Dern near ever'body's workin' down on the south side of town at the fortifications. Ain't nuthin' anybody's talkin' about except the Yankees is comin'. "

By midnight, Caleb had finished the pile of dishes and curled up in a corner of the pantry for the night. At daylight, he set out for the work going on south of town. In addition to what Mr. Lucas, the bartender, had said, Caleb had overheard the men playing cards in the saloon. They were all talking about the fortifications being built on the hills surrounding Vicksburg especially those south of town to defend against the Yankee Navy that was bound to be on the way upriver from Baton Rouge. The artillery surrounding Vicksburg was set up so that it could fire on boats coming and going on both arms of the long loop the river made here as well as directly abreast as they made the bend. This provided a great advantage since the guns on the boats would mostly be mounted on the sides and could not be brought to bear except in the bend of the river. Additionally, the height of the hills placed the Reb guns out of the reach of the boats' guns.

Caleb quickly got a job carrying drinking water to the men digging trenches. He had lied to the lieutenant to get the job. He had said he was sixteen after reading the sign outside the lieutenant's tent that clearly said no one under sixteen would be hired. The pay wasn't great but they would feed him and, at the end of two weeks, he would have the dollar he needed for the ferry across the river.

There were three other boys working with Caleb, hauling water and running errands for the work crew. They were brothers and nearly the same size as Caleb but a few years older. Johnny was seventeen while the twins, Luther and Billy, were sixteen. The four of them shared a small tent provided by the army. It wasn't great but it kept the rain off while they slept. As the eldest, Johnny took a leadership role with the younger boys.

At the end of work the first day, Johnny said, "Let's take a walk into town after supper. I know a place where we can watch the dancin' gals from a tree outside the window at Millie's Saloon."

"I'm too derned wore out to walk anywheres," said Luther. "I bet I toted a thousand gallons of water up that hill today. I'll be lucky if'n I can make it through supper before I fall out. You fellers go if'n you want but I'm goin' to bed right after I eat."

"I'll go," said Billy. "I'm pritnear tuckered out myself but I could stand to see them hoochie dancers."

"How's about you, Caleb," said Johnny.

"I guess a look or two won't hurt," said Caleb. "But I won't stay too long 'cuz I'm tuckered, too."

Supper consisted of a plate of black-eyed peas, a piece of cornbread and a cup of weak coffee. Luther dozed off while they ate. "Wake up, little brother, before you drown in your derned plate of peas," said Johnny.

They finished their meal and washed off their spoons, bowls and cups. Johnny said, "Luther, tote our stuff back to the tent with you. We're headin' for Ms. Millie's."

Luther shuffled off with the stack of utensils and the other three headed into town. They hadn't gone far when Johnny asked, "How much money you got, Caleb? I can buy us a bottle of beer or two out the back door if'n you have a couple of nickels."

"I don't have no money," said Caleb. "Why in the heck do you think I'm breakin' my back totin' water all day? If'n I was rich enough to be buyin' beer, I'd be ridin' in a buggy 'stead of wadin' in this mud."

They all laughed at the thought of Caleb riding in a buggy up to the front steps of Millie's Saloon. It was pitch dark by the time they reached Millie's place. Cigar smoke and piano music poured from the doors and windows of the place. The boys climbed a big oak growing at the right of the building. They clambered along a big limb until they could see the stage at one end of the saloon. Three tired-looking, painted-up women kicked their legs up above their heads as they danced more or less in time with the piano.

"Is that what we walked all this way for?" asked Caleb. "Them 'gals' are older than our Maws. And, I've seen more whilst skinny-dippin' with the Ledbetter gals back home on White Oak Crick than what these three are showin'. I'm headin' back to the tent with Luther."

Just as Caleb swung down from the tree limb, a pistol shot cracked and Billy fell from the limb. Johnny started screaming and crying. Meanwhile, all tarnation broke loose inside of the saloon. Several more shots were fired, the men began shouting and the women shrieked. In the light that shone out from the saloon window, Caleb looked down on Billy and saw a dark round hole in his forehead. A pool of blood spread on the ground beneath Billy's head. Johnny staggered around, dazed and crying.

"Stay with Billy!" shouted Caleb. "I'll go get help."

The noise in the saloon had stopped except for a continuing wail from one of the women. Caleb raced to the front door and peeked in. One of the poker tables was upset and a man in a pea green frock coat with maroon lapels lay on the floor. The wailing woman rocked back and forth cradling the dead gambler's head in her arms. Three men who stood with their backs to the bar restrained a grizzled-looking farmer. A big pistol and a little two-barreled derringer lay on the floor. Blood seeped from two bloody holes in the farmer's shirt.

"He was cheatin' me!" cried the farmer. "I caught him dealin' from the bottom and he threw down on me with that little pea shooter. His first shot went right through my hat and out th' winder. His second shot hit me here in the shoulder. That's when I pulled my gun and shot him."

"One of you killed Billy!" shouted Caleb.

Everyone turned his way. One of the men holding the farmer said, "Who th' heck are you and who's this Billy?"

"Billy's my friend. He's layin' dead outside that window," said Caleb. "We was just climbin' a tree outside to see what was goin' on in here when someone shot him."

Two men from the saloon ran outside and brought Billy and Johnny back inside. They laid Billy on one of the poker tables.

"Dang bad luck," said one of the men. "I looks like that gambler's little derringer popped this youngin' right through the head."

A woman came down the stairs that ran down the wall to the left of the stage. Her lips were painted bright red and her eyes looked to Caleb like they had clumps of daddy longlegs glued to them. She asked, "What is going on down here?"

"Millie, Nathan says that Jessie was cheatin' him and they shot it out," said the bartender. "When I heard the shots, I pulled my gun from behind the bar and shot Nathan before he could kill anybody else. It appears that Jessie's shot went out the window and killed that boy layin' on the front table."

Most of the rest of the crowd nodded in agreement. Mille said to the bartender, "Wally, you'd best go get the sheriff and explain what happened. Sarah, you and Betty get Lizbeth up off the floor and take her to her room." She turned to Johnny and Caleb and said, "Who's this boy? Where's his folks?"

"He don't have nobody but me and Luther," said Johnny. "Our Ma died of the consumption five years ago and we run off last month 'cuz our Pa gets drunk and beats us."

"Where are you boys living?" asked Mille.

"We work for the soldiers and they give us a tent to live in," said Johnny.

"Well, you and Luther had best go back to your tent," said Millie. "I'll see that your brother gets buried proper."

"He ain't Luther," said Johnny pointing to Caleb. "He's our friend Caleb. Luther's back at the camp. Where you goin' to bury Billy?"

"We'll bury him in the town cemetery tomorrow. If you want to come to the burial, be at the cemetery around ten o'clock," said Millie.

"No, ma'am, " said Johnny. "We have to work and poor Billy's beyond help. I 'spec we'll just be goin'."

"Good night, boys," said Millie.

Caleb and Johnny walked back to camp without another word and climbed under their blankets. The next morning broke gray and foggy. Luther cried all morning after learning about Billy's death. He gave Johnny a long hard look after Johnny told him the news but said nothing. The look said all that needed to be said.

The boys returned to their tent each night after supper. No one had much appetite for trips to town anymore. Johnny and Luther had decided to join the Confederate Army. The lieutenant said that they could sign up on the first of next month. Captain Holmes would be in town to muster a new regiment and they could enlist then. Caleb said he still planned to seek his grandfather and would be heading west across Louisiana as soon as they got paid. The work was hard but the two weeks flew by. Tonight Caleb would get his dollar!

Suddenly, there was a flurry of shouts followed by the boom of artillery all around him. Once he had gathered his wits, Caleb saw a group of gunboats steaming up the river. Huge geysers of water shot up around them but none of the shells found its mark. The gunboats put about and anchored downstream out of the range of the Reb guns.

The Union command had decided that Vicksburg was key to dividing the Confederacy and denying Confederate forces supplies and reinforcements from the west. The fall of New Orleans, Baton Rouge and Natchez to the south and Memphis to the north meant that only Vicksburg stood in the way of Union plans. The surrounding terrain made the prospect of a land assault unsavory. Therefore, a naval assault was attempted.

The excitement of the firing had the soldiers renew their

digging at a frenzied pace. By the end of the day, Caleb was exhausted. He collected his pay, said his goodbyes to Luther and Johnny, and headed for town. He planned to check with Mr. Adams at the ferry to find out when the next trip across would be and collect his valuables from their hiding place.

"Ain't nobody crossin' th' river 'til the Yankee boats leave," said Mr. Adams. "And, word is that more Yankee boats is comin' down from Memphis. Colonel Autry's sealed the riverfront. There's armed guards posted all along to keep anybody from stealing boats or any of these supplies piled up. You ain't goin' nowheres 'til th' Yankees leave, dollar or no dollar."

Caleb wandered back up the hill into town. 'Back to haulin' water, I guess,' thought Caleb.

Two days and hundreds of water buckets later, big Union warships up from New Orleans joined the gunboats downstream of the Confederate emplacements. The talk around town was that there would be a siege of Vicksburg, which could last months. The town was well provisioned and the terrain was such that it could be easily defended. Everyone seemed confident that the Yankees would eventually give up and leave. 'Eventually!' thought Caleb, 'I need to get out of here now or I'll be trapped for who knows how long.' He said his goodbyes to Luther and Johnny again, and walked north back through town.

Caleb dug up his valuables and headed up river. He had been told that the Yazoo River entered the Mississippi from the east just a few miles upstream. Maybe he could find a boat before he got there.

Later that morning, Caleb spotted a young man working his way across the mouth of the Yazoo in a small skiff. The man removed catfish from a trotline and re-baited the hooks with chicken gizzards as he went. Caleb called out to him as the boat neared the shore, "Hello, mister, looks like the fishin's pretty good."

"Yup," replied the fisherman. "Grab the front of the boat for me, will you?"

Caleb grabbed the bow of the skiff and held it while the fisherman clamored out. "You want to buy some catfish?" asked the fisherman.

"No thanks," answered Caleb, "but I'll pay you a quarter to paddle me across the Mississippi."

"A pup like you don't have no quarter! 'Sides, look how fast the big river's runnin'. It'd be awfully dangerous to cross in my little boat."

"I got the quarter," said Caleb. "I figured you'd be too skeered to cross the big river."

"I ain't skeered of no river," said the young man. "Make it four bits and you got yourself a deal."

"Deal," said Caleb.

"Les see the money," said the fisherman.

Caleb held up the two Yankee coins for him to see. The fisherman's eyes got big and he said, "Les go." They climbed in and each took a paddle. Caleb sat up front and the fisherman in the back. The fisherman said, "When we hit the current of the river, paddle hard as you can and watch sharp for trees and such in the water. We'll run with the current and angle across."

They paddled out of the Yazoo onto the Mississippi. It looked like a long way across and the water rushed past them. Once they hit the current, the skiff shot downstream like a runaway horse. The river made a hissing sound and a low, dull roar as it rushed along. It smelled of mud and rotting vegetation. Here and there huge logs and whole trees rushed along. Every now and then a log or tree would disappear below the water only to shoot violently up yards downstream. Caleb was terrified in the tiny boat out in the huge powerful river. They paddled furiously and gradually angled across to the far bank. The current had swept them several miles south. They could see the Vicksburg landing just downstream on the east bank. Caleb paid the fisherman and thanked him. The fisherman started back across, paddling like mad.

'Made it!' Caleb thought.

IV

Crossing the Mississippi had been a lark compared to what Caleb found to the west of the river. The Mississippi was now the highest it had been in memory and the bottomlands west of the river were flooded for twenty miles.

After fighting his way through the tangle of willows at the riverbank, Caleb spotted what must be the road leading west from the ferry landing across the river from Vicksburg. From the little rise on which he stood with the rushing river behind him, he could see that everything was flooded in front of him. Caleb knew his grandfather could not have made it across that with the three wagons. In spite of what the ferryman had told him, his grandfather must have made his way down the Mississippi to the Red by boat. That, or else they got through before the bottoms flooded. Caleb tightly tied up his pistol, powder and caps in a piece of oilcloth and put it in a leather pack he wore on his back. The soldiers at the fortification site had given him the leather pack and the oilcloth. *Well, ain't nothing to be done but wade west*, thought Caleb.

The first mile was the worst. He waded in water anywhere from knee to chest deep. And, there was a fair amount of current that he had to fight to keep from falling. He could see the tops of bushes sticking up out of the water. The surface of the water was littered with leaves and sticks and other flotsam. Since most of the bottomland was heavily farmed, it was hard to tell where the road was under the lake of thick muddy water. But, by feeling his way along, he kept to the roadbed as much as possible.

His first mistake came about a half-mile in as he reached a tree line. He plunged in over his head and nearly lost his pack before he scrambled out of the creek. The water was too muddy to see even an inch into and he had waded into a submerged creek that crossed the roadbed. *How stupid!* he thought. *Any dummy knows a crooked tree line in bottom lands marks a creek.* He cut a stick about six feet long to use as a walking stick and to probe ahead for deep holes and such.

After the next mile or so, there was little current and from time to time, he came to sections of the road that were just above the water. His feet were heavy with mud and he had lost his shoes in the first hour. The high spots, here and there, were covered in varmints, snakes, ants, and the like all trying to escape the flood. He used his stick to clear them out of his way as he went. The trees and bushes were alive with flood escapees as well. It was almost sunset and he had only come a few miles. A middling sized hickory tree stood off to itself beside the flooded roadbed. He climbed up into its branches, knocked all the snakes he could see into the water and settled in for a long, cold, hungry night.

The going was excruciatingly slow. Caleb had waded off and on for three days before he finally reached higher ground. All that wading and struggling had only gotten him twenty miles west of the big river. All of the roads behind him, across the low land of eastern Louisiana, were under water. Caleb wasn't about to cross all that water and swamp again. He didn't know what lay ahead but surely it couldn't be as bad as what he had just crossed. He would continue on to the Indian Nations and hope for the best.

Every few miles he had to cross a creek or a small river. As long as he stuck to the roads, he would find a bridge or a ford or, sometimes a ferry. The ferry at the Tensas River had no one around, so he pulled himself across. He hopped off and the ferry began to work itself back across the river propelled by the slow current. Whoever owned it, knew his business, obviously, since he had set his pull rope so that the ferry would return itself by the force of the river.

Caleb arrived at the town of Monroe late one afternoon. The muddy road through the middle of town was heavily rutted. He slogged through the mud and stopped outside of the first saloon. It had too many rough looking characters hanging out in front, so he stepped up onto the boardwalk in front of the second saloon and peeked inside.

The smell of stale beer and cigar smoke poured from the door. Three men sat at one of the tables playing cards. A drunk slept on the floor in the back corner of the dimly lit room. The bartender was so short that Caleb could just see the top of his head over the bar. Everyone in the place jabbered away in a language that Caleb did not understand. Except for the passed out drunk, of course, who snored in plain English. Caleb had a bad feeling that this town might be trouble for him and that he had best move on.

He decided to move on to the river and see if he could get across. The Ouachita flowed along the west side of town, although there was a bit more town on the west bank. The river fairly bustled with a couple of small steamboats and dozens of canoes. The rough characters that Caleb had seen in town looked like preachers compared to the men he saw along the river. Most of them appeared to be trappers, since the docks had piles of furs stacked here and there. The ferry at the Ouachita was a little steam-operated boat covered in rough wooden planking. Caleb had to split a pile of firewood in return for a crossing. He didn't want to spend his last coins unless absolutely necessary. The old man who ran the ferry was grouchy and filthy.

"Where're you coming from, pup?" snarled the old man.

"I came from Vicksburg," replied Caleb.

"You're the first person to come from that way since the big river got up. How'n the heck did you get across all that water?"

"I just kept wadin' and walkin'," said Caleb.

Caleb kept at the stack of wood until he had split it all. The old man sat on the porch of his shack sipping whiskey from a pottery jug watching Caleb work. Every now and then, the old man would squirt a stream of brown tobacco juice into the dirt in front of him. When the wood was split and stacked, the old man stood up and scratched his belly.

"I'll take you across as soon as I get a full load wantin' to cross," he snarled.

Caleb glared at him and said, "I've split your stack of wood and I want to cross now. That was our deal." He set his pack on the floor of the little ferry and said, "Either you take me across or I do it myself."

"Why, you no more know how to run that steamer than a spotted dog," snarled the old man. "If you git fresh with me, I'll whup the tar outa you."

Caleb picked up the ax that he had been using to split the wood. He said, "I don't need to run the steam engine to git across. I can chop these moorin' lines and let it drift across. Sooner or later, it'll reach the west bank as I drift downstream."

"You chop them lines and I'll skin you alive," snarled the old man.

Caleb raised the ax over his head and prepared to chop the first of the two mooring lines. Before he could chop the line, the old man shouted, "Now wait a minute. I'll take you across. Just put that ax down."

The old man got up from his chair and shuffled down the ramp to the ferry. Caleb lowered the ax and backed to the far end of the ferry. The old man stepped onto the ferry and made a rush toward Caleb. He nearly turned himself inside out stopping his charge as he heard the pistol cock and looked down the barrel of the big Colt revolver that Caleb had whipped out of his pack.

"Lordy, don't shoot me boy!" said the old man.

"I'll blow you to Kingdom Come if you try anything," said Caleb. "Now git me across the river like you promised."

The old man backed to the mooring lines and let them slip. He fiddled with a couple of valves on the little steam engine and the ferry began to back across the river. It wasn't more than two hundred yards to the far side. Caleb kept the pistol pointed at the old man.

"You wouldn't really shoot an ol' man like me, would you?" said the old man.

"I'll do what I have to, and you'd better believe it."

The old man could see from the fire in Caleb's eyes that he meant what he said. As they neared the west bank, the old man adjusted a valve or two and pulled a lever. The paddle wheels on the sides of the ferry reversed directions and the boat bumped into the ramp. Caleb hopped off and waved the barrel of the pistol back and forth.

"Good riddance to you," shouted the old man as he chuffed back across the river.

Caleb uncocked his pistol and stuck it back into his pack. He walked up the ramp into the little community on the west bank of the river. He couldn't get away from the old grouch soon enough.

A week west of Monroe, Caleb stopped at a farm to ask directions from a man who was planting corn in a newly plowed field.

"Hello, sir," said Caleb.

"Why hello, who're you and whar you goin'?" asked the

man.

"I'm Caleb McDougal from Tennessee and I'm on my way to th' Nations to meet up with my Grandpaw. Is this the road to Shreveport?"

"Well, it's in the right direction but you're still a good fifty miles away. My name's Charley Benson and this here's my place. My wife died havin' our first youngun and the baby died too. So's I'm pretty much by myself here. Why don't you rest here a day or two? I'd appreciate the company and you can eat some of my cookin'. It wouldn't hurt you none to clean some of that mud offin' you either. You look like a derned mud turtle."

Caleb hadn't thought much about his appearance but he was indeed muddy from head to foot. He was now convinced that he wouldn't catch up with his Grandfather before reaching the Indian Nations anyway. A day or two off the road would be good. He could help out Mr. Benson to pay for his food and shelter. It would also be good to just talk and listen a bit after a week without any human contact other than the old grouch at the ferry in Monroe.

"Okay, I'll stay a day or two. What can I do to help around here? I won't eat your food for free."

"It's a deal. You see that stand of pines to the north?'

"Yessir."

"I want to clear it to add to this field I'm plantin'. Two can cut down trees a whole lot easier than one. If you help me for a coupla days, I'll feed you and give you some food to tote with you on your trip."

"Deal, where's the ax?"

"You just go down to the crick and git yoursef cleaned up while I finish up these last few rows. Then, we'll go check my fish lines and fix us up a mess of catfish for supper. We'll get to the tree cuttin' tomorrow."

An hour before dawn, a hoot owl woke Caleb. He got up and went outside to get some fresh water from the well. Crickets and frogs made a racket. Whippoorwills called in the woods around the cabin. The pine forest looked black in the darkness. Caleb could smell magnolias blooming somewhere. It was peaceful sitting in the starlight listening to the critters and night sounds. This farm wasn't all that different from Caleb's family farm. He used to get up early and sit on the old porch just like he was doing now. He was sad and happy at the same time. It was a curious feeling. To the east, false dawn was just fading to black before the glory of the real thing. He stretched a time or two, yawned and leaned back against the front of the cabin. A thick fog began to settle in around the farm. It made everything wet and drippy. The sky began to lighten in the east when he heard Mr. Benson stirring in the cabin.

"You're up early. I thought you'd run off," said Mr. Benson.

"No sir, Mr. Benson," said Caleb. "I've always been an early riser and I was just enjoyin' the comin' of the dawn."

"Call me Charley," said Mr. Benson. "Ever'body else does and when you start that Mr. Benson stuff I keep lookin' around for my Pap. Of course, he ain't no wheres around here."

"Yessir, Mr. … I mean Charley."

After breakfast of grits, bacon, and leftover cornbread, they set into the work of felling the pines. Charley wanted to clear the five acres between his existing field and the creek. They notched the big pines with axes to direct their fall and then used a two-man buck saw from the opposite side of the notch to fell the trees. Once a tree was down, they had to trim the branches and use the mules to drag the heavy logs to a spot just beyond the cabin. Charley said he planned to use the logs to enlarge the one-room cabin.

It took them three full days to cut down the fifty big pines, trim them, and clear out the small stuff growing beneath them. Of course, the stumps would need to be pulled before the field could be plowed and planted. They had two huge piles of limbs and brush that they set afire with some coal oil on the third night. They sat out under the stars after supper and watched the red sparks rise up from the bonfires. Each time the fire popped another shower of sparks was sent up.

"Thar's somethin' comfortin' about watchin' a fahr," said Charley. "I like t' look at the glowin' coals and see faces and critters and such in them."

"I like that bright blue color of the flame on some of the coals," said Caleb. "My Paw called it blue fire. He said it was the hottest."

"I expect he was right. I reckon you'll be leaving come mornin'," said Charley.

"Yes, I'd best be on my way if I'm ever gonna git there,"

said Caleb.

"It'd of taken me two weeks or more to clear that patch by myself. I sure do 'preciate your help. I'll work on them stumps off 'n on and have that patch ready for plantin' next season."

Caleb set out west right after breakfast. He was a bit sore from the hard work but he felt good overall. Charley had given him a pair of old boots to protect his feet and some corn meal and beans to put in his pack. Caleb whistled as he walked down the muddy road and the miles slid by. The pine forest smelled fresh and clean. Crows cawed at one another as he came near them. Occasionally, he would meet someone coming his way or would be overtaken by a rider heading west, but generally he kept to himself. He was at the east bank of the Red River by mid-afternoon of the third day.

V

Shreveport was a bustling place filled with all sorts of rough looking characters – black, red and white. Piles of furs and bales of cotton stood in sheds along the riverfront. Boats of every size and description were being loaded and unloaded. Stores and saloons lined the muddy streets. Folks milled about like a stirred up ant nest.

After an hour of asking about, Caleb found work loading furs and cotton onto a steamboat heading south. He concluded that by working on the docks he would find someone going up river who needed him to help with their work. After a week and a half, Caleb found a job with a group of traders heading up the Red River for the Indian Nations. They were a rough group but not as bad looking as the trappers and downright outlaws he saw everywhere.

"We'll take the *Marybelle* as far as Jefferson," said Mr. Arceneau. Phillipe Arceneau was the leader of three traders who moved back and forth from the Indian Nations to Louisiana. They traded pots and pans, mirrors and such to the Indians in exchange for furs that they sold in New Orleans. With New Orleans now under Union control, they stored their furs in a big warehouse in Shreveport until the war ended. The *Marybelle* was a sixty-foot stern-wheeler that made the run back and forth from Shreveport to Jefferson, Texas. The Red River was blocked above Shreveport by a logjam that stretched more than one hundred miles up the Red River. Therefore, river traffic was diverted to Jefferson, Texas via Twelve Mile Bayou, Caddo Lake and Big Cypress Creek.

"We'll load all our trade goods onto our wagons in Jefferson and then head on up to Doakesville near old Ft. Towson. We always do a good bit of trade with the Choctaws there," continued Mr. Arceneau.

Caleb's ears pricked up at that. They would make it to Choctaw country at last. His duties were to help load and unload the trade goods and furs and to drive one of the wagons.

The other two members of Mr. Arceneau's outfit were a former fur trapper, Bob Skinner, and a teamster named Jody Turnipseed. Bob had broken his back in a fall with a horse out in the Rocky Mountains. He walked in something between a limp and a lope and was bent forward at a forty-five degree angle from the middle of his back up. Jody was bald as an apple and covered in freckles. Both Bob and Jody were dressed in leather from head to foot. Each had a long knife handle protruding from his right boot, a pistol tucked into his belt and a big bore buffalo rifle in hand. Mr. Arceneau wore a black felt hat with a broad flat brim, a bright red silk shirt and fringed leather trousers. They were a sight to behold!

Mr. Arceneau said to Caleb, "Son, you're not going to last in those rags you're wearing. Let's fit you out with something a bit better for our trip."

After a trip to Mr. Arceneau's storehouse, Caleb didn't look much like a Tennessee farm boy anymore. His shiny black hair had grown longer, to his shoulders. He was now outfitted in a leather shirt and buckskin trousers. His feet were shod with buckskin moccasins. On top sat a broad brimmed tan leather hat. His skin had darkened even more until he looked like the other Indians working along the Shreveport docks. Only his blue eyes betrayed his half-breed ancestry. He had picked up a bit of a swagger and didn't look to be a boy to be messed with. He had a big knife strapped to one hip and the hog-leg Colt in a holster across his belly. No one would guess that he was just shy of fifteen. More likely, he looked seventeen or eighteen.

Jody had cut the leather flap off of the top of Caleb's holster. It was embossed with a big 'U.S.' and was a dead give away that it had been taken from a Yankee soldier. Likewise, he switched the holster's buckle for a plain brass one. Jody had said that there was no sense drawing the ire of partisans on either side.

Caleb, Jody and Bob unloaded their trade goods from the wagons to the docks and watched as the goods were lifted onto the deck of the *Marybelle*. At three o'clock, the *Marybelle*'s whistle blew and they chuffed out into the river. Caleb was elated; he had never been on a steamboat before and the throb of the engine, splash of the paddle wheel and rush of the tomato red water was exhilarating.

They stopped at Mooringsport for the night. Mr. Arceneau had a cabin on the boat although he spent most of the night at the card table in the main salon. Caleb, Bob and Jody slept on the deck next to their pile of trade goods. They took turns standing guard against the thieves that wandered the dock. Just after full sun the next day, the boat pulled away to cross the lake and enter Big Cypress bayou just above the little town of Uncertain. They reached Jefferson just before sunset.

Bob, Jody and Caleb went off to the livery to fetch their wagons and Mr. Arceneau's black gelding while Mr. Arceneau supervised the unloading at the dock. Four mules pulled each wagon. Caleb had his team hitched and ready just after Jody had finished hitching his team. They both helped Bob who was hampered by his bad back. Once they had the goods loaded onto the wagons, they set out due north. Mr. Arceneau wanted to get clear of Jefferson before they stopped for the night. He said they would be less likely to be struck by thieves if they got away from town. Three hours north of town they drove the wagons into a dense woods off to the side of the road to camp for the remainder of the night.

Caleb awoke from a sound sleep at the first gunshot. He banged his head on the bottom of the wagon under which he had been sleeping, scrambled out into the clearing and looked about with eyes as big as saucers.

"They're tryin' to steal the wagons!" shouted Jody who had been on watch. Jody fired again at movement in the moonlight and his target let out a groan. Someone started shooting from Bob's wagon and then all tarnation broke loose.

A big man on horseback charged out of the dark towards Caleb. Before he could think, Caleb drew the Colt and fired. All of his blue fire hatred for the Yankees had been unleashed on the charging man. The horse brushed by without its rider. The big man was hit but he got back up and pointed his gun at Caleb. Both shot simultaneously and the big man went down for good. Caleb felt the big man's bullet pass through his leather shirt and just barely graze his left side. He dived to his left just as another man rushed him from the woods. The man was thrown on top of Caleb by the force of Bob's 50-caliber buffalo gun.

A scream came from near Mr. Arceneau's tent. Caleb scrambled to his feet and ran toward the sound. He found Mr. Arceneau pulling his knife out of a dead man at his feet. Caleb could hear the sound of horses running away through the woods to the south.

"Well, we kilt four of 'em and the rest run off," said Jody. "Anybody hurt?'

Bob had a big wooden splinter in his cheek from a near miss that hit the wagon he was shooting from behind. Caleb had a knot on his head and a scratch on his side but the main casualties were two dead mules. The thieves had accidentally shot the mules during the battle.

"Dang!" exclaimed Mr. Arceneau. "I didn't think we'd been followed. At least none of us is incapacitated. We'll have to buy another pair of mules when we get to Linden. It's only an hour until daylight so we may as well get our breakfast, hitch up and go."

They removed the weapons, boots, and anything else of value from the bodies of the thieves, dug a shallow hole, and piled the bodies in.

"Better 'n they deserve," said Bob.

"Ol' Caleb stood his ground in the fight and pistol fought that bigun toe to toe," Bob said to Jody. "I'll pardner up with him anytime we get in a scrape, by Gol! He whupped that big horse pistol out before you could blink and popped that feller right outa th' saddle. Then just stood there calm as Miz Ellie's milk cow and shot 'im clear through the heart and paid no never mind to the bullet whizzin' at him. I ain't never seen nothin' like it."

The fire began to fade from Caleb's eyes as he grinned from ear to ear. He felt like he was a man among men and respected by his comrades. Inside, he knew he hadn't been brave at all. He just started shooting at what came at him out of reflex more than any act of courage. His pistol was out, cocked, aimed and fired almost by itself. *How did I do that?* he thought.

They redistributed the loads so that the two-mule wagon would have less weight and then started up the road to the north. By early afternoon, they had passed through Linden. Mr. Arceneau had bought the needed mules and told the blacksmith about the attack and where the dead were buried.

"Sounds like Big Bill Murphy's bunch," said the blacksmith. "This country'll be a sight better off with him dead. You say that young pup killed ol' Big Bill in a pistol fight? Boy howdy, that youngun must be somethin'. I'll tell Sheriff Parker where they're buried when he makes his round through town. He'll be glad to be shut of that bunch."

From Linden they traveled west to Hughes Springs without

further incident. From time to time, they would stop near a farmhouse and sell a few items of cookware. Mr. Arceneau was well known in the area to be a fair trader with quality goods.

In Hughes Springs, Mr. Arceneau had a lady friend named Nellie Fitzhugh who ran the sporting house next to the Last Dollar Saloon. Old Bob and young Jody seemed to be in good spirits when they returned to the wagons where they had left Caleb camped.

"Th' boss's stayin' in town," said Bob. "You're quite a celebrity, Caleb. Ever'body in town is talkin' about the man what shot down Big Bill Murphy. Caleb McDougal's a name that ever'body in this country will know!"

"Yep," said Jody. "Once-t Ol' Bob told the story at the Last Dollar, it spread like lightnin' through the town. "Course, Bob flavored it up a bit. He had you and Ol' Big Bill emptyin' your shooters at each other at ten paces. And, of course, he had to tell how he saved your hide with his buffalo gun, afore Big Bill's brother could kill you."

Caleb just laughed and shook his head. "You boys can sure tell some whoppers," he said.

After supper, the three of them sat around the campfire while Bob told a tale of his adventures in the Rocky Mountains trapping beaver. "I was up in th' headwaters of th' Platte back in '58 with a Blackfoot named Big Hands," said Bob. "We was trappin' beaver and had a passel of skins cached in a little cave up on the north side of th' river. I was cookin' our beans at our little camp when I heard Big Hands runnin' like the devil was on his tail through the bresh. All of a sudden he busted past me with a grizzly b'ar snappin' at his backside. That ol' b'ar was, runnin' an' lookin' back over his shoulder at me when he run smack dab into a big fir tree trunk. Well, that took most of th' starch outta his britches. He sat up on his hind end shakin' his head and moanin'. He took one more look at me and then lit out up the mountainside like he thought I'd whack him agin or somethin'. Big Hands came slinkin' back and wanted to know what I'd done with his b'ar. I tolt him that I ran th' booger off with a willer switch for upsettin' my peace and quiet."

Jody said, "I wouldn't believe too much of Bob's tales if'n I was you, Caleb."

Bob and Jody were passing a bottle back and forth when suddenly they heard someone moving around in the brush about fifty yards off to their right. All three were belly down under the nearest wagon with their guns at the ready in a heartbeat.

"Who's out yonder in them bushes?" shouted Bob. "If'n you don't come out with your hands up we're gonna shoot!"

"Don't shoot!" called out a young voice. "We didn't mean no harm. We're comin' out."

Out slunk five boys between eight and ten years old.

"We just wanted to get a look at the gun fighter what kilt Big Bill, that's all," said the boldest of the group.

"I ain't no gun fighter," said Caleb. "Now you boys run on home to Mama before we skin the lot of you."

The boys scattered like quail while Bob and Jody roared with laughter.

"Caleb, I swear if you ain't a corker," said Jody. "When you came bilin' up from under th' wagon, those boys jumped like they was snake bit. I think two of 'em wet their britches."

"You need to stop spreadin' these tall tales about me," said Caleb. "Before you know it, somebody will believe it."

"Tain't ever'body what kilt a man at your age," said Bob.

"Two," said Caleb.

"What?" exclaimed both Bob and Jody.

Caleb told them the story of the Yankee at the farm and his trip across Mississippi and Louisiana.

"Why laws sakes, ain't you th' thumper," said Bob. "I thought I was a bull of th' woods by goin' to th' mountains at age seventeen. But here you've bested me and you ain't even sixteen yet."

"I ain't but fourteen," said Caleb.

"Lordy!" said Jody. "You shore fooled me. I'd a guessed sixteen or seventeen or maybe a runty eighteen. You gonna be a regular lobo wolf by the time you gets growed."

"I'd appreciate it if you kept my age and the dead Yankee to yourselves," said Caleb. "Mr. Arceneau might not keep me on if he thinks I'm too young and the Yankees don't need to be lookin' for me out here."

"Swear," they both vowed.

It took two days to reach the Sulfur River crossing. The land was swampy and the heavy wagons wallowed through the muddy road. The air was thick with mosquitoes and stank from the rotting vegetation.

"This here's the stretch I hate the worst," said Bob. "Dern skeeters bleed you dry whilst the mud and the stink just sticks to your innerds."

"Quit your fussin',' said Jody. "You're gittin' to sound like an ol' woman. 'Sides, we're all sufferin' just like you."

Caleb chuckled to himself. Jody and Bob bickered almost constantly even though it was obvious what good friends they were. Mr. Arceneau was quiet most of the time. He wasn't unfriendly but seemed reserved. Caleb thought that he must be what his Paw had called a gentleman. At least, he was a close as Caleb had ever come to meeting one.

The river crossing went off without a hitch. Three miles north of the river, they climbed a hill and were free of the swamp. The sky was so blue that it almost hurt to look at it. The sun was bright and the country was completely covered in wildflowers. Most of them were bright yellow but a few red ones and blue ones were in patches here and there. The fragrance of pines was a blessing after the stench of the swamp. Caleb dozed on his wagon seat as the mules plodded along. This was the first time he had felt at peace since he had left the family farm.

That night, they set up camp just outside Dalby Springs. Mr. Arceneau said that the springs were medicinal and they could sell some of the water to folks further north. The town that had built up around the springs was typical of small towns across the south. Mr. Arceneau and Jody went into town to arrange for the jugs of water while Bob and Caleb set up camp and got supper going.

"Stir up the fire under that pot of beans, Caleb," said Bob. "I'll go fetch us some water from the crick."

Bob worked his way through the dense woods toward the creek. He wasn't more than fifty yards from the campsite when someone hit him along the side of his head with a pistol barrel. He was out cold before he hit the ground.

"So, you're the famous pistolero who shot Big Bill Murphy?" said the young man who stepped into the clearing. Caleb squatted beside the fire adding some cut up salt pork to the pot of beans. Caleb lowered the lid of the pot and stood up slowly. There were two of them standing twenty feet away. The one on the left was six feet tall and skinny as a snake. The short fat one on the right avoided Caleb's eyes and seemed nervous. The skinny one continued, "I bet you ain't near as quick as they say."

"I don't want no trouble, " said Caleb. "We're just passin' through and fixin' our supper. The boss and the others'll be back any minute."

"Your compadre's sleepin' down by the crick and there ain't no one else around but you," said Skinny. "Bill Murphy was my Ma's cousin. I'm Johnny Hanks and I'm here to settle the score." With that, he reached for his pistol.

Caleb's hog leg was out, cocked and aimed square at the middle of Skinny's chest before Skinny could clear leather. Skinny let the pistol fall back into its holster and let out a squeal. "Dang, I'm sorry. Please don't kill me."

"What in the heck is going on here?" said Mr. Arceneau as he stepped into the clearing.

"This feller and his pal just showed up and said they wanted to shoot me. I think they may have killed Bob," said Caleb. "He went to fetch water and never came back."

"Jody, go take a look," said Mr. Arceneau. "You two drop your weapons and lie down on the ground over here. Caleb, pick up their weapons and put them in the wagon."

Bob rubbed his head as he and Jody returned from the shadows. He had a knot on the side of his head and a little blood running from his left ear.

"Who whopped me?" said Bob.

"He did," said the fat boy.

"Shut up!" said Skinny.

"Get up," said Mr. Arceneau. "Pull off your boots and strip down to your drawers. "

They did as ordered.

"Jody, tie up their clothes and boots and tie them to the saddle of that bay pony,' said Mr. Arceneau.

Jody did as told. Mr. Arceneau smacked the bay and the paint on their rumps and the horses raced off to the east.

"Your horses will be home without you and your families will be worried. I'll leave your knives and guns with the Postmaster in Dalby Springs. If we ever see you again, we'll shoot you on sight. Now you boys get on home," said Mr. Arceneau.

After the young men had run off, Mr. Arceneau said to Caleb, "Son, you're getting to be a liability through no fault of your own. Would you have shot him?"

"I didn't want to but I'd have shot them both if they'd cleared leather," Caleb said. "I didn't come all this way to be killed by some outlaw's kin."

The next morning at breakfast, Mr. Arceneau said, "I think it would be best if you take off that pistol and change out of those buckskins. And, maybe we should call you by another name, Caleb. That way, we can tell anyone that we meet that Caleb is no longer with us and that you took his place. I think it would be safer for all of us."

"How about 'Buck'," said Jody. "No offense, but you look like an Injun Buck and it's a common enough name."

"All right by me," said Caleb. "I don't want no more trouble."

Caleb shed his buckskins and put on a pair of canvas trousers and a plaid shirt. He tucked his hair up into a straw hat and put a pair of plow boots on his feet.

"Why, look at you," laughed Jody. "If'n I hadn't watched you change clothes, I'd of thought we had a new farm boy amongst us."

They all had a good laugh, hitched up their teams and set off up the road.

A week later they set up camp outside old Fort Towson just north of the Red River. They had sold a little of their stock of goods to farmers and town folk along the way but had saved most of it for trade with the Indians for furs.

"This is where we part ways," said Mr. Arceneau. "I wish you well, Buck."

"Thank you, sir," said 'Buck'. "I sure am going to miss y'all."

"I'm sure we'll cross trails again someday," said Bob.

Buck bought a buckskin mare, saddle and bridle from the man at the livery stable.

"She neck reins real good," said the man at the livery. "Be careful around dogs, though. She'll buck and kick if a dog gits aroun' behind 'er."

"I'll mind the dogs," said Buck. "How far to Durant?"

"Durant's a good sixty, seventy miles west," said the man. "I expect it take you two, three days. The road's purty good but there's road agents about. You'd best keep your eyes peeled sharp."

"Thanks, I'll stay alert," said Buck. He gave a wave and rode off to the west.

The trip to Durant was uneventful. He rode into town and dismounted outside the blacksmith's shop. He tied 'Chigger' to the rail and walked into the livery.

"I see Billy sold you that dog stompin' mare," laughed the blacksmith. "She's got a good easy gait but she's heck on dogs. What can I do for you?"

"I'm lookin' for my Grandpaw. He's a Choctaw and should be settin' up a store somewheres around here. He should have come in from Mississippi in the last month or so."

"Is his name *Ofi Humma*?" asked the blacksmith.

"That's him," replied Buck excitedly.

"Him and his crowd are building their store on the Washita River about twelve miles west of town," said the blacksmith.

"Thanks," said Buck as he remounted Chigger.

It was just before sunset when Buck rode into camp. A young Choctaw man stepped away from the fire toward Buck and said, "Evening, what do you want here?"

Buck introduced himself and said, "I've come all the way from Tennessee to find my Grandpaw. His name is *Ofi Humma*. Is he here?"

"Welcome cousin! He is my grandfather, too. I am *Isuba Lusa*, Black Horse. I am also called James, which is my Christian name. I will take you to Grandfather."

PART II

Indian Nations – Fall, 1873

VI

Eleven years had passed since Buck first came to live with his grandfather. At twenty-five years of age, Buck had grown to six feet two inches tall and he weighed a solid one hundred ninety five pounds. His size and his deep blue eyes marked him as different from his neighbors but otherwise he was completely accepted by the rest of the community. Though he was reserved and somewhat of a loner, he had gained the respect of almost everyone for his skills at hunting and tracking. He was by far the best marksman that anyone knew and could outrun everyone but his older cousin James. He liked the name, Buck, and had kept it.

Building the store and a house and getting to know his Choctaw relatives consumed the first year. Since then, he had learned the business of running a store and helping his grandfather with whatever needed doing. Most of the neighbors were farmers and life was not a great deal different from what he had known in Tennessee. Also, almost everyone was a Choctaw but they didn't really seem to be any different from the neighbors back in Tennessee. Of course, he was now a storekeeper instead of a farmer. Buck, James and James' younger brother, Luke, worked together in the store and had become fast friends.

Last year, Buck and James had both fallen in love with Becky Griffin. It was Buck's second love, but Sarah had just been 'puppy love', Becky was different. She was a small, pretty twenty year old who lived nearby with her family. She kept her raven black hair in bangs across her forehead and cut straight off just above her shoulders. James eventually won out in the courtship duel. Buck understood that her family's preference for someone of pure Choctaw blood weighed heavily in her choice. Buck was best man at the wedding and truly was happy for them both.

Buck's former employer, Phillipe Arceneau, had prospered in the years following the Civil War. He now remained in New Orleans and directed a large trade business throughout Louisiana, east Texas, Arkansas and the Indian Nations. Much of the business was devoted to supplying the general stores found in the towns and villages throughout the region. Thieves had murdered Bob Skinner during a trip to deliver a wagonload of supplies to Ft. Smith, Arkansas, but Jody Turnipseed was still active in the company.

"James, go get Grandfather. I see Jody's wagons comin' down the hill," called Buck from the front of the store. "It's a good thing, too, since we're running low on tinned goods and sugar."

"I'll see if he's finished burning that hog," laughed James. James went out the back door to where Luke and Grandfather were pit-roasting a pig.

"Grandfather, Jody's coming down the hill in his wagons. Buck thought you'd want to order some supplies from him," said James.

"Luke, start digging the dirt off the top of those coals. When we get the pig out, I want you to cut off a hind quarter and take it over to Becky's folks," said Grandfather.

"Yes sir," said Luke

The old man then said, "James, let's go see Jody."

Buck stepped off the porch and waved to Jody. "Howdy, Buck!" shouted Jody. "It's good to see you agin. This here's my new helper, Sam."

"Pleased to meet you, Sam. Jody, you got anything left for us out here in the sticks?" said Buck.

"You betcha," said Jody. "Whatcha need? Oh, how do, Mr. Gibson." Grandfather and James had just walked up. Grandfather's Christian name was Dan Gibson.

Grandfather pulled a piece of paper from his shirt pocket and unfolded it. "Here's my list," he said.

Jody looked over the list and said, "I've got everthin' on here but the two hunert pounds of eight penny nails. I only got one hunert-pound keg left."

"One keg'll have to do, then," said Grandfather. "James and Buck will help you and your helper unload. Come on back out under the oaks when you're finished. I've got a hog cooking and need to dig him out of the pit. You can join us for lunch."

Buck, James, Becky, Jody, Sam and Grandfather sat under the trees at a big plank table eating barbequed pork, turnip greens and corn bread when the Comanches struck. There were eight of them led by White Elk. The raiders rode in at a full gallop. Sam slumped over dead on the table, killed by the first arrow before anyone realized that they were under attack. James grabbed Becky and pushed her to the ground behind him while trying to shield her with his body. The move saved her life but cost him his.

Grandfather made it to the back of the store before one of the raiders ran a lance through him. Jody pulled one of the riders and his horse down but was clubbed unconscious by another Comanche. Buck pulled one of the Comanches off of his pony, threw him to the ground, and killed him with a shovel before a shot from White Elk's rifle knocked Buck flat on his back. Then, in one move, White Elk spurred his pony, leaned over and snatched up Becky as his horse ran past the overturned table.

Though dazed, Buck sat up in the blood stained dirt. He could hear some of the Comanches ransacking the store. They ran out carrying all of the weapons and ammunition they could hold. The store began to burn as Buck crawled over to where Grandfather lay. The old man was dead. Buck could hear Becky's screams as she bounced along across the neck of the horse White Elk rode. The Comanches were riding off to the west in a cloud of dust when Buck blacked out.

From far off, Buck thought he heard someone calling his name. "Buck, look at me! Can you talk? We saw the smoke and heard the shooting," said Ben Green. Ben and Mary Green were the nearest neighbors. They lived only a quarter mile east of the store.

Buck willed himself out of the darkness as Ben continued, "We got the fire put out before too much was burned. Who was it that attacked? I pulled a Kiowa lance out of poor old Dan. The arrows in James and that white man over there look Comanche to me."

"We were making so much noise joking and laughing that we didn't hear them coming," said Buck. "There were eight of them riding Medicine Hat paint ponies. I killed one, but they shot me and killed the rest of us. Except Becky, they took her and must have carried off the dead Comanche."

"They didn't kill all of you," said Ben. "Mary's got Jody over there by the table. He's alive but his head's all busted up. I don't know if he'll make it or not. That bullet went right through your chest but it looks like it missed your vitals.

RICHARD WILLIS

The pain in Buck's left shoulder came in waves, each more intense than the last. "I think I've gotta lay back down," said Buck. He slumped back in the dirt as blackness closed in again.

VII

White Elk knew that he was a respected leader among his people. He had first proved himself against Kit Carson and the white army at the Battle of Adobe Walls back in the winter of 1864. The whites had claimed a big victory but the Comanches and Kiowas thought otherwise. Had they not driven the white army away in full retreat? True, the Indian loses were heavy, but their weapons were inferior to the howitzers of Carson's forces. Did not the Comanches and Kiowas now roam where they wished? White Elk's small band raided throughout New Mexico, Kansas, the Indian Nations, Texas and Mexico. The Comanches had been nearly run out of Texas before the war that the whites made on themselves. The Texas Rangers had driven them as far as the Palo Duro Comancheria but the Yankee whites had defeated the Texans in their great war and the Yankee Army had disbanded the Rangers.

The white army was powerful but slow. White Elk and his warriors were quick and among the best light cavalry ever to exist. They were unsurpassed in their abilities to hunt and to fight from horseback. In battle, they struck and moved on. Their raids on the whites, Mexicans and other Indian tribes secured for them horses and women. Their own villages were small and mobile. The white army's tactic of destroying their villages had led to the need for new tactics. They moved often and only felt safe in their stronghold in Palo Duro Canyon.

White Elk and his people hated everyone who was not Comanche or Kiowa, their long-term allies. They showed little mercy on those they came across. Carson's men had killed White Elk's family as they slept in their tepees. White Elk's family had been camped with a group of Kiowas on the day of the great battle at Adobe Walls. Carson and the Army had attacked the Indian village just west of the old fort. They had destroyed the lodges and had killed or run off everyone. The news of the massacre traveled quickly to the thousands camped at Palo Duro. The Comanches and Kiowas poured out of their stronghold and attacked Carson's forces repeatedly throughout the day. White Elk killed one of the soldiers and wounded several. He rode in and out of their ranks and showed them that he did not fear their bullets. If it had not been for the howitzers, White Elk was certain that the Comanches and Kiowas would have killed all of the invaders. As it was, they had to keep their distance and make only small quick strikes against the enemy. By late afternoon, the whites were on the run back to the west. White Elk led a small group that attempted to block the retreat by setting the grass of the Llano on fire but the whites were able to offset that by building backfires of their own.

White Elk considered the whites to be his mortal enemies and he considered any of the Indians who lived in peace with the whites to be traitors, including these Choctaws living in the Nations. This young Choctaw woman flopping on the neck of his horse would bring a good price from the Comancheros down south. He was confident that he and his men would not be followed. The loss of Little Feather was a blow but White Elk was certain that all of the whites and Choctaws had been killed. How could they have been eating together and without any guards or weapons at hand? There was little glory in defeating enemies as weak as these. There would be no song of this raid to sing at the fire, especially since they had had to leave their fallen comrade. They stopped briefly to bury Little Feather before continuing west.

Lord, but it's hot, said Jed Holloway to himself. He moved along the rows picking sweet corn in his field. He had bought this farm from the Chickasaws two years earlier. The deep red soil here along the Red River was fertile and he had a good young team of mules. Martha and little Jed were back at their cabin. The boy was eight and becoming more useful with the work. In fact, the boy was hauling water for Martha right now. Jed was proud of the new room he had built on the back of the cabin. A three-room cabin was prosperous by his accounting. If the folks back in Arkansas could see him now!

Ol' Bugler, his redbone hound, had been snuffling around the rows of corn. *He's smellin' a coon, no doubt*, thought Jed. Suddenly, Ol' Bugler started growling. The hair stood up in a ridge down the middle of his back. The hound started backing toward the cabin two hundred yards away.

"What's gotten into you, you fool dog," said Jed as he picked up the basket of roasting ears. "You smell a b'ar, or whut?"

BLUE FIRE

Jed started for the wagon at the end of the field. Then he heard the horses coming. Jed dropped the basket of corn and ran for the wagon and his rifle. Just as he jumped for the wagon, a Henry rifle cracked. The heavy .44 caliber bullet hit him just to the right of his spine, shattering his shoulder blade and ruining his right lung. He dragged himself up by the wagon wheel and grabbed his rifle. The second bullet smashed into the middle of his chest. He slumped back down as darkness closed in on him. *I must be dyin'*, he thought. And he was.

White Elk saw Black Hand race toward the wagon, leap from his pony and quickly cut away Jed's scalp. He held the bloody trophy high and yelled, "Ye-Ye-Ye!" in delight. He immediately swung back onto his pony's back.

A shotgun roared from one of the cabin windows and buckshot rattled through the corn. Martha screamed, "Little Jed! Get back in the cabin!" Little Jed sprinted from the well into the back of the cabin.

White Elk shouted in Comanche, "Badger, circle the cabin and set the roof on fire! The man is dead. If we can capture the woman and boy, we will have more to sell to Quintana."

The cabin was well built of stout logs. The windows were shuttered with heavy planks with a cross cut into each set of shutters. The cross was not there for religious purposes. It was so that a rifle could swing right or left, up or down without exposing the cabin occupants to much in the way of incoming fire. The roof was covered in thick sod.

Badger and Long Tooth dug furiously through the sod with their knives. White Elk and the others rode back and forth outside of the effective range of the shotgun. Occasionally, they were harmlessly pelted with shot as the woman kept up a steady volley. The boy was plinking away from another window with a small caliber rifle. Deadly enough if he managed to hit a vital spot. Badger piled dry brush on the spot in the roof where he and Long Tooth had been digging. He set the pile on fire and stepped back. Soon smoke began pouring from the windows' gun ports.

Martha was desperate. She knew that Jed had been killed. The choking smoke was intolerable. "Little Jed, we're going to burn in here. When I say, jump out the back door and run for the barn.

Take your rifle and all the shells you can tote."

"Yes ma'am," said Little Jed. He stuffed his pockets with shells and checked to make certain that his rifle was fully loaded.

"Now!" shouted Martha as she fired both barrels at the circling Indians.

Martha reloaded the shotgun as she bolted out of the back door of the cabin. One of the Comanches ran after Little Jed. She snapped the breech closed and shot from the hip at the Indian. Little Jed flew forward from the impact of two barrels of double ought buckshot. He had darted back right into her line of fire.

Martha stood stunned from the sight of just having killed her own son. Badger jumped down from the cabin roof and ran toward the woman. Martha regained her senses just as Badger got to her. She whirled on him in a fury, cracking him in the side of his head with the shotgun. He fell to his knees and shook his head to clear it. Long Tooth shot the woman through the heart just as she was about to crush Badger's skull with the raised shotgun. Overwhelming these settlers was not as easy as they had thought it would be. Now that the band was better equipped with the new repeating rifles, they had been a bit overconfident and careless.

"She fought like one of our women," said Badger rubbing his head. "Too bad you killed her."

"If I had not killed her, you would be the dead one," said Long Tooth.

"Take the ponies from the barn, then burn it," said White Elk. "We have no use for mules, kill them. Cut some meat from the young mule. It will be good to eat. Tie this Choctaw woman to one of the ponies." He dropped Becky from the neck of his pony. Badger dragged her to one of the dead farmer's horses and lifted her onto its back. He checked the rawhide strips on her wrists to make certain that they were secure. He cut a strip of bloody hide from one of the dead mules, looped it under the horse's belly, and tied each end to her feet. White Elk grabbed the reins of her horse and set off to the west.

VIII

Becky was stunned by the events of the day. She had been wrenched from the arms of her dying husband and carried off. She felt a mixture of horror, grief and terror but mostly she just felt numb. In fact, she felt as though she were watching herself from some distance away in an almost dream state. As she had watched the slaughter at the Holloway's farm, she nearly lost consciousness.

During the initial ride from the store, she had tried to slip off the neck of the Comanche's horse but he had rapped her repeatedly on her back and head with the barrel of his rifle until she quit struggling. White Elk's pony had a smooth gait but her position, lying with her belly across the pony's withers, had bruised her ribs and belly. Now she rode along bareback with her feet tied to one another under the belly of this horse and her hands painfully tied together. It was all she could do to stay on the horse and hold tightly to a handful of its mane. The rawhide thong at her wrists had rubbed her arms bloody, likewise the one hobbling her ankles. Without a saddle or blanket, the insides of her legs were being rubbed raw. The dead farmer's horse had a choppy gait that bounced her terribly. She wanted to cry and feared that she would slip off the horse's back and be kicked to death beneath the horse's belly. There was nothing to do but hang on as best she could.

By late afternoon, they had left the scrubby oak forest and loped along across a rolling, almost treeless plain. The grass was belly high on the horses. Meadowlarks scattered before them while an occasional hawk soared overhead. The river ran parallel to their route just to the south of them. The stream was a half-mile wide expanse of rusty red sand with a meandering course of tomato red water snaking back and forth through the sand. White Elk kept up a steady pace all afternoon. Becky feared that they would ride all night too. She knew that if they did, she would surely fall and die.

To her surprise, they stopped for the night along the riverbank a good distance west of the lunchtime slaughter. Becky was given some bitter, muddy water to drink and a piece of roasted mule to eat. White Elk tied her to a little sumac at the edge of the little camp they had made. The men talked among themselves and laughed when one pointed to Becky and said something. She understood almost nothing in Kiowa or Comanche but had an idea that they did not intend to kill her now. *Why else would they have kept her alive this long?* She tried not to think about that too much. Soon, exhaustion overcame her and she fell into a fitful sleep.

She awoke sometime in the middle of the night. The fire had burned down to coals but she could see that one of the Comanches was awake and guarding the horses. Becky was no fool and she well knew what the Comanches did to the women they captured. She had heard stories of their cruelty all her life. Her chance of escape was nil. Even if she slipped away from the camp, the Comanches would quickly find her. Besides, she was tied so tightly that she couldn't free herself. She drifted back into a restless sleep. At dawn, she was awakened, given more water and tied back on the horse. Off they went following the north bank of the river ever westward.

Just before dark of the tenth day, they entered Palo Duro Canyon and arrived at a large Comanche village. Becky was taken into a tepee by two women and tethered to a short wooden post next to a bed made of skins. She was not treated roughly but the women weren't friendly either. That night, one of the Comanche women untied Becky's hands and feet and rubbed the raw skin with buffalo fat. A blond white woman dressed in Comanche clothing was brought into the tent.

"I am called Yellow Hair,' said the woman in broken English. "I became one of the People when I was a small child. If you try to escape or if you give us trouble, your hands and feet will be tied again and you will be beaten."

"What is to happen to me?" asked Becky.

"You belong to White Elk. He will tell you when he is ready," said Yellow Hair. "Be quiet now and sleep."

At daybreak, four women including Yellow Hair took Becky to the river's edge. "Take off your clothes and wash yourself," said Yellow Hair. One of the women took Becky's blue dress while the others divided up her undergarments and shoes. She was given a plain buckskin dress and a pair of moccasins to wear.

"Come, you must help us gather firewood," said Yellow Hair.

Becky spent all of that day and the next performing various

chores to which she was assigned. She had not seen White Elk or any of the others who took her since she had arrived at the village. At night, she was placed back in the tent along with an old woman who slept across the entrance to the teepee. There was no way to get past the old woman and the sides and back of the tepee were staked too tightly to slip under.

On the third morning, White Elk appeared at the entrance of the tepee and spoke to the old woman. The old woman left and White Elk entered the lodge. He surprised Becky by speaking to her in English.

"I have fasted and purified myself and the spirits have spoken to me. It is time for us to ride south while my *puha*, my medicine, is strong. You will be taken south and sold to Quintana Gomez. If you give me no trouble, you will not be harmed by me or by my warriors. If you try to escape or if you give me trouble, you will become entertainment for my warriors and will still be sold to Quintana. The choice is yours."

Becky was taken outside and tied back onto the pony. This time, her wrists were not so tightly bound, though her feet were still tied together by a leather thong beneath the pony's belly. Also, this time, her legs were protected by a blanket across the pony's back. White Elk and four of the others from the raiding party that had attacked the store set off south, leading her up out of the canyon.

IX

Buck awoke to find his younger cousin, Luke, asleep in a chair next to the bed. It took a moment to determine where he was and to remember what had happened. Lordy, but his mouth was dry and his shoulder hurt like all thunder. The shoulder throbbed with a deep pain at each heartbeat. He moaned as he sat up. His moan caused Luke to open his eyes with a start. "How long?" asked Buck.

"Five days," said Luke. "Miz Green's been takin' care of you and I've just been waitin'. They killed everybody but you, Jody and Becky. Jody's head is all messed up and he ain't woke up yet. I wanted to go after Becky but everybody convinced me to wait until you could go too."

"Do you know which way they went when they left here?" asked Buck.

"They headed west. Everybody thinks they'll take her back to the Comancheria," said Luke.

"Get me my britches and see if Miz Green can fix me something to eat," said Buck.

Buck struggled to control his rage. *I couldn't avenge my Maw and Paw nor my brothers by killin' all of those Yankees*, he thought. *But, by gol, these Comanches will pay. I'll follow them through the Devil's own fire if I have to.*

Early the next morning, Buck and Luke were mounted, provisioned, armed and on their way. Buck's shoulder hurt but it was manageable. It had loosened up a bit after he was up and moving about. He had managed to keep down a plate of eggs and grits but he felt weak and a bit shaky. He decided that their best hope of killing the Comanches and recovering Becky would be to catch the band before they got her to the Comancheria. He hoped that the Comanches had taken their time stealing horses and raiding farms on their way west.

Buck was mounted on his big black Morgan stallion and Luke had James' bay gelding. The Morgan wasn't the fastest horse around but he had plenty of bottom and could be counted on for the long haul. Buck borrowed two additional horses from Ben Green and Grandfather's best young mule. Grandfather's mule was faster than many of the horses around and had won several races. With two mounts each, one to ride and one to lead, they could hopefully keep from running the horses to death. Buck and Luke were well armed since the Comanches did not get everything from the store. They each carried a new Henry rifle and a new Model 3, .44 caliber Smith & Wesson revolver. In addition Buck carried his old cap and ball Colt. The mule was packed with provisions and grain for the horses.

By switching mounts every hour or so and alternating periods of walking and loping the horses, they were able to cross the border into the Panhandle of Texas and cover the distance to the edge of the Palo Duro in eight days. They had stopped on the first day at the Holloway farm and buried what was left of the bodies they discovered there. They had fed their animals and added a bit more grain from Holloway's bin to what the mule was carrying.

For the last several days, they had ridden across a flat treeless expanse of brown grass. They had been slowed due to the necessity to search for water in this dry country. Occasionally, they would see a small group of antelope or scare up a jackrabbit or two, but mostly there wasn't much to see other than grass and clear blue sky.

Palo Duro Canyon is invisible until one is almost to the edge. It plunges straight down from the grassy plain with a startling suddenness. Its walls are a rainbow of colored rocks and clays. The floor is strewn with colorful spires, hoodoos and other formations. The little trickle of the Prairie Dog Town Fork of the Red River meanders through the red sand of the canyon floor. As Buck and Luke arrived at the rim, they reined in their horses; both they and their horses were pretty well spent. They camped for the night in a little draw that poured off the rim into the canyon.

Before dawn, Buck shook Luke gently. "You stay here and keep the horses quiet," whispered Buck. "I'm goin' to scout northwest along the rim on foot and see if I can locate the Comanche village."

"Okay," said Luke. "How long do you think you'll be gone?"

"Long as it takes but I'll be back before dark tonight for sure. Keep yourself hid and watch sharp," said Buck. "If you hear me shootin', come runnin' with the horses."

Buck eased off into the dark. He found the Comanche

village at mid-morning. There were many little clusters of tepees strung out along the trickle of the river running on the floor of the canyon. People milled about going through their normal routines. The villagers were too far away to identify individuals but he assumed that Becky would still be wearing the blue dress she had on when she was taken. No blue dresses in sight. In fact, there was nothing but blankets and buckskin in sight. If she was down there, she was probably in one of the tepees.

Buck was pretty certain she had made it this far. As they followed the trail of the raiders west, he had found signs of their attack on the Holloway farm and their nightly camps. And, Becky, bless her, had left a little scrap of the hem of her dress tied to a bush at each campsite. She obviously knew or at least hoped someone would be coming for her. Recovering Becky was important but she would also lead him to the Comanches who had killed his people. He planned to kill them for what they had done.

There was no way to know where Becky might be held and any attempt to ride into the camp would be stupid and fatal. In fact, he and Luke were lucky that they had not been discovered when riding to the canyon rim yesterday. After an hour of watching the village, Buck spotted two men mounted on paint ponies and carrying brand new Henry rifles. The shiny brass frames of the Henrys were like a beacon in the sun. Those had to be two of the rifles stolen from Grandfather's store. The riders headed southeast away from the village.

Buck crawled back from the edge of the rim and began running back to where Luke and the horses were hidden. As he neared the draw, Buck stopped and gave the "come covey" call of a quail hen so as to alert Luke that it was he who approached. Luke answered the call twice as prearranged.

"Two of the men who raided the store are ridin' out of the canyon to the south," said Buck. "If we can catch them alive, maybe we can get some information about Becky. The village I found is too big for us to sneak into and find her without bein' discovered."

Buck and Luke rode hard for two hours, keeping well back from the canyon rim. They found an obvious trail down into the canyon and then they rode back upstream to hide in a stand of cottonwoods along the riverbank. Buck was certain that they had gotten ahead of the two riders if, indeed, they were still coming this way. Buck left Luke with the horses. He took his horsehair riata and his rifle and set out upriver on foot to find an ambush site. The water course was about fifteen feet wide and five or six inches deep as it meandered across the half mile wide red sand of the river bed. Here and there were cottonwoods and willows or a pile of logs and other flotsam from the last big flood. Buck selected a log pile with a half-mile view up river into the wide canyon. He would have a good view of anyone coming down the canyon and a clear field of fire if needed.

Badger and Long Tooth were delayed in joining White Elk and the others. Their families had needed meat and they had remained behind to hunt for a couple of days. Now that their family obligations were satisfied, they hurried to catch up with their comrades. They joked as they rode along about the whiskey and horses that they would get for the woman. Quintana Gomez had a big appetite for pretty young women and was generous in his trades, especially if the woman had not been badly used. They had to hurry to catch up to the others but there was plenty of time. Quintana's group ranged about in Old Mexico and up and down the Pecos River from northern New Mexico to the Rio Bravo, Rio Grande the whites called it. The Comancheros often stayed at their big camp in the canyon where the Pecos joined the Rio Bravo and that was many sleeps ride to the south. White Elk and the others would not be moving too fast because of the woman.

They stopped just beyond a big bend in the canyon to let their horses drink. Badger motioned to his friend. Something reflected the sun from a spot in the sand near that log pile a few hundred yards downstream from them. They slowly rode toward the bright, shiny, brass object.

"I think it's a rifle like these we carry," said Badger. "Do you suppose White Elk or one of the others left it there?"

Badger jumped down from his pony and ran toward the rifle lying in the sand. As he reached to pick it up, the sand around him erupted as a noose leapt from the sand and jerked his feet out from under him. At almost the same instant, a rifle boomed and Long Tooth fell from his pony with a crimson bullet wound in the middle of his forehead.

Badger's rifle was just out of reach but he pulled his knife in an attempt to cut the braided, horsehair rope from around his legs and he spun toward the direction from which the shot had come. As he looked up, the big man was on him. He looked like the same man that White Elk had shot when they took the woman. *How can he be here? Surely, he is dead,* thought Badger. But this man was not dead. In fact, Badger was surprised by the strength of the man. This man seemed as large and strong as the great humped-back bears that lived in the mountains far to the west. For the first time since he was a child, Badger was frightened. The big man's blue eyes flamed with rage.

Buck tore the knife from the Comanche's hand and lifted him clear of the ground with his hands clamped around the Comanche's throat. Luke came riding up just as Buck released the gasping Comanche.

"Gather up their weapons and catch their ponies," said Buck. "Let's see if we can get any information out of this one."

Buck bound the Comanche's upper arms to his sides, tied his hands behind his back and hobbled his feet. He dragged the Comanche to his feet and pitched him belly down across one of the ponies, then tied his feet and hands together under the pony's belly. Buck swung up into his saddle and headed back toward the stand of cottonwoods leading the pony with the Comanche on it. Luke followed on his gelding leading the other pony.

Buck untied the rope under the pony's belly and dragged the Comanche off the pony and to a spot under one of the big cottonwoods. He threw Luke's rope over a limb ten feet up in the cottonwood, slipped a noose around the Comanche's neck, drew the rope tight and tied it off to the trunk of the tree.

Buck didn't speak but a few words of Comanche but he knew enough Kiowa to get by and he was fairly certain this man understood some Kiowa.

"Where is the woman in the blue dress and the ones who killed my people?" asked Buck.

The Comanche spit in his face but said nothing.

"You can die easy and as a man or hard and as a woman," snarled Buck in Kiowa.

Luke gasped but said nothing. He had never seen Buck act this way. His normally quiet and gentle cousin was a wild-eyed stranger to him. His huge size and his full long black hair made him look like a raging bear. Buck's eyes blazed like blue fire.

"If you can't stomach this, go tend to the ponies," said Buck with an angry glance in Luke's direction. "I aim to get what I want out of this one." Buck turned back to the Comanche.

Badger thought that he might get the big man to kill him quickly if he could enrage him enough. Badger was not a coward but he wanted to die as a man. He had sworn during his vision quest as a youth that he would honor the spirits and his ancestors by keeping his hair long, as was proper. Only Comanche women cut their hair. Also, he feared that the big man might remove his manhood and send him to the Shadow Land as a woman. Or worse, if he were hanged by this rope, his spirit could not get out to the Shadow Land. He would be doomed to wander the earth forever as a woman. Badger kicked out with both feet at the big man and spat out a curse. It was like kicking a tree. The big man did not move.

The big man slapped Badger across the face with the back of his hand and said, "Again, where is the woman in the blue dress?" The big man drew his knife and in one quick move sliced the leather band that held up the Badger's breechclout and leggings. He stood bare from his pipe-bone chest plate to his leggings now tangled around his ankles. "Talk or join your ancestors with the hair and body of a woman," snarled the big man.

His tormenter grabbed one of the Badger's long braids and moved the knife to it.

"She has been taken to Quintana Gomez and his Comancheros for sale," spit out Badger. Badger knew that White Elk would avenge him by killing this man. *Why die as a woman for nothing,* he thought.

"Where?" asked the man.

"Where the Pecos meets the Rio Bravo," spit out Badger.

Buck severed the Comanche's throat in one swift slash with the sharp knife. Luke was ashen and weak kneed as he turned away from the bloody scene. Buck walked to the water's edge to wash the blood from his arms and chest.

"Luke, I appreciate your help so far but I think it's best if you head back home. You can tell the neighbors what's happened to

Becky so far and that I'm on her trail. I'll keep my horse, the mule, and the two Comanche ponies and you can lead both of Mr. Green's horses back. He'll be needin' them. All you need do is follow the river along the north bank. This fork will join up with the others to form the main body of the Red and then just follow it home. I'll take most of the provisions we brought and all of the grain for the horses. You don't have that far to go and you needn't be in a big hurry once your well away from the Comancheria."

Luke was only sixteen but he felt he was man enough to stay. "I think I should stay to help," he said.

"It's not goin' to be pretty from here on," said Buck. "What you saw today might just be a taste of what is to come. Plus, the folks back home need to know what's happened to Becky. If I don't make it, they'll know to search down among the Mexicans for her. Besides, your trip back ain't goin' to be no slice of pie either. You've got to manage three horses and keep from gettin' caught by more Comanches and hunt game to eat. I trust you can do it."

Luke could see that there was no use in arguing and they were wasting time as it was. Buck was obviously anxious to get on the trail after Becky. "Okay, I'll go," said Luke. "But I'm not happy about it."

They shook hands and then embraced before mounting their horses. "Take care, cousin," said Buck. He spurred his mount and headed off to the south with the two Comanche ponies and the mule in tow. Luke rode east to follow the river back home.

X

Running Bird, Red Horse, Lone Tree, Bear Killer, Water Finder, and Little Wolf sat on their ponies on the ridge top. After several days riding southeast from the Comancheria, they had swung to the south to avoid a troop of soldiers from Ft. Concho and now looked down on a little farm at the confluence of Lipan Creek and the Concho River. Running Bird could see a woman bent over picking string beans which she deposited into a basket. Two small children played along the edge of the shallow creek. The man was busily sawing lumber next to a shed that he was building. From their dress, the farmers were obviously Lipan Apaches, mortal enemies of the Comanches.

'Angry Who Runs Far' had settled into the life of a farmer after his years as a Scout for the Texas Rangers working the border country west and north of Laredo. To him, working with the whites seemed more sensible than fighting them like many of his tribe did. Life as a scout for the Rangers had been exciting. The Civil War and its aftermath had resulted in the dissolution of the Rangers and the loss of his job. He had drifted to San Antonio and worked as a guard on the mail route to El Paso but the work was boring and he quit. He had then moved northwest of Austin where some members of his tribe were farming. He worked as a horse wrangler on a ranch just outside of the little town of San Saba for a year, where he met Yellow Bird. She worked on a nearby large cotton farm as a nanny to the farmer's children. After a brief courtship, Angry had married Yellow Bird and they had moved up the San Saba River to Ft. McKavett. The fort was being rebuilt after a ten-year abandonment.
Angry was immediately hired on as a Scout and Yellow Bird was given a position as cook's helper. The Army pay was steady, if not particularly good. Two years and two babies later, they had been able to save enough to buy a small piece of fertile land a few miles to the north where Lipan Creek spilled into the Concho River. They had built a small house using native limestone and mortar made from water and baked caliche. Angry had dug a series of aquacetas to divert some of the creek water to his fields. Fort Concho and the

town of Santa Angela were only a few miles away. Life was good and they were beginning to prosper in their modest way.

Angry was building a chicken coop in an attempt to keep his chickens safe from varmints at night. The foxes and coyotes were constant visitors as were raccoons. *I should get a dog*, thought Angry. *A dog would be good to protect the boys from snakes and to keep the raccoons and other varmints away from the house. The next time I go to the soldier fort, I'll look for a puppy*, he thought.

He heard Yellow Bird shrieking to the boys and guessed that they had cornered a snake. The little one was just toddling and followed his older brother everywhere. *How could a two year old and a three year old get into so much mischief so quickly?* He thought.

Angry stepped around the shed to see six Comanches racing toward Yellow Bird and his sons. Angry's rifle was propped against the splitting stump behind the house fifty feet away. As he ran for the rifle, one of the Comanches reached Yellow Bird. She stood between the charging Comanche and the boys with her knife in her hand. The Comanche leapt on her from his horse just as Angry reached his rifle. Before he could shoot, the Comanche stood up holding Yellow Bird's bloody scalp high over her limp body. Angry shot him dead where he stood. Another Comanche had killed his sons with a war ax and raced toward Angry.

Angry turned to face the approaching riders and the one on foot. He snapped off a shot that killed the lead rider. That stopped the charge and gave Angry time to run for the cover of the house. The four remaining Comanches including the one who had murdered his sons rode their horses down into the creek and took cover behind the creek bank. Angry fired a few shots in their direction to no effect. At the moment of his last shot, a bullet from one of the Comanches smashed into the loading gate on the side frame, effectively ruining Angry's Winchester. Instead of attacking, the Comanches chose to collect their dead comrades and their ponies. They then rode off to the west after stealing Angry's two horses. Angry was sick at heart and stunned by the death of his wife and sons. He had always hated the Comanches but the death of the remaining four attackers would be his reason for living.

After burying his family, Angry sang the death song. He built a small fire of juniper branches and purified himself with the smoke and the ashes. Then he quickly prepared for his pursuit. He carried a water bag and a pouch of venison jerky on a strap over his left shoulder. He was a short man but strong. He had a big chest, muscular arms and a broad, almost flat, face. His straight hair was cut above the shoulders and tied back from his forehead with a leather band. He wore leather leggings over the tops of his beaded buckskin boots and a long leather shirt cinched at the waist with a red sash. Long days in the sun had tanned his skin to a deep walnut hue. His only weapon was a long bone-handled knife held at his hip by a thin rawhide thong around his waist. Angry was born to a tribe with a long heritage of running. As a young man, he had once run over one hundred miles in one long day while scouting for the Texas Rangers. And, that was in the harsh desert west of Laredo. His leggings would interfere with the long run ahead so he stripped them off. His powerful brown legs were now bare below his breechclout. Angry set off at a steady lope west along the creek.

After three hours, the tracks of the Comanches veered away from the creek to the west and after another hour led north. Angry's pursuit led him across the South and Middle forks of the Concho. He stopped briefly at each to drink and to rest. When the tracks reached the North Concho, the Comanches had turned northwest to follow the river. *They are heading for the Llano Estacado and the Comancheria*, thought Angry. He stopped at the river and rested until first light before continuing on.

XI

"Haa ma ruawe," called out Running Bird as he, Red Horse, Lone Tree and Little Wolf rode into White Elk's camp.

"And hello to you all as well," replied White Elk. "I see you have captured some ponies, but are not these two the ponies of Water Finder and Bear Killer? Where are they?"

Running Bird slid down from his pony and said, "We attacked an Apache farmer and stole his ponies. He was a fighter and he killed the ones of whom we do not speak. We killed his woman and his sons but he escaped us. We have come here to the Big Spring for water before returning to the Comancheria. Why are you here? Do you take the War Trail south or do you return home?"

"We have stopped here for a few sleeps to rest the horses where there is plenty of good water. Soon, we will ride south to sell that woman over there to Quintana and then to raid Mexico for ponies," said White Elk. "We captured this woman and killed many whites and weak Indians in a raid to the east. We also captured many ponies that we gave to our people in the Comancheria. Why don't you join us in our raid?"

"I will speak to the others," said Running Bird. "As is our way, each warrior can choose for himself. For me, I say yes."

Becky had always been quick to pick up new languages. So far she had only managed to learn a few words of Comanche since her capture but she was learning fast. She had no idea of the full content of the discussion between the new arrival and White Elk. But, it was obvious that the newcomers had captured some horses and were excited to see White Elk. After an animated exchange of bragging, it was clear that these four decided to join White Elk's group for the ride to the Rio and then maybe a raid into Mexico.

The whole group was up and on its way before dawn the next morning. Becky rode along without a word in the heat and the constant, gritty, arid wind. Surprisingly, the men had left her alone. It was obvious that White Elk's word was to be strictly obeyed. White Elk himself was harsh in his manner but had not struck her since the first day of her capture. She had no doubt that he would kill her in an instant if she gave him trouble. Each night, Becky was careful to walk in soft soil or near the water holes or springs so as to leave a track or two in case someone followed. She had no reason to believe she would be saved but somehow she felt a presence drawing closer.

After two brutally dry and long days a-horseback, they entered an area of bright sand piled high in great dunes. Then, amidst it all was a stand of a few willows and a bit of a spring, though the Comanches had to dig a hole several feet deep to get enough water to drink and to meet the needs of their horses. Even though it was only mid-afternoon, the Comanches set up camp. *It must be too far to the next water,* thought Becky.

White Elk dragged her off of her pony and pushed her toward the willows. Once the Comanches and their horses had all the water that they wanted, Becky was allowed to drink. She cupped her hands and drank the bitter alkali water. When her thirst had been slaked, White Elk tied her to one of the willows. He and eight of the men mounted and rode off to the west. She was left with the Kiowa named Black Hand. He was not happy to be left behind while the others went hunting. Becky pretended to be asleep while Black Hand stared holes through her. After an hour, he got up from where he sat and moved near her. He smelled of smoke and sweat and leather. She squeezed her eyes tightly shut and gritted her teeth when he reached over and touched her. Suddenly there was a clatter in the brush behind her and Black Hand jumped back like he was snake bit. It was only a big lizard scuttling through the dry willow leaves but Black Hand's reaction told her that White Elk would not be pleased if she were molested. Black Hand moved back to his spot in the shade and continued to stare at her. Becky sat up and stared back. After an hour or so, they both tired of staring and dozed off to sleep.

The sun was low in the sky when the hunting party returned. They had killed two antelope does and four jackrabbits. The meat was soon roasting on spits over the fire. After days living on jerked meat, the sizzling feast smelled wonderful. The Comanches and the Kiowa were excited, too. They kept checking the meat and fussing about the fire. Black Hand had busied himself with scraping the backsides of the antelope and rabbit hides with his knife. He would smoke the antelope hide a bit over the fire to partially cure it so that it could be used to tie up any leftover roasted meat for the remainder of their journey. Black Hand tied the rabbit skins to the scalps and other small animal skins adorning his pony.

White Elk carved off pieces of cooked meat for himself and each of his men. He then gave a piece to Becky. It was delicious. They all ate ravenously until they had had their fill. Soon, all Becky could hear was the sound of the men snoring. She lay back in the warm sand and looked up at the sea of stars spread above her. Tears ran from the corners of her eyes as she thought about her dead husband. Had everyone else been killed? She tried not to think about what would happen to her when they reached the end of this journey. She was certain that she would to have to fend for herself. No one could have survived the attack at the store and neither her family nor her neighbors could possibly find her so far from home. Her earlier feeling of possible rescue was now gone.

Angry had always been a man of simple needs. He sought little from others and attended to his own business. His years with the Rangers helped to toughen him and to hone his tracking and survival skills. The Rangers were tough men who dealt with brutal enemies harshly. If the Comanches or bandits they chased were not killed during capture, they were promptly hanged. Courts and judges were often too far away and the Rangers saw no need for the delay. There were always more bandits to catch or Comanches and Kiowas to kill.

Angry's toughness overlay a deep tenderness for his wife and sons. The few years with Yellow Bird and then the boys were the only period since childhood that he had been truly happy. Their murder by the Comanches intensified his hated for these traditional enemies. He knew that to extract his revenge, he would have to catch them before they reached the Comancheria. Once they got there, hundreds, perhaps thousands, of their tribe, would protect these Comanches.

After a quick breakfast of jerky and water, Angry again ran along the tracks leading northwest. Except for the creek and river bottoms, the land was a sea of grass with an occasional motte of small oak trees. The sun was so bright that everything on the land seemed to be bowed by its force. The sky was deep blue with a few wispy high clouds off to the north. Running became easier as the rock-strewn ground gradually gave way to sandy soil and tall grass. Small clouds of grasshoppers scattered before him as he ran. Their chirping was the only sound other than the wind and his own breathing. Occasionally, a hawk or buzzard circled overhead. Angry loped at a steady pace all day. At dark he made camp beside the trickle that was the river. He made no fire for it was still warm even though winter approached. He was dog tired and fell into a fitful but replenishing sleep.

By noon of the next day, there was no Concho left to follow. The tracks of the Comanches veered to the west. *They are heading to the Big Spring before turning north to the Comancheria,* thought Angry. The tracks were getting fresher so Angry knew he was gaining on his enemies.

Late in the afternoon of the following day, Angry heard a horse nicker and he quickly dropped to the ground. He had best be careful lest he give himself away. His only hope against the superior numbers of the Comanches was to surprise them. He felt a bit weak and light-headed. His jerky supply had run out the day before and he had not wanted to delay his pursuit to take time for hunting. He crawled slowly through the tall grass until he could see two Comanche ponies, a mule, and a big black stallion grazing just below his position. The mule was puzzling but perhaps the Comanches were planning to eat it somewhere along their route.

Becky awoke to the song of a Canyon Wren. The cheerful bird flitted from bush to bush along the edge of the spring. She could not help but smile at the little bird's antics. She had always thought of wrens as her favorite birds. In fact, she had once raised a pair of orphaned wren chicks and set them free.

After a hasty breakfast of cold roasted antelope, Becky was tied back onto her pony. The band headed due south and was soon out of the sand and onto a parched stretch of scrub desert surrounded by hills and small mountains. White Elk had told her that they would reach the Pecos River today. At noon, they topped a small rise and there, below them, was a green stripe of vegetation that had to mark the river. At the river, there was an obviously much-used crossing. There were horse skulls scattered about and two stuck up on poles at the top of the riverbank. The Comanches let the ponies

74

drink but only a little of the brackish water.

"This water kills ponies if they drink too much," explained White Elk as he motioned to the bones scattered about. "My people have lost many of the ponies that we have taken from the Mexicans when the ponies drink too much here. We have learned to let them drink only a little at one time. We will leave the War Trail here and follow the river to meet Quintana. The War Trail south to Comanche Springs is now blocked by a fort filled with Buffalo Soldiers. The black white men are fierce warriors and we do not have time to kill them all now. Besides, Quitana's camp is on this river and not on the War Trail."

It seemed like an idle boast to Becky. The thought that these nine men could wipe out a fort full of soldiers was almost funny. *No lack of swagger*, she thought. As much as she hated them, there was something exciting and maybe even admirable in the way they faced life. Although the slaughter at the store and at the Holloway farm was still fresh in her mind, she had not been abused as she had expected to be. In fact, all things considered, she had been treated fairly well. White Elk had control of his group as far as her physical welfare was concerned. The new additions to the party seemed to know that she was off limits. In other matters, the members of the band seemed to share responsibilities with no obvious command structure. Lone Tree was the scout who led the way. Bright Arrow was the hunter who found them game and so on. Their ease on horseback was amazing. They seemed to be almost an appendage of their ponies or vice versa. On foot they were not impressive, a bit short and bandy-legged. But on horseback, they knew no equals. The women back in the Comancheria had seemed healthy enough. While she saw that the women were expected to perform most of the work, they were not abused. Maybe life with these people wouldn't be too bad? Maybe she could convince White Elk not to trade her to the Mexicans?

The river meandered off to the southeast. The cold water of the river was sixty to seventy feet across and, except for here at the crossing and occasional riffles, seven to ten feet deep. It was bracketed by high earthen bluffs that were cut straight down to the tangle of green brush along the riverbed. Scattered among the brush were cottonwood trees but they were few and battered. Obviously, from time to time, great floods roared down the river. It was far too brushy to ride along the river's edge and White Elk said the river itself was too deep and full of quicksand in the shallow sections to ride in it.

They rode along the desert, back from the bluffs through a broad valley that was bracketed by flat-topped mountains. The trail was narrow and not much used. The rough rocky ground was covered in small brush and cactus and an occasional mesquite tree. Every leaf and twig was armored with thorns. Bees and flies buzzed continually. The sun was relentless and almost a physical weight pressing down on them. The wind was hot, dry and constant. Dust and grit pelted them. Occasionally, a rattlesnake would buzz its warning from the shade of a creosote bush or a patch of prickly pear cactus. Now and then a few quail or doves would scatter before them. They plodded slowly along. This was no country to be pressing the horses too much. There were few places where they could get the horses down to the river and the water was salty and bitter. There wasn't much relief to be had from drinking it. Its only merits were that it was wet and cold.

They stopped for the night at a place White Elk called Galvez Crossing. It was an ancient and little used crossing but there was a small stand of cottonwoods along the eastern bank that would make a good campsite. It was clear that no one had camped here for a long time. The group settled into their normal evening routine. Bright Arrow and three of the others went off hunting. The horses were hobbled and set loose to browse. A fire was made and the men sat in the shade and talked or dozed. Becky was tied to some salt brush under one of the cottonwoods. Although the days were scorching hot, the nights were now cold. Becky wished for a blanket but the men did not offer her one. She shivered herself to sleep.

White Elk looked haggard. He had not slept well. For the past three nights, he had had the same dream. In the dream, the spirits showed him the big blue-eyed Choctaw coming for him through the darkness. During the daylight, White Elk was certain that he had shot the big man through the heart and that he was dead. But, late at night, he was not quite so certain. Perhaps the man's spirit was strong and his spirit came each night to drive White Elk crazy. This was known to have happened in the past when one of his people killed an especially powerful enemy. But the big man did not seem to be much of an enemy. True he had killed Little Feather, but with a shovel, not with a warrior's weapon. And, the big man wore white man's clothes and was unarmed when they had attacked. Even the white men who were fierce warriors always wore their guns. This dream was troubling though. What could it mean? He would have to speak with one of the elders when he returned to the Comancheria. They had experience in such matters. Perhaps he would need to purify himself with a new vision quest?

XII

The Llano Estacado stretched south and west. From Buck's vantage point, the Llano was totally devoid of useful landmarks. Navigation was by sun and stars and gut feel. As far as the eye could travel, there was nothing but scrub grass and occasional patches of cholla cactus. From time to time, he came to huge prairie dog towns that covered hundreds of acres. He had to swing wide to avoid them so as to prevent his horses from stepping into one of the burrows. He quickly learned to anticipate the towns by watching for red-tailed hawks circling overhead. Each 'town' seemed to have its own hawk contingent gliding above looking for the slow or sick. Just before dark, Buck chanced on a faint trail in the grass heading off to the southwest. He decided to stop for the night lest he lose the trail in the dark.

Buck hobbled his horses and the mule to keep them from wandering off, he strung them together on his rope and tied one end to his knife, which he stuck into the ground up to the hilt. Then, he settled down for a meal of muddy water from his canteen and dried beef jerky. He did not want to risk a fire as he didn't know how far ahead Becky's captors were and who might be following along behind. Coyotes began their evening sing somewhere off to the west. The sky was filled with so many stars that the whole area was dimly visible. The west Texas wind had been blowing hard all day but now it calmed a bit.

Buck stretched out on his blanket with his head propped on his saddle. He thought about how far he had come from the farm in Tennessee. His teen years had been filled mostly with good times. The work at the store had been relatively easy compared to working on his family's worn-out farm in Tennessee. He and his cousins had ample time to roam the woods and rivers to hunt, fish and trap. His grandfather spent a lot of time with the boys teaching them the 'old ways' and the values of his people. The Choctaws were living in two worlds. They valued their traditions while adapting to the realities of the white man's world. Since Buck was truly of both worlds, he had struggled to decide if he were white or Choctaw or somewhere in between. As he looked up at the sky filled with stars, he concluded that he had basically 'turned Injun', as they used to say back in Tennessee. A member of the civilized tribes but an Indian no less and now he hunted other Indians. His adversaries were known for their skills and their ruthlessness throughout all the tribes, including the whites. Was Becky unharmed? How far ahead were they? Would he alone be able to wrest her away from five warriors? Would he even catch up to them before they sold her to the Mexican? Was he on the right trail? How would he make the Kiowa who killed grandfather and the Comanche who took Becky suffer enough? He drifted off to a restless sleep with these questions churning in his head.

At first light, Buck picked up the faint trail and headed west. In a little over an hour, he came to what had to be the Comanche War Trail to Mexico. It was a well-worn trail heading south through the Llano. He turned south and rode hard, switching mounts by leaping from one to another, every hour or so. By nightfall of the second day, he had reached Yellow House Canyon and its spring. There were signs all around of the many campers who had spent nights here over the years. One campsite looked fresh. The ashes were cold but hadn't been there more than a few days. Buck knew in his gut that this is where they had camped with Becky. A thorough search turned up a woman's footprint in the sand next to the Yellow cliff. It just had to be Becky's.

Buck had repressed his deep feelings for Becky once it became apparent that she would wed his cousin, James. But now, his love for her had shifted in his mind from that of a brother back to that of a suitor. The loss of James and Grandfather tore at him as well. His hatred for the Comanches grew until in seemed to have a life of its own. He vowed to himself that he would not rest until all of the attackers lay dead. And if Becky were harmed, he would make war on the entire Comanche Nation. He drifted off to sleep with the bitter taste of hatred on his tongue.

Buck was up and moving before daylight. There was enough starlight to keep from riding into a gully or a patch of cholla. His inclination was to push the horses so as to catch up to Becky. But he realized that they had their limits and he had used almost all of the grain he had brought to supplement what they were able to browse. He forced himself to keep a steady pace that the animals could tolerate. It took two days to reach Big Spring. Plenty of good water and grass here. He was out of the Llano now. He could see a few hills and mesas about from his perch on the caprock escarpment above the spot where the spring issued.

He climbed back down from the bluff and examined the area around the spring. He was certain that these were Becky's tracks in the mud. From the freshness of the footprints and the ashes of the campfire, Buck knew that he was no more than two days behind. There was still a lot of country to cross but he thought he could catch them if his luck held out. He decided to let the horses and mule graze and get some much-needed rest. He could not afford to cripple his mounts and they needed rest. This was a pretty place compared to the vastness of the Llano. Frogs croaked at the far edge of the little pond below the spring. Insects darted above the surface of the water. Birds chattered in the bushes along the escarpment. The horses were hobbled but he had set the mule free. The grain was depleted and he had no further use for the mule. It could live well here by the spring if it chose to stay when he left.

Buck dozed a bit as the rabbits he had killed earlier roasted slowly on the sticks he had angled over the campfire. Every so often, he would rotate the sticks so that a different part of the rabbits faced the coals. A coyote slinked up to the edge of the water for a drink. The coyote could smell the meat cooking and knew that a man must be nearby but he couldn't see Buck sitting in the shadow of the overhang. The coyote's better judgment overcame his hunger and he trotted off to the west. A red-tailed hawk screamed from overhead as he soared in big lazy circles. *A man could live a good life here*, thought Buck. But, the rabbits were ready and there were miles more to travel. But, perhaps he could afford a day of rest for the horses. It was difficult to be patient when he felt that he was nearing the Comanches and Becky. Logic had to prevail over heart.

Buck ate his supper and then went for a walk along the top of the bluff. He could see that the trail he had been following no longer continued south but veered sharply off to the southwest. *That must be the way to the next water*, Buck thought. He turned his focus back toward the north and looked down on the meadow where the horses and mule grazed. There was an Indian crawling belly down through the tall grass toward the horses!

Buck scrambled down from the bluff and started running toward his horses.

"HEY, YOU THERE!" he shouted.

The horses shied away from Buck, frightened by the shouting. The mule brayed and kicked out its heels as it ran into the brush. The man stood up. He appeared to be dazed. He took a staggering step toward Buck and fell face down in the grass. Buck dragged him to the water's edge and splashed some water over his face. The man drank a little and then sat up.

"My name is Angry Who Runs Far," said the man. "I am *Tindi Dine*, what the whites call Lipan Apache. My enemies, the Comanches, killed my woman and children and left me for dead. I smelled the water and your fire and saw the Comanche ponies. I thought you were Comanche, too."

"My name is Buck McDougal and I'm part white and part Choctaw. I'm trailing a band of Comanches and Kiowas who killed some of my family and stole a woman. Here, eat," said Buck as he handed a piece of roasted rabbit to the man.

Angry took the meat and ate it ravenously. He looked pretty much played out but he seemed to revive by the minute.

"How did you get here?" asked Buck. "Where's your pony?"

"I ran. The Comanches took my ponies in the raid. My home is on Rio Concho just east of Santa Angela and Fort Concho. I followed the Concho on the trail of the Comanches until there was no more Concho to follow. The trail led north and I am here."

"Well, from the tracks, it appears your bunch joined up with the bunch I'm trailin'," said Buck. "The tracks head off to the southwest from here. I aim to set out after 'em after resting my horses a day."

Angry eyed the three Henry rifles propped against a rock next to Buck's bedroll. "I could go with you and help you kill the Comanches. I spent many years as a Scout for the Rangers. I know this country and I know our enemy."

"The main thing is to get the woman back safe," said Buck. "If I can kill all of the sumbucks, that's so much the better. But you must help me rescue the woman, no matter what else happens."

"Yes, I would want that too, if they had my woman," said Angry.

"I've been gainin' on 'em by switchin' mounts but if I let you ride one, there won't an extra for you to switch to. I've got a mule out yonder in the brush. He's as fast as these horses but I set him a-loose. If'n we can catch him, you can ride him and the third Comanche pony, but I don't have an extra saddle and bridle," said Buck.

"I need no saddle and can make a hackamore from a piece of your rope. If we cannot catch the mule, I can rest the pony the Apache way. Each time you switch ponies, I will tie my hand to the pony's neck and run beside him. You will be faster but I will not fall far behind."

"If you're gonna run half the day when we leave, you better eat some more. We're all out of rabbit, eat some of this jerky and get some sleep. I'll stand watch for a while."

Somehow Buck knew he could trust the Apache. In a way, they were on the same mission. Plus, the Apache said he knew the country and looked like he could more than hold his own in a fight. Angry's nut-brown skin bore a number of scars that could only have been made by bullets and arrows.

Buck climbed up onto the bluff and looked around him. A small herd of buffaloes grazed a mile or so off to the east. If there were time, it would be a good idea to kill one for meat but it would take a couple of days to sneak up close enough for a shot, butcher the carcass and smoke the meat. He just didn't have that time. The sun was a bright red ball at the western horizon. The sky was pink with a deep violet band just above the rolling hills to the west. Above and to the east, the sky began to fade to pale blue before it darkened to black. Venus shone brightly above the eastern horizon. *There will be a little moonlight tonight*, thought Buck. He carefully scanned the horizon in all directions looking for more Comanches. Satisfied that they would have no visitors, Buck descended the bluff and settled in across the campfire from the sleeping Apache.

When Buck awoke, the Apache was gone! The ponies were still here. They stood head down, dozing in the tall grass. All of Buck's possessions were exactly were he had left them. *I'm surprised he didn't take one of the ponies and one of the rifles*, thought Buck.

If he has gone on ahead, I'd best be on my way too, thought Buck. He got up, gathered his belongings and saddled his horse. Just as he was ready to mount, Angry appeared over the bluff rim carrying a dead buffalo calf draped over his shoulders. Angry had been unable to catch the mule and they decided not to waste time trying to chase it in the heavy brush.

They skinned and butchered the buffalo calf. Angry ate half of the raw liver and offered the other half to Buck. "It will make you strong," said Angry.

Buck ate a little and gave the rest back to Angry. "Thanks, but liver ain't my favorite," he said.

They split the meat, rubbed it down with a heavy dose of salt, wrapped it in pieces of the calf's hide, tied the bundles to two of the horses, and set out to the southwest. Angry had made a strap from a piece of the buffalo calf's hide to use as a sling for the rifle that Buck had given him. He slung the gun over his back and grinned from ear to ear. "Let's go kill some Comanches," he said.

Angry had told Buck that there was a spring at some willow trees among the large sand dunes that he would soon encounter two suns ride in the direction of the Comanche tracks. Late in the afternoon of the second day, Buck followed the Comanches' trail into a large expanse of shifting sand dunes. Some of the dunes were over fifty feet tall and comprised of loose shifting white sand. At the top of one of the dunes, Buck thought he could see the fringe of something green in the distance to the southwest.

Riding through the soft sand was difficult and he finally had to dismount to get his horses through. Sure enough, there was a spring of sorts and a stand of willows. He could see where the Comanches had dug a shallow pit in the sand to expose water. Buck would have bet twenty Yankee dollars that there was no water in all this sand. But not only was there water, there were coals of a campfire that were still hot enough to restart a fire. Also, there were tracks all around – including the woman's tracks he had been seeing at the other campsites. *Only a day behind*, thought Buck. He gathered some dry willow sticks and built up the fire. Once he had a bed of red coals, he skewered some pieces of the buffalo meat onto willow sticks and angled them over the coals. About the time that the meat began to sizzle, Angry appeared from over the top of the dune.

"About time you showed up," said Buck. "I was about to have dinner without you."

Angry led his pony to the water and let him drink. "Drink plenty here," said Angry. "We can dig more if we need to. We will reach the Pecos tomorrow. The water in that river is no good. We will be several sleeps on bad water."

"They camped here last night," said Buck. "This fire is from their coals. From the tracks, there are at least nine or ten of them plus Becky. We're goin' to have to be real careful to be able to best them and get Becky away unharmed. I know the ones that I was trailin' all have Henrys like these we're totin'. How were the ones that attacked you armed?"

"I killed two but four escaped with my ponies. One had an old Springfield and one had an old flintlock pistol. They all had bows."

"Well, it's our three Henrys and my two pistols against at least five or six rifles, their bows, and a pistol. We'll have to see if we can whittle 'em down a little to improve our odds. From the tracks I spotted at each of their campsites, I can see that two or three wandered off – huntin', I expect. Since we're gettin' close, I expect we should see if we can take care of the hunters while they're away from the main group. Where are the likely camp spots for each night from here to the Rio Grande?"

"We will reach Horsehead Crossing at the Pecos tomorrow morning. The Comanche War Trail continues south but Fort Stockton and the Buffalo Soldiers will block their way. Also, that way will not lead to the place where the Pecos meets the Rio Bravo, or Rio Grande, as you call it. I think they will follow the Pecos to old abandoned Fort Lancaster at the San Antonio Road Crossing and then on to the Rio Bravo. They will probably camp at the fort since the creek there has sweet water, then maybe three more sleeps to the Rio Bravo. From here on, we cannot travel fast, like today, or we will kill our ponies. The land is arid and rough with little for the ponies to eat and the water of the Pecos is not good for them. I do not think we will gain much on the Comanches. Your ponies are good but the Comanches always ride the best ponies."

"Well, we can try," said Buck. We're gettin' more moon ever night. Maybe we can ease along a bit later each day and catch 'em before they reach the Comanchero camp. Odds are bad now and will be worse once they get to Quintana."

"Quintana is a very bad man," said Angry. "I scouted for a company of the Texas Rangers under Captain Rip Ford in the old days and we tried to catch him. His band killed five Rangers and wounded all of the rest of us." Angry pointed to two puckered scars on his upper chest. "We were lucky to escape. I fear that the woman you seek will be treated badly by Quintana and his men before she is sold as a servant in Mexico. That is the nature of his business."

That confirmed Buck's fears and made him more resolute to catch the Comanches before they reached the border. Catching up to them would mostly be dependent on the strength and endurance of their horses. The Comanches had not been pushing their mounts as hard as Buck had his. He decided to adopt Angry's system of riding, running, riding to spare the mounts as much as possible. He didn't want to get too far in front of Angry now anyway. He would need him when the fighting started.

"Let's get some sleep," said Buck. "I want to get started early so we can cover some ground before it gets too hot."

The quarter moon lit their way as Buck and Angry set out to the south. A few hours later, the sun was just rising above the flat-topped mesa to the east as they reached the Pecos at Horsehead Crossing. They let the horses drink a little of the brackish water and then followed the river to the east. The trail left by the Comanches was clearly visible and fresh! Buck urged his horse forward at a lope.

Angry had warned that the trail would be rough and his warning was if anything an understatement. Just before noon, Buck's big Morgan took a misstep on a rough stretch of rocky ground and they went down in a heap. Buck jumped clear and only had a few scrapes and a dozen or so cactus spines in his left arm. The horse, on the other hand, had broken his right foreleg. Buck didn't want to risk a shot since he didn't know how far ahead the Comanches were, so he severed one of the big jugular veins in the horse's throat with his knife. Angry said nothing but gave him a look that said, 'I told you we would have to go slow.'

Buck cursed himself for his stupidity. *Here we are almost up to the Comanches and I go and kill one of our horses!* He thought. He said to Angry, "You were right, I should have been more careful."

Angry only grunted.

Buck stripped his saddle and bridle from the dead horse and

put them on one of the Comanche ponies. The tack was unfamiliar to the pony and it took several minutes to get the saddle cinched and to set the bit in the pony's mouth. The pony bucked three or four times without being able to unseat Buck. Then he settled down. Buck and Angry were now down to only two mounts. Buck said, "I'll be careful with this one."

The Comanche pony was smaller but seemed more surefooted than Buck's Morgan had been. Still, it was a shame to waste such a fine horse. Within the hour, they passed the smoldering campfire where the Comanches had spent the night. *We could catch up to them tonight,* thought Buck. *Then what?*

XIII

White Elk and his group reached the place where Live Oak Creek spills into the Pecos late that afternoon. They followed the creek to the east a mile or so to the old fort at the base of a tall mesa. There was plenty of green grass along the creek and the water was sweet compared to the Pecos. From the tracks and fresh droppings, it was clear that a small herd of buffalo had been here within a day. The tracks led around the mesa and up into the mountains to the northeast.

Fort Lancaster had been built to guard the "lower" road from San Antonio to El Paso where it crossed the Pecos River. The Union Army had abandoned it at the start of the Civil War. In the early years of the war, the Texas Mounted Rifles briefly reoccupied the fort. Following the war, it remained unoccupied for several years. Its main purpose had been to guard the mail route from San Antonio to El Paso but the mail route had been moved north to the "upper" road and the fort was no longer needed. The lower road was now unprotected and not much used.

"Bright Arrow, go find where the buffalo have gone so we can hunt them tomorrow," said White Elk. "We can use fresh meat and this is a good place to rest. There is plenty of grass and good water for the horses. There will be little grass and poor water for the next three sleeps once we enter the canyons of the Pecos. We will make a camp while you are gone."

White Elk had tied the rope from Becky's feet to a large boulder that had tumbled down the mesa eons ago. The rope was long enough to give her some freedom of movement but the knots were tied tight enough to prevent her from quickly freeing herself. Mesquites and junipers grew up the steep side of the mesa. Compared to what they had been crossing, this was a pretty spot.

Bright Arrow returned just before dark. "The buffalo are in a big meadow less than one hour up the canyon where the creek makes several branches. The buffalo will not leave such a good meadow for several sleeps unless chased," he reported to White Elk.

"Good, we will have fresh meat and can dry more for our journey. Once we have done business with Quintana, we can raid the villages to the south and east in Mexico. We will bring many horses north with us when we return," said White Elk.

Buck and Angry topped a little rise, reined in their horses, and looked to the southeast. Angry pointed to the base of the largest mesa on the horizon.

"Look, something shines," he said.

The low sun on the western horizon was indeed reflecting from a golden mirror at the base of the mesa off in the distance to the southeast. *Not a mirror*, thought Buck. "It's one of the Henry rifles," said Buck. "The Comanches must be camped at that mesa."

"That is the location of the old abandoned soldier fort," said Angry. "We are much closer to them that I thought. We must be careful or they will see us or this dust that the ponies are kicking up as they walk."

"Let's slip back behind this ridge and wait for dark," said Buck. "We'll have plenty of moonlight to slip in a little closer tonight."

"Maybe we should cross over to the northeast to try to get around behind that mesa. I don't think they will expect anyone from that direction," said Angry.

"Okay," said Buck. "We'll just settle for jerky and have a cold camp for supper tonight."

Little Wolf was the youngest of the four that rode out of camp in the predawn light. Bright Arrow had selected him and two others for the buffalo hunt. Little Wolf intended to prove himself worthy of the respect of the older men. They rode along the creek bank and talked of their hunting prowess. The flat-topped mountains around them bracketed a deep blue sky. Along the western horizon, a line of angry dark clouds was just barely peaking over the distant mesas. Swallows flitted along the creek catching insects. The ever-present wind whispered through the scrubby junipers. The creek wound its way up into the surrounding juniper covered mesas.

Little Wolf said, "This new Henry rifle will kill many buffalo. The rest of you can rest until it is time to skin them."

The older men laughed.

Bright Arrow said, "Be careful that you do not let your

tongue wag like the coyote's and get you into trouble, little brother, and remember that the rifle you carry belongs to White Elk, take good care of it."

They continued their banter as they rode along the shoulder of the mesa. They topped a little rise as they cleared the shadow of the mesa. Squinting into the sun, they could see the buffalo below them along the creek to the north.

Just as they got near enough to rush the herd, a volley of rifle shots rained down on them. Bright Arrow and the other two were killed with the first shots. Little Wolf's pony was shot from under him. He lay dazed on the rocky ground wondering who could be shooting at him. He regained his wits and his feet at about the same time. He snatched up his rifle and ran for the creek. He could hear two men shouting to each other as they came down the side of the mesa. The high creek bank concealed him and he decided to run back toward the camp at the old fort.

Buck and Angry were up before dawn and preparing to sneak around the big mesa when they heard voices below them to the southwest. Angry slipped down the side of the hill to see who and how many were coming.

"There are four of them," he said when he got back to Buck. "I think they are coming to hunt those buffalo down in that meadow," he said as he pointed to the north. "Two of them carry Henrys and the other two, bows. Two of them were among those who killed my family."

"Let's slip down behind those rocks and see if we can surprise 'em," said Buck.

Buck and Angry positioned themselves one hundred yards apart behind large boulders just above the trail that the hunters would obviously take. The hunting party rode down the little rise to the south and was concentrating on the buffalo herd when Angry and Buck stood up and began shooting.

"I only see three of them!" shouted Angry as he ran down the hillside. "Where is the other one?"

"I don't know if he's hit or not!" shouted Buck. "Just as I shot at him, his pony shied and I hit the pony in the head."

They ran to the fallen horse and Angry said, "Look where the rider fell. His tracks lead to the creek. I will follow him while you catch the other ponies. We do not want him to warn the others at the camp"

"OK," said Buck. "But watch yourself. The one that got away has one of the Henrys. This one had the other Henry. I'll be along as soon as I fetch our mounts and catch theirs."

Buck gathered up the weapons and ran back to his horses. It took less than ten minutes to gather up the Comanches' three ponies and string them together behind Angry's pony.

As Little Wolf ran down the creek bed, a bullet hit him in the back of his left shoulder and ripped out of his upper chest leaving a hole the size of a walnut. He dived to his left into a small gully entering the creek. He quickly scooped up some mud from the creek bank and stuffed it into the wound in his chest. The blood flow ebbed to a trickle. He could do little about the entry wound in his back. The pain was almost unendurable but he managed to stand up. His left arm was useless but he was able to lift the heavy rifle to his right shoulder with his right arm alone. He aimed and fired at the Apache but the pain in his chest, the unsteadiness of holding the rifle with one hand, and his nervousness caused the shot to hit the water five yards in front of his pursuer.

Little Wolf could not see the Apache but he levered another round into the chamber and fired from the hip down the creek toward his pursuer. He then darted out of the gully and ran along the wall of the creek bed toward White Elk's camp. He knew the Apache would be coming either along the creek or from above the high bank. He could hear thunder booming off to the west and smell rain on the wind.

Angry leapt behind a boulder before the Comanche's second shot came whizzing by. He could no longer see the boy but he knew he had hit him with his own shot. Angry crawled up over the creek bank and slipped downstream toward the little gully into which the Comanche boy had ducked. A line of tall black thunderheads swept toward him. He could see lightning striking the ground all along the edge of the storm front.

A quick peek over the creek bank confirmed that the boy was no longer in the gulley. Angry dropped down into the gulley and looked for sign. Here were the boy's tracks but only a small amount of blood. *I guess I only nicked him*, thought Angry. He peeked around a big rock to see if the boy waited in ambush. He saw nothing but tracks heading off downstream. From the spread of the tracks, the boy was obviously at a full run, but staggering.

XIV

Willard Roberson had loaded his family and possessions into a wagon and set out for California from San Antonio three weeks ago. He had studied the maps and decided that he would take the shorter lower road. It was less used and not as well protected but the man at the livery had assured him that most of the Indians and bandits had been tamed or killed. In fact, they had hardly seen anyone since they left Fort McKavett twelve days ago. They had camped last night between two big mesas. His maps indicated that he should reach the Pecos River crossing this morning and he wanted to get across as soon as possible. *I don't like the look of that line of clouds*, he thought. *Best get across the river before the rains hit.* The road wound steeply down between the two mesas as it headed west toward a bright green line of brush in the broad valley below. *That must be the Pecos*, thought Willard.

"Billy, why don't you take the mare and ride on ahead of us a ways and see if you can kill us a deer or something," said Willard. "The river's supposed to be just down yonder a few miles. See that line of green brush off in the distance. That's likely the river."

"Sure, Pa," said Billy. He was happy to be out away from the wagon and to be hunting. He easily became bored just walking along beside the wagon as it slowly creaked and rumbled down the road.

As the boy neared the river, he spotted a flock of turkeys crossing the road ahead of him. He took careful aim with the old rifle and shot the big tom trailing the flock of hens. *Ma will be happy to see this*, he thought. They had been living on rabbit, raccoon, and armadillo for days. A turkey would be a treat. He decided that he wouldn't get a shot at any of the other turkeys as they had scattered into the thick brush along the river when he shot. He picked up the turkey and climbed back up onto the mare. He gave the mare a cluck or two and dug his bare heels into her brown sides. She responded by starting to plod back up the hill toward the wagon.

White Elk could hear Bright Arrow and the others shooting at the buffalo up the creek to the north but who was this shooting to the south? "Running Bird, you and Walks Alone see who fired a shot down that way," said White Elk as he pointed to the south.

In less than five minutes, Running Bird and Walks Alone came racing back to the camp.

"There are a man and woman in a wagon on the road heading toward the river," said Running Bird, as he and Walks Alone returned to camp. "A boy is hunting turkeys down near the river. It was his shot that we heard."

"Black Hand, you stay and watch the Choctaw woman," said White Elk. "We will kill the man and boy and steal the woman in the wagon. We will take anything we can use and burn the rest."

"Come,' said White Elk to the others as he mounted his pony.

In a heartbeat, the air was filled with the whoops of the attackers and their bullets and arrows. Willard couldn't believe his eyes. One moment his grinning boy was riding up holding a big tom turkey and the next the boy was falling off the mare with two arrows in his chest. Billy had just rounded a bend in the road and was in sight of the wagon when the arrows struck him. The boy managed to spur the horse forward before he died.

"Git down low in the wagon!" Willard shouted to his wife. He lashed the mules and raced the wagon down slope toward the river and his dead son. Mary started shooting out of the back of the wagon. She killed one of the Indians and was reloading the rifle when Red Horse leapt onto her from behind the wagon. As Mary and Red Horse struggled, White Elk leapt onto Willard and threw him from the racing wagon. Willard barely gained his feet before he was cut down by a shot from Running Bird's rifle. The bullet had shattered his femur just above the knee. He struggled to rise but was shot through the heart and lungs with Running Bird's next shot. He died watching his wagon race down the road.

White Elk had never driven a wagon and didn't know how to stop the running mules. His sharp jerks on the reins only frightened the mules into an even faster gait. Meanwhile, Mary fought like a wildcat. By the time that Red Horse had managed to gain control by pinning her arms behind her, his face and arms bled from scratches and bites. She continued to snap at him with her teeth and squirm in his grasp.

"White Elk, help me! This one fights like a panther!" Red Horse shouted above the noise of the rumbling wagon. The team and wagon hit the river with a splash. At least that stopped the mules.

White Elk jumped into the back of the wagon to help Red Horse with the squirming, shrieking woman. They finally managed to tie her arms and legs with a horsehair rope White Elk found hanging on a hook on the side of the wagon. She continued to wriggle like a catfish and scream like a banshee.

Running Bird rode into the shallow river crossing and grabbed the harness of the right lead mule of the wagon team. He led the team and wagon up on to the high ground above the west bank of the river.

"Walks Alone is dead," Running Bird said to White Elk who was climbing down from the wagon.

"Lead the wagon back across the river and to our camp at the old fort," said White Elk. "I will catch my pony and Walks Alone's pony. Put Walks Alone's body in the wagon and take him back to our camp." Turning back to the wagon, he said, "Red Horse, stop that woman from screaming. She is making my head hurt."

Red Horse placed his hand over Mary's mouth and shook his head. She bit his hand and stopped screaming. He removed his hand and she screamed again. He slapped her hard across her face, replaced his hand across her mouth, and shook his head again. This time she didn't bite and she stopped screaming. Instead, she spit in Red Horse's face, and began to cry softly.

White Elk gathered the turkey, Billy's mare and rifle, and Walk's Alone's pony and followed the wagon back to their camp. They hurried in advance of the coming storm. Just as they arrived at the ruins of the fort, big drops of rain began to hammer the dust. Becky and Black Hand had moved the group's blankets into one of the buildings that still had a roof and sat near a little fire that Black Hand had built.

Thunder shook the ground and a violent wind howled around the buildings. While Running Bird hobbled the horses, White Elk carried Walks Alone's body into the fort. Red Horse followed dragging Mary behind him. He tied her to an iron ring hanging from the wall at the corner of the room.

Little Wolf came struggling up from the creek with a wild look in his eyes. He collapsed at White Elk's feet. White Elk knelt beside him and asked, "Where are the others? Why are you bleeding?"

"We were attacked," said Little Wolf. "The Apache that we fought at the Rio Concho and another man hid in the rocks above the buffalo. See, I have been shot. They killed Bright Arrow and the others and they are coming."

"We are safe inside this solder fort," said White Elk. "Besides, they are only two and we are five. Look at the storm outside. Even we could not attack in such rain. They will wait until the storm is gone before they attack."

Becky had overhead Little Wolf but had learned only a few words of Comanche. She gathered that Apaches had attacked the group of hunters and that all but Little Wolf had been killed. She had heard tales of the Apaches and their fierceness but maybe they would kill the Comanches and release her. At least, she now had a glimmer of hope. Of course, the Apaches might be worse than the Comanches. And, she was dressed like a Comanche woman. The Apaches might think that she too was a Comanche.

While the men talked and the storm raged, she moved over to where Mary was tied. Mary gave her a wild, frightened look.

"What is your name," whispered Becky. "I am a captive, like you."

"But you're an Injun," whispered Mary. "Ain't you one of them?"

"No, I am Choctaw and was taken from my family in the Nations," whispered Becky. "They are Comanches, except one who is Kiowa. They are taking me to someone named Quintana to sell me to him."

"No talking," said Black Hand. "Stay away from her." He grabbed Becky by her hair and dragged her to the opposite side of the room. He said to White Elk, "They were whispering to each other. I don't trust these women."

"The Choctaw seems tame enough," said White Elk, "but the white one is a fighter. Be careful around her. Look at Red Horse's face and arms. He looks like he has been chewed by a wolf." They all laughed at Red Horse's expense.

Black Hand laughed, "Maybe Red Horse is inexperienced with white women. Women with spirit need an experienced man. I can tame this one if you wish."

"Leave her alone, for now. The women can wait, we have these Apaches to consider," said White Elk. "When the storm passes, you should go on top of the fort and watch for them."

XV

The wind had picked up with a vengeance. Sand pelted Buck as he struggled to keep control of the ponies. He heard a strange buzzing sound just before he was slammed off his pony and onto his back on the ground.

His first thought was that he had been shot but no, he was only stunned. Lightning had struck a juniper next to him and killed the Comanche pony that he rode. The air was thick with the smell of ozone and burning horsehair. The other ponies had scattered like quail. Before he could regain his feet, rain pored down in torrents. The suddenness and intensity of the storm was amazing in such dry country. Buck couldn't see ten feet in the heavy downpour. The lightning and thunder continued, along with gale force wind. Buck struggled down slope toward the creek.

As Angry eased down the east side of the creek, the lightning began to strike the mesa off to his left. He could hear the roar of the coming storm and knew he had to get out of the creek bed before the storm hit. A creek could become a river in minutes during one of these storms. Just as he climbed up onto the top of the creek bank, he saw lightning strike the hillside fifty yards upslope from him and then, four ponies came racing past. One of the ponies had the Henry rifles tied onto its back. The ponies splashed across the creek and ran west toward the river. *Where is Buck?* Thought Angry.

Buck had barely made it to the creek bank when the hail started. He spotted an overhanging bank a few yards upstream on the east side of the creek and splashed his way to it. He squeezed himself into the little overhang so that at least his head was protected. Hailstones half the size of hens' eggs hammered down on his back and legs. The roar of the storm was deafening. Meanwhile, Angry had found a bit of shelter from the hailstorm in a thick clump of junipers. They didn't know it at the time but they were only two hundred yards apart.

Mercifully, the hail only lasted a few minutes, though it seemed much longer. Now the rain fell as though poured from a big bucket. Buck crawled up over the creek bank and ran toward a big clump of junipers. There, under a big one, squatted Angry.

The storm had stalled over them and it continued to pour. After three hours, the rain finally slackened as the storm began moving off to the east. The creek was a raging river of churning, brown muddy water filled with all sorts of debris.

"There's no way we can get across until the water runs off," said Buck.

"The boy I shot is either drowned or made it back to the fort," said Angry. "If he made it back to the others, they will be waiting for us. We can't get across this creek to catch our ponies so we can't attack them anyway. As soon as we can cross the creek, let's see if we can find our ponies."

Buck walked back to the lightning-killed pony and retrieved his rifle, saddle and bridle. He carried them down to the creek bank and stashed the saddle and bridle up in a mesquite tree. He and Angry walked upstream looking for a place to cross. Three hours later, they found a place where they could jump from the creek bank to a large boulder and then to the opposite creek bank. The rain had wiped out any tracks, but the horses had run toward the Pecos and might not be too far away.

Late that afternoon, Angry gave a whistle. Buck loped over to where Angry stood. There in the brush along the now raging Pecos was a tangle of the four horses. Angry's pony and the three that Buck had tied to it were ensnarled around a little mesquite tree. They had apparently tried to pass the tree on opposite sides and gotten the rope tangled in the thorny branches. 'What luck that the rifles and gear were not bucked off,' thought Buck.

"Let's make camp here for the night," said Buck. "We can't get the ponies across the creek until tomorrow anyhow."

White Elk had slept fitfully all night. He again had the dream of the big man with blue fire in his eyes. In his dream, the big man came for him and he was powerless to stop him. For the first time in his life, White Elk was afraid. He told himself that his fears were foolish. He had killed the big man at the Choctaw store. And besides, even if the man were alive and came near, White Elk would kill him as he did all of his enemies. However, the loss of the hunting party and Walks Alone was troubling. Perhaps, his medicine was no longer strong. If there were only time, he would purify himself to strengthen his power.

While Red Horse and Running Bird were outside the fort burying Walks Alone, as was the Comanche custom, White Elk motioned for Little Wolf to come to him. Little Wolf groaned as he rose from his blanket and slowly and painfully walked to where White Elk sat. He sat down opposite the little fire and waited for White Elk to speak.

"Little Wolf, tell me about the two men who attacked you," said White Elk. "Describe the attack to me."

"We were just above the buffalo on a small ridge when suddenly shooting began from the mesa above us," said Little Wolf. "Bright Arrow, Lone Tree and Sparrow were killed immediately. My pony was shot from under me. I picked up my rifle and ran for the creek. I could hear two men shouting to each other in the white man's tongue. One of them chased me and shot me in the shoulder. He was the Apache that we attacked many sleeps ago near the Rio Concho. I only saw the other briefly and at a distance. He looked to be a big man with long hair. He spoke in the white man's tongue and he looked too tall to be an Apache, but he was far away and I only saw him for a moment. As I ran down the creek, the storm began and I was back at the soldier fort with you. That is all there is to tell."

Surely, this could not be the same man from the Choctaw store, thought White Elk, but he was not certain. When Red Horse and Running Bird returned to the fort, White Elk said, "Burn the wagon and bring the women. We leave now to take them to Quintana."

The others were surprised by White Elk's decision to leave without killing their enemies. Even though there was no formal command structure among the Comanches and each warrior was free to decide for himself, they all respected White Elk's wisdom, especially in matters of battle. White Elk was a leader in the true sense that a leader is one that others willingly follow.

The seven of them mounted their ponies and rode off to the southwest toward the Pecos. The black smoke from the burning wagon rose straight up in the clear blue sky. The storm had even taken the ever-present wind away. Becky tried to comfort Mary as she and Mary were secured to their ponies in the middle of the line of riders.

It was only a few miles down to the Pecos. The flood was still in progress though the water level had dropped considerably from its peak. The river had stripped much of the brush along its edge and eroded the sandy clay banks so that there were fresh scars along the edge, twenty feet above the river below. As they crossed the old San Antonio road, a flock of buzzards rose from something on which they fed just up the hill. Mary let out a wail when she realized that the buzzards were feasting on her son and husband's bodies. Black Hand rode up along side and slapped her sharply twice.

Becky was in anguish as to what to do. She had no way to comfort Mary or to protect her. During the previous night Black Hand and two of the Comanches had repeatedly used Mary. Only White Elk and the wounded boy refrained. White Elk had made it clear that they were to leave 'the young one fresh for Quintana', but he put no such restrictions with respect to Mary. Becky could only pretend to sleep in the dark as she heard Mary's sobs and the grunts of Mary's tormentors. And now, Becky had no way of helping Mary in her grief. Both women rode along sobbing to themselves.

White Elk set a course parallel to the river but a few hundred yards east of its bank. The earth was soft and subject to collapse too near to the river. White Elk knew that the water would run off quickly and the soil would dry to a hard surface before the day was out. By nightfall, only the scoured-out riverbed would show evidence of yesterday's storms. A huge benefit would be the freshness of the river water for a few days, as the flood would have flushed much of the alkali-laden water downstream.

XVI

Buck crawled out of his bedroll and walked down to the river's edge. Both the Pecos and the creek were still too deep and swift to cross. He walked back to where Angry was rekindling last night's fire. Buck said, "The way I see it, we can either set here all day waitin' for this dern creek to run down or we can head up into the mesas and see if we can get our ponies back across further up the creek. Either way we'll lose the day but I ain't much for just settin' around. I'd like to come at that fort from above anyways. I expect they'll be figurin' that we'll come at 'em from below along the creek. Maybe we can surprise 'em."

"Yes, let's go," said Angry. We can hunt along the way and maybe kill a deer or a buffalo calf. That herd of buffalo ran up into the mesas when we started shooting at the Comanches. Maybe they are still up there."

"We can't be shootin' or we'll let the Comanches know where we are," said Buck.

"Oh yes, we can," said Angry. He held up one of the Comanche bows and a quiver of arrows and grinned like a mule eating briars.

Buck laughed out loud. "Ain't you the one," he said?

They had a hasty meal of the last of their venison then rode into the hills to the northeast. Little rivulets poured off the mesa tops and ran down watercourses that had been long dry to join up with the creek. The soil of the area could change from loose dusty sand to clinging soft mud to hard-packed crust depending on water content.

Due to the rain, the surface consisted of the soft sticky mud form and it made the going difficult. The ponies constantly slipped and slid as they made their way up the steep slopes at the base of the mesas. The air had been washed of its usual dust and was sweet. The plants were already beginning to revive and show a burst of green. Within two more days the whole countryside would be lush green and covered in flowers. It wouldn't last long but the effect of rain on this parched country was always amazing. The sky was so blue that it was hard to look at for long. The sun blazed down with a withering brilliance. The rock of the mesa shone with newly washed colors, red and brown and yellow and black. Insects buzzed and chirped and birds sang from every direction. All of nature rejoiced in the sweet, precious gift of water.

At noon, they found a place where they could get across the creek. Along the way up the mesa's side, Angry had managed to kill a doe with his bow. After crossing the creek, they stopped to cook some of the venison and to eat it. They were both hungry since they had eaten little during the last few days. Buck gathered some sagebrush so that Angry could quickly smoke the remaining venison. The wind was up again and from the west so they knew that their smoke would not be smelled or seen by the Comanches down below them and around the mesa to the southwest of their campfire. They had decided to wait to attack the fort until after dark. It would take them most of the afternoon to sneak down to position anyway and darkness would help them in attacking the superior numbers of the Comanches.

"Let's tie the ponies here and ease down to the fort on foot," suggested Buck. "If our horses get wind of the Comanches' ponies, at least one of them will nicker for sure. And, we can't keep all four quiet with just the two of us."

They were approximately two miles from the fort and up on the shoulder of the mesa. They worked their way around the mesa until they were directly above the fort but still a good mile away.

"It's strange that they have no fire," said Angry. " And, I see no ponies."

"Maybe they're hid out in one of those buildings and we just can't see them from here," whispered Buck.

Maybe, thought Angry. *And maybe they're gone.* But he kept his thoughts to himself.

"I'll ease down from this direction," whispered Buck while pointing to the south. "Maybe you could sneak down through that little gully over there." He pointed to the northwest.

They each set out slowly and quietly. It took them an hour to sneak down to the hillside just above the old tumbledown fort.

"They're gone," Buck called out to Angry.

"I feared as much," replied Angry. "Their tracks lead south. It looks like there are seven mounted and a few other ponies with them."

"Look here at this burned-out wagon," said Buck. "They

didn't have a wagon before. They must have come on some travelers."

"Let's go get our ponies and spend the night here," said Angry. "Their muddy tracks will be easy to follow in the morning and maybe we can figure out the wagon mystery when it is light."

"Ok," said Buck. "How about you get a fire going and I'll go fetch the ponies."

A little over an hour later, Buck returned with the ponies and the venison. "We best eat as much as we can and sleep deep," said Angry. "The land gets much steeper and harder to cross from here on. The Pecos enters a steep and narrow canyon about one sleep south. The travel will be difficult for the ponies and we will have to ride slowly."

"All right," said Buck. "Let's get that deer meat over the fire."

The sun had risen, though they were still in the deep shadow of the mesas to the east, when Buck and Angry found Walks Alone's fresh grave.

"Maybe that boy you shot died," said Buck. "They buried someone here. They left his bow and quiver on top of the grave."

"Maybe, but I don't think the boy was hurt that bad," said Angry. "Maybe another one of them was killed by whoever was in that wagon?"

Part of the mystery was solved when Buck discovered what was left of Will and Billy Roberson. The full sun poured over the mesa rim as they finished the two graves.

"A long way to come to be slaughtered by Comanches," said Buck. "Kinda odd that just a man and boy would travel alone in a wagon. I wonder where their woman is. There ain't no buzzards hoverin' around the brush. So, I don't think they shot her and she crawled off to die. These pilgrims should have been on the upper road where there are soldiers."

"Yes, but even there is not completely safe. My family was killed only hours from the soldiers at Fort Concho by some of these same Comanches," said Angry. "Life is a delicate thing in this country. And even your family was killed in the 'safe' country."

"You're right, of course," said Buck. "Let's git a little move on."

They mounted their ponies with the two extra Comanche ponies in tow and headed down the road toward the Pecos. The Comanche tracks trailed south along the east bank of the river, clearly visible, though now hardened in the dried out mud. Buck and Angry trailed south at an easy lope. They wanted to gain ground on the Comanches but not run right into them unexpectedly.

XVII

Becky had been surprised that they had left the fort so abruptly. *The Comanches must be afraid of the Apaches,* she thought. *I wonder if the Apaches will follow. Perhaps they only wanted the buffalo and killed the Comanches by chance. The Apaches would have no way of knowing about White Elk and this group and they might have decided that chasing after Little Wolf was not worth the effort, especially with the storm.* Her ray of hope dimmed again.

They were entering a country that abruptly changed from the broad river valley that they had been riding through to ever narrower and steeper canyons. The easiest route would be down along the Pecos riverbed but that wasn't possible now because of the high water. Their current route required considerable meandering to find ways to cross the side canyons entering the Pecos. By noon they had left the mud and passed out of the areas affected by the rain. At least that helped their progress somewhat.

To Becky, White Elk seemed restless and kept mostly to himself. She saw that the others had noticed also because they looked at him with side-glances and spoke softly to one another. Little Wolf's wound caused him to groan from time to time and it had begun to fester.

At nightfall, they made camp where the Pecos made a big loop to the northwest. Becky and Mary were tied next to one another against the riverbank. Black Hand brought them food and water and then returned to his comrades.

Black Hand made a poultice of mud and ground up lichens that he had scraped from some of the boulders along the canyon floor. The boy seemed to be in a good bit of pain and had the glassy eyes of someone with high fever. Black Hand shook his head and muttered as he worked on the wound.

When Black Hand finished tending to Little Wolf's wound, he joined Running Bird and Red Horse for another turn at Mary. Mary no longer made a sound. Becky inched as far away as the rope that secured her would allow. The Kiowa and the Comanches seemed to ignore her presence just a few feet away. Becky was disgusted as well as horrified but was helpless to intervene.

"Maybe if you do not fight them, they will leave you alone," whispered Becky after the men had returned to the campfire. "They have not touched me and I have been their captive for weeks."

Mary looked at her with a blank stare as though she did not understand a word Becky had said. The shock of the last two days' events had overwhelmed Mary's ability to cope. She no longer seemed to care what happened to her. Will and Billy were dead and left to the varmints. Last night, these savage Indians had repeatedly violated her. Her only wish was to die and, if possible, take one or two of the Indians with her. This Indian girl was of no comfort. They were all savages as far as Mary was concerned. The sooner they were all dead, the better in her mind. But her mind was slowly slipping away from her. She had lengthening periods where she seemed to float above herself. During those periods, she looked down on herself with only mild interest.

White Elk spent another restless night. He dreamed that he looked up into a clear blue sky with the big man standing over him while he was helpless to defend himself. It was the helplessness that frightened him. White Elk had always been self-sufficient and a man of action. He could not bear the thought of being helpless at the hand of an enemy. He had often thought that he would die in battle but during a valiant fight not while lying helplessly at an enemy's feet.

"Are you awake?" asked Black Hand.

"Yes, of course," answered White Elk. "What do you want?"

"It's Little Wolf," said Black Hand. "His wound is not serious of itself but he now has the fever sickness. I do not know enough medicine to heal him. Badger was to have joined us but has not come. He knows the proper songs and herbs. I do not."

"I, too, find it strange that Badger and Long Tooth did not join us," said White Elk. "They were to remain at the Comancheria only a sleep or two before following. They should have easily caught up two or three sleeps ago and certainly by the time we reached the soldier fort. As for the boy, do you think that he can travel?"

"He can travel but not well and he may fall from his pony," said Black Hand. "We could tie him to the pony but someone will need to watch him closely."

"Red Horse is the brother of Little Wolf's father," said White Elk. "Show Red Horse how to make the poultice and he can remain here with Little Wolf. When Little Wolf is stronger they can return to our people or follow us as they wish."

Becky had been given a bit more freedom to move about. It was clear to her that any attempt to escape was futile. Where would she go? Besides, they would track her and quickly find her. She walked along the water's edge in the pre-dawn light. The flood had scoured the riverbed clear of brush for fifty yards or more from either side of the watercourse. Here and there were tangles of debris piled up around the base of a big cottonwood tree or a large boulder.

She walked across a mixture of rounded stones and sand. A great Blue Heron rose before her, squawking his disapproval. The bird had been stalking minnows in a small eddy along the far edge of the river. *I wonder if the Apaches will follow?* She thought. *And will the Comanches and that Kiowa ever leave poor Mary alone? I think she may have lost her mind. What can I do to help her?* The world was a dangerous place with men like these Comanches roaming about.

"Come," called White Elk. "It is time to leave."

Becky walked slowly back to the campsite. She was tired of traveling day after day and to a destination that she feared. She helped to lift Mary onto her pony. Mary was as limp as a rag. She had no fight left in her and probably no hope either.

"White Elk, I will stay with Little Wolf until his strength returns,' said Red Horse. "Black Hand has shown me the poultice and I will sing the medicine song of my father. Leave me some of the dried meat to make a soup for him. If he is well soon, we will rejoin you. If it takes more than two sleeps, we will return to our people."

"We go," said White Elk. And with that, White Elk, Becky, Mary, Black Hand and Running Bird rode off south along the river's edge.

Becky was exhausted. White Elk had driven his party hard all day. They stopped for the night at the place where the river canyon began to narrow and deepen. From that point until the Pecos pours into the Rio Grande, the canyon walls are ever taller and the river more confined. The river is intermittently shallow, fast running and strewn with boulders followed by deep stretches of clear green water.

"We should reach Quintana in three sleeps or less," said White Elk in English.

Becky nodded her head. She understood. She knew that escape was futile and that her destiny was likely to be terrible. While the men made camp she walked along the river and cried silently. If her hands were not bound, she would leap into the river and chance swimming across and running back to the road by the old fort. But her hands were tied and she could not swim far, if at all. Mary was alive but no longer in this world. Her mind seemed gone completely. Black Hand dragged Mary from her pony and tied her to a bush. She did not struggle anymore. The men seemed to have lost interest in her and now left her alone. In fact, the men seemed to be somewhat afraid of Mary now that she had that strange look in her eyes and made odd sounds. Becky wet a small piece of cloth in the river and used it to wipe Mary's forehead and to clean her face. It seemed the least that she could do.

That night, White Elk's dream returned. Again he was helpless and at the feet of the big man. His companions lay dead around him. The sun burned brightly and insects buzzed loudly. Now the big man appeared to be covered in blood but did not seem injured. How could this be? What was the meaning of this strange dream? What were the spirits trying to tell him?

White Elk awoke lathered in sweat though the night was cool. He could no longer sleep. He arose and walked along the river's edge. The night sky was filled with stars. Even without a moon, there was enough light to see dimly across the gurgling river. The canyon walls loomed on either side of the river as it disappeared into darkness downstream. He washed his face in the cold water. *These dreams are foolish*, he thought. *Let the big man come, if he still lives. I fear no man.*

RICHARD WILLIS

Becky had heard White Elk tossing in his blanket and saw him get up and walk off toward the river. She sensed that he was worried. Was it the Apaches? Quintana? It seemed strange that he would be so restless now after his calmness through most of the trip.

At daybreak, Black Hand added more dry wood to the campfire and passed around some roasted venison and the last of the turkey that they had taken from the Roberson boy. They mounted and entered the canyon. A narrow trail followed the river's edge. Occasionally, small side canyons entered the main canyon from one side or the other, but mostly the sheer cliffs were close by or even overhead. Here and there, the rocks along the canyon walls bore pictures made by the ancient ones. This canyon was a forbidding place. All of them seemed a bit edgy, even the ponies. The wind played tricks as well, blowing from one direction and then another. Sometimes it swirled in a giant eddy that danced across the surface of the river and blew coarse sand in their faces once it had skittered ashore.

At noon, they reached a spot where there was a natural crossing. There was a bit of a break in the canyon wall on both sides of the river and a plain trail led down to the water from east and west.

"We must leave the canyon here," said White Elk. "The way further downstream becomes too narrow for the ponies."

"There are deer tracks heading up the east trail," said Running Bird. "I will hunt for some meat for us while you continue on. I will find your camp tonight."

White Elk, Black Hand and the women splashed across the shallow river and followed the narrow game trail up the side canyon to the west. They stopped as they reached the top of the canyon rim. They could see Running Bird heading east up the game trail to look for deer.

White Elk led his group due south across the dry terrain. They rode up and down a series of ridges across extremely rough country for the remainder of the day. By late afternoon, they came to a place where the river canyon looped back before them. They urged their ponies down a side canyon to the main river canyon and stopped on a rock ledge just above the rushing river.

"Build a fire. We camp here for the night," said White Elk.

While Black Hand and White Elk were busy with the fire, Becky spent the better part of an hour walking along the river's edge. The gurgle and splash of the river was calming. Becky sighed deeply and looked up into looked up into the deep blue sky. Down here in the canyon, the sun was already gone from the sky though darkness was more than an hour away. A Canyon Wren sang out its tune from the far canyon wall. Tomorrow, or the next day at the latest, they would reach the camp of the Comancheros.

Running Bird rode up with two rabbits and a doe tied across the neck of his pony. The men cleaned the game and began roasting it over the fire. They all ate heartily before settling in for the night.

"I sense that we are being followed," said White Elk. "See that tall rock on the east rim? It will serve as a good lookout upriver. We will take turns watching tonight."

Black Hand and Running Bird nodded in agreement. "I will take the first watch," said Running Bird. "I, too, feel someone is following. It is the Apache and the other man, I'm sure. If it were Red Horse and Little Wolf, I would not feel this uneasiness. I think that the spirits are warning us." He picked up his rifle, waded across to the east bank and began his climb to the top.

XVIII

At mid-afternoon, Angry reined up and held up his hand. "Look, there near the river, smoke!" he said. "Someone is camped there, it must be the Comanches. The ground between us and them is open with no cover to hide our approach."

Buck could see that what Angry said was true. The brush that covered the plain was only two or three feet tall. It was tall enough to crawl through unseen but not for walking upright and certainly not on horseback. The smoke rose over the riverbank one-half mile ahead before it was quickly swept to the east by the relentless west wind.

"I don't think they've seen us yet," said Buck. "We could charge at 'em but they'd likely cut us down afore we kin git in amongst 'em. How's about you cross the river over yonder and make a ruckus comin' at 'em from the west side? I'll follow you to the river and ease along behind that tall brush on this side. When they make a move to deal with you, I'll have at 'em from this side. If'n we kin surprise 'em, we might just kill 'em all."

"This is a risky plan," said Angry. "What if they kill the woman?"

"I don't think they'll kill her unless they think we're tryin' to rescue her. My guess is that they'll think were after the horses once-t they see you comin', said Buck"

"Okay, let's get to it," said Angry.

They checked their weapons and eased down into the brush above the riverbank. Buck tied the two spare Comanche ponies to some brush as Angry made his way across a shallow section of the river. Buck walked along the top of the riverbank leading his pony. He had tied his sweat-soaked bandana across his horse's nose to keep the horse from smelling the Comanches and their ponies.

After an hour, Buck mounted and looked to the west. There came Angry riding full out and whooping his war cry. Buck waited a minute to give the Comanches a chance to see and hear Angry. Then, Buck charged the riverbank at the spot where the smoke rose.

His horse jumped the bank and skidded down the soft dirt of the riverbank popping brush along the way. Buck whipped out his

Colt and shot Red Horse as he rode at him. Buck wheeled his horse left and right looking for the other Comanches. There was only a boy lying by the fire wrapped in a blanket. Buck leapt from the saddle and ran toward the boy. The boy was too sick to stand but raised his rifle to shoot. Buck kicked the rifle aside and whacked the boy along the side of his head with the big revolver. About that time, Angry came splashing through the river.

"That's the boy I shot," said Angry. "He and this dead one were among the attackers at my farm. The boy looks very sick. I do not think he will live."

"Kill him or leave him. Your choice," said Buck.

"It is already late in the day. Let's make camp here by their fire. Perhaps, in the morning, the boy can tell us of the condition of the woman?"

Buck set Little Wolf's and Red Horse's ponies free and chased them back up river, away from the camp. They already had two good mounts each and additional ponies would just add to the bother. Little Wolf's fever heightened. Just before dawn, he began mumbling something in Comanche, then gave a long sigh and died.

"Saved me the trouble of killing him," said Angry.

Buck and Angry were up on their horses and on the move early. Buck had tied the two Henry rifles that the Comanches had carried beside the extra one on his packhorse. "These extra rifles may come in handy somewhere down the line," said Buck, "besides they were stolen from Grandpaw's store. They're mine anyways."

Angry rode on ahead following the trail left by the Comanches. They reached White Elk's campsite at the head of the canyon shortly after noon.

"They followed the river into the canyon," said Angry as he knelt over the smooth limestone rock. "See where their ponies have marked the rock? This canyon can be followed for only a few hours before it becomes impassable to ponies. I think we should ride along the west rim from here. Our way will be shorter and easier on the ponies. There is a good river crossing ahead used by my people for many years. Ponies cannot go much further down the canyon from that point. My guess is that the Comanches may camp there for the night. We might surprise them there."

"You know this country and I don't. I'll follow your lead,"

said Buck. "But lets ease up on that spot where you think they might camp. I don't want to alert them that we are coming."

Angry mounted his pony and then splashed through the gravelly riffle to the west bank. Buck followed. They each led their spare pony as they topped the west rim and turned southeast. Angry set a course more or less parallel to the river. They wound around the shoulders of a series of mesas and down and back up numerous small side canyons. They traveled at least forty miles to gain fifteen as the crow flies. They reached the crossing just before dark. The men and their horses were completely exhausted. They carefully scanned the crossing and the riverbank from the top of the rim.

"They are not here," said Angry. "See those deer drinking in the shadow to the right of the big rock? If people were there, the deer would not be."

"Do you think we got ahead of 'em?" asked Buck.

"Maybe, but we should go down and look for sign," said Angry.

Wearily, they trudged down into the side canyon leading their horses behind. When they reached the trail heading west, Angry squatted to examine the dust.

"Four of them passed this way several hours ago and the fifth one, sometime later. I think the last one stayed to hunt. See, he rides one of my stolen ponies. I know its track. My pony makes a deeper track than what we have been seeing and here are drops of blood. The fifth one must have killed a deer and be carrying it to the others," said Angry. "Also, two of the ponies make a lighter track. I think there are now two women or else your woman and a child. Maybe the second one is a woman from the wagon at the old soldier fort?"

"Maybe so," said Buck. "I thought it was strange that the man and boy had no woman with them."

Angry then said, "Wait here for a little. I will see if I can kill one of those deer that we saw for our supper."

Buck waited thirty minutes before slowly leading the four horses down the steep trail. By the time he reached the river, Angry had a fire started and was skinning a young buck. After their meal of roasted venison, Buck asked, "How much farther to the Rio Grande?"

"Two sleeps. Maybe one and one-half," replied Angry.

"And the way will be as difficult as this afternoon or worse."

"Then, we will not catch them before they reach Quintana's camp," said Buck.

"True," said Angry. "When I saw that they were not here, I knew we would not stop them in time. I did not wish to cause you to lose hope."

"How big is Quintana's camp? How many men do you think he has?" asked Buck.

"It is hard to say," replied Angry. "I would guess at least fifty and maybe as many as two hundred. His men steal horses and cattle as well as women and children over a large part of Mexico and south Texas. Sometimes, even into New Mexico. He is a very bad man but his men are loyal. It is said that he shares with them generously provided that they remain loyal. Those who are disloyal are soon dead."

"We've killed three of the Comanches who attacked your family," said Buck. "Well, technically the boy died on his own but it was your shot that made him sick. We can't kill the last one or the ones who killed my folks and took Becky and the other woman before they reach Quintana and there's no way to get them in Quintana's camp. Do you wish to abandon the chase?"

"I will kill the man who killed two sons," said Angry. "He is the one who rides my pony. But I will not catch him this week. When they are finished at Quintana's camp, they will either continue into Mexico or they will raid back to the east through Texas. I cannot enter Quintana's camp for I am known to them. Many of them remember me from my time as a scout for the Rangers. I think that we should cross the river tomorrow and travel southeast to the town of San Felipe del Rio. It is near a major crossing of the Rio Grande into Mexico. If this Comanche group raids into Texas or Mexico, we will get word there quickly."

"How large is this town?" asked Buck. "If it has a bank, I can arrange to have some of my funds sent from the bank back in Durant and then maybe buy Becky from Quintana. Once she's safe, we'll be free to kill all of the Comanches."

"The town is small. I do not know if it has a bank but buying your woman is a possibility," said Angry. "If that is your plan, we must not be seen together. Quintana has eyes and ears everywhere in this town. If we are seen together, he will suspect that you are a lawman. If the town does not have a bank, you will need to ride east, maybe to San Antonio. The road east is good. If you ride hard and have a good pony, you can reach San Antonio in two sleeps from San Felipe del Rio."

XIX

Quintana's camp was located in a little side canyon just east of where the Pecos poured into the Rio Grande. Becky could see several adobe-plastered jacals scattered along the canyon sides. A large rock hacienda sat up on a broad ledge overlooking the rivers. A wagon road had been cut into the canyon wall leading up out of the canyon to the east. Men armed with rifles were positioned at several spots along the rim to serve as guards. The camp itself was basically a small village with chickens and small numbers of goats, burros, cattle and other livestock scattered about. At present, Quintana and eighty of his men along with assorted wives, children, whores and slaves occupied the camp.

Becky rode quietly as White Elk led his party down the steep narrow trail from the west rim to the Pecos. They splashed across the river under the watchful eyes of Quintana's sentries. As they rode up into the camp, Black Hand leapt to the ground and embraced a fat, dark Mexican standing next to a small goat pen.

"Gordo, *mi hermano*, it is good to see you are still fat," said Black Hand.

"And you, *mi companero*, I see you have not been killed by the blue coats or the Texans," said Gordo. "*Hola*, White Elk and you too, Running Bird. I see you have brought two presents for El Patron. Come I will take you to him. He will be glad to see you."

White Elk and Running Bird slid down from their ponies and joined Black Hand and Gordo. Becky remained on her pony and looked about her at the dusty scene. Mary was slumped on her pony singing softly to herself. Becky had decided that Mary's mind was completely gone. The sun blazed down with a fury matched only by the swirling wind kicking dust and sand everywhere. White Elk reached up and dragged the two women down from their ponies and roughly pushed them to the ground.

"You will do everything that you are told or you will be killed," he said harshly. "Follow us."

Gordo led them up through the camp to the wide veranda along the front of the hacienda. Becky pulled Mary along with her.

"Wait here," instructed Gordo. He then disappeared into the

house.

"*Mis amigos*!" called out a muscular man as he stepped out onto the veranda. Quintana Gomez looked more like a Spanish nobleman than a Mexican bandit. He was well dressed and had the light complexion and sharp features of a Castilian. His jet-black hair was short as was his mustache. He made a grand bow with a sweep of his broad brimmed hat and indicated that the men should be seated in the heavy wooden chairs set along the front wall of the hacienda. He looked at Becky and Mary who stood before him with their heads bowed and their wrists bound. Mary continued to sing to herself and seemed to be oblivious to her circumstance.

"What have we here," asked Quintana?

White Elk pointed to Becky and Mary then spoke, "We have brought these women to trade for ponies. I took the young one from a Choctaw town in the Nations. She has been untouched by us. I kept her fresh for you. As you can see, she has not been treated badly and she will make a good worker. The other, we found along the way to you. My men amused themselves with her until she got the head sickness. Now they are afraid of her."

"*Ay, y una muy bonita y una muy loco*," said Quintana. "Consuela!" he shouted toward the door of the hacienda.

"*Si*," said a female voice from the darkness inside.

"Take these women. Wash them and feed them. After the young one is clean and has eaten, take her to the room next to ours. I will see to her after my friends and I have had a chance to dine and relax."

A short, pretty young woman led Becky and Mary inside.

White Elk stood next to Quintana surveying the area as though expecting trouble. He motioned for Black Hand and Running Bird to join him. All three looked about for any sign of treachery.

"Gordo, have Carlotta prepare food for my friends and bring it to us here on the veranda," said Quintana.

"*Si, Patron*," replied Gordo as he hurried into the hacienda.

"On the table, there is water in the pitcher and tequila in the bottle, help yourselves," said Quintana to Black Hand and Running Bird. "White Elk, come walk with me and we will talk of this trade," said Quintana.

As Quintana and White Elk walked to the south end of the veranda, Black Hand and Running Bird poured tall glasses of tequila for themselves.

"This time you come with only two warriors," said Quintana. "Where are the others? You have come a long way to be so few."

"We have many enemies," said White Elk. "Many of my party were killed along the way. We lost some in the raids but an Apache and another man attacked our hunting party at the old soldier fort where the old road to San Antonio crosses the Pecos. They killed several of my men there. For a time, I thought they were following us but I no longer feel that they come."

"*Si*, the trail from the Comancheria is difficult and dangerous. I hear that there are bad men traveling about," Quintana said with a wink followed by a deep laugh. "But enough of bad news, I will give you twelve good ponies for the women," said Quintana. "When they no longer amuse me or my men, I will sell them in Mexico. I know several who would buy the young one to warm their ranchos. The other one will not fetch as good a price."

"The young one is worth fifteen ponies, at least, and the other I will give to you for only five," said White Elk. "I will not take less. If you do not want them for twenty ponies, I will keep them for myself."

"You always bargain for more," laughed Quintana. "Twenty ponies it is. You and your men can rest here tonight and take your pleasures from our whores. Then we will ride to my rancho across the Rio Bravo and you can select your ponies from any in my remuda. Now, let us eat."

Gordo had brought heaping trays of roasted meats and steaming vegetables to the table. White Elk and his men ate heartily. Black Hand and Running Bird were fairly drunk by the meal's end. White Elk did not drink any of the tequila or any of the wine offered. He knew that Quintana could easily have them killed and take the women, if he so desired. White Elk thought that he should remain alert so that he would live to get the promised ponies.

Consuela led Becky and Mary through the hacienda and out to a small building in the back. Becky had never seen anything like the opulence of the hacienda. The rooms were huge and well furnished. The floors were made of large clay tiles that were polished to a brilliant shine. On the walls hung brightly colored woven rugs and an array of large paintings. *How could all of this be here in this arid wasteland?* Thought Becky.

A small building out back of the main house was the kitchen for the hacienda. Consuela spoke to two women in Spanish. The women scurried to heat large pots of water on the iron stoves. They appeared to be frightened of Consuela. They did not look directly at Becky or Mary.

Just beside the kitchen was a small shed with a bathtub. "Take off your clothes and get into the tub," said Consuela. "Do you speak Spanish? English?"

"Yes, English" said Becky as she pulled the Comanche buckskin dress over her head and stepped into the tub. Becky actually spoke Spanish passably well but decided that it might be best to keep that information to herself, at least for now.

"*Bueno*, good," said Consuela. "The women will bring you warm water. There is soap beside you. I will get you something to wear." Then to Mary, she said, "You come with me."

The bath was wonderful after so many days on the trail in dirt and sand. A small Indian woman brought towels and clothing. After Becky was outfitted in a bright yellow dress, she was led into a small room in the rear of the hacienda and given food. Consuela had disappeared and Becky was left with one of the women from the kitchen.

"I am called Blue Flower," said the frail dark woman. "I am Tewa but was stolen from my people as a child."

"My name is Becky. I am Choctaw and was stolen from my home just a few weeks ago. The Comanches and a Kiowa killed my husband and his family. What will happen to me? Why am I dressed so well? Where is Mary, the woman who came with me?"

Blue Flower replied, "So many questions! Because you are pretty, you will be treated well for a while, provided that you please *El Patron*. You are lucky that Consuela is here. She is the wife of *Señor* Quintana. He is not likely to molest you in her presence but be careful. If he comes to you in Consuela's absence and you resist him, he will use you anyway and then give you to his men. In any case, you will either be sold as a slave in Mexico or in New Mexico or you will remain here as a slave like me and my sister. The other woman who came with you has been taken to Gordo. He will decide her fate. Do you want more food?"

"No," replied Becky, "I've had enough. Thank you."

Blue Flower said, " I must go now. Consuela will have me beaten if she sees me talking with you."

XX

Buck stirred the ashes away from the coals, added some dry grass and small twigs. He soon had their little fire blazing. He put on a few pieces of mesquite. Angry walked up from the river with the coffee pot. The coffee had run out days ago but they had parched the last of the corn that Buck had brought for the horses. Parched corn made for a poor substitute for coffee but it was better than nothing. Buck took a sip, winced a bit, and said, "I think we should go on to this town of San Felipe. The sooner we can get there, the sooner I can have my money sent to the bank, if there is one. Elsewise, I can light out for San Antonio. We can ride together until we get close to the town and then split up."

"We will come to the old road from San Antonio to El Paso Del Norte between Quintana's camp and San Felipe del Rio," said Angry. "We must split up before then in case we encounter anyone."

"You just tell me when," said Buck.

After breakfast, such as it was, they crossed to the east bank of the river and rode up the steep trail out of the main canyon. They followed a narrow side canyon all morning before topping out on a relatively flat plain that stretched south-southeast. The sun beat down with blistering heat. The scrubby brush was dry and brown. Huge patches of prickly pear cactus had to be circumvented. The ponies kicked up a cloud of acrid white dust from the rock and caliche-covered ground. A lone buzzard circled high overhead hoping for a meal.

"Dang, it's hot," said Buck. "Even this wind don't cool me off any."

"Yes," replied Angry. "It will take us one or two more sleeps to cross this to San Felipe del Rio."

"I'm sure glad you had the good sense to make a water bag out of that deer hide. We're gonna need ever drop," said Buck as he dismounted.

"Do not worry," said Angry. "Tonight we will reach the Devil's River. There will be good water from place to place along it and the traveling will be easier tomorrow and the next day."

Buck took a drink from his canteen and poured some in his hat, which he offered to his ponies. They each drank a share.

"Let's walk awhile and give the ponies a rest," said Angry. "They look exhausted. We cannot afford to lose them."

As they plodded along, Buck thought about Becky and wondered how she fared. He concluded that she would reach Quintana's camp tomorrow night or the next day. If he had to ride to San Antonio and back for the money, it would be a week or a little more before he could buy her. He knew that she was strong in spirit and could weather most anything. He just hoped that her temper would stay in check. It apparently had so far or the Comanches would have killed her. Of course, they may have broken her will through continual abuse. If the Comanches were still in Quintana's camp, they would likely recognize Buck. He tried to put those thoughts out of his mind. *Perhaps, I can come in a bit of a disguise,* he thought. *The Comanches have only seen me with long hair and in my rough clothes. Maybe, just maybe, I can pull this off and get her out without them knowing who I am. Or, who knows, they may have left already.* He loosened his gun belt a notch and looked south across the rocky terrain. *Them Comanches and Becky are down that way somewhere,* he thought. *Hang on Becky, I'm comin'.*

The sun began to slacken its assault as it had noticeably dropped lower in the sky. They were out of the dust and walking across hard, stony ground. Ahead the land began to slope to the east.

"The Devil's River is just ahead in that canyon," said Angry. "We can find cool water and some grass for the ponies. I know of a spring just a few miles downstream where we can camp."

"Great!" exclaimed Buck. "My feet hurt and I could stand a soak in a cool pool. I'm sure these ponies would go for some grass. They haven't had much to eat except this scrubby brush for the last few days."

At first light, they rode off down the canyon. At noon, Angry said, "I think we can reach San Felipe del Rio tonight. This river will lead us to the road that is only a few miles west of the town."

What's off to the due east of us here?" asked Buck.

"There's an old trail that once led from San Felipe del Rio to old Fort Terrett. But, the fort has been abandoned for many years. I do not know if the trail is much used anymore,' replied Angry.

"Since you say that Quintana's men may know you, perhaps we should split up now," said Buck. "I can slide over to that trail by headin' up this little draw to the east. You can keep goin' south and come into town from the west. How would you feel about camping here for a day or two so's we don't hit town on the same day? I'll leave all our meat with you and you can rest up a bit."

Angry replied, "I think that is a wise plan. I will ride south a bit more to a place I know where the old ones lived in caves. I will stay there two sleeps before going to town. When I was a scout for the Rangers, I knew a Ranger named Cal Watson. He was a trusted friend. I have heard that he had opened a small store in San Felipe del Rio. If he is still there, we can pass messages to each other through him. Be careful, my friend."

"We'll meet again once I've got Becky back, if not before," said Buck. "Watch out for Indians," he laughed as he rode into the river and up the side draw.

Buck rode into the town from the east just as a dust storm began to blow in from the west. He tied his ponies to the corner post of the gallery on the front of Watson's Store, or so the sign said. As he stepped inside the door, a tall, lean man with a big drooping mustache said, "Shut the dern door, podner, before you let half of west Texas blow in."

The man stuck out his hand to shake and said, "I'm Cal Watson. I own this here place. What can I do you for?"

"My name's Buck McDougal. I'm down from the Nations trailin' some Comanches that killed some of my people and stole a woman. I've been ridin' a piece with a feller that says he and you used to Ranger together. His name's Angry."

"Why, heck yes, I know that cuss," said Cal. "He's the best dern scout I ever saw. Why, I once seen him track a patch of Meskin bandits acrost bare rock for near to eighty miles. Where is he?"

"We split trails a few miles up north so's we could hit town on different days from different directions. Except for you, we don't want folks knowing that we know each other. I plan to try and ride into Quintana's camp and buy the woman back as soon as I can get some money sent down from my bank," said Buck. "Is there a bank in town? I couldn't see much with the dern dirt blowin' in my face.

I figured you'd know the lay of the place and could tell me what I needed to know."

"No, we ain't got no bank," said Cal. "Ain't got no telegraph neither. This here little fart of a town's only got my store, a little adobe cantina and Ol' Jesus's blacksmith shop. Plus some shacks and houses, of course. If'n I was you, I'd light out for San Antone first thing in the mornin'. You can spend the night here with me and my wife, Maria."

"How much do you think it will take to buy a woman from Quintana?" asked Buck. "I don't have no experience in woman buyin'."

"Depends on the woman, of course," answered Cal. "If'n she's young and pretty and a good worker, she might fetch as high as four or five hunert dollars. I heard of a gal sellin' for that much last year. So's the story goes, she was a yaller-haired gal about seventeen or eighteen and Quintana sold her to some Grandee down Chihuahua City way. Seems this feller wanted a yaller-haired gal for a wife so's he could have yaller-haired youngins. Why anyone one thinks yaller-haired youngins is special, I do not know."

"*Buenas tardes*," said an attractive Mexican woman as she descended the stairs at the back of the store.

"This here's my Maria," said Cal. To Maria, he said, "This feller's called Buck and he's a friend of one of my old compadre's. He'll be stayin' the night with us."

"Welcome to San Felipe del Rio, *Señor*," said Maria. "We are happy to have a guest in our home."

"Why, thank you, ma'am," said Buck. "I've been on the trail for weeks and I probably smell like it. As soon as this storm lies down, I'll git down to the river and have a wash."

"No need to go all the way down to the river," said Cal. "I built me a little aquaceta from the spring and we got fresh water runnin' right out behind th' back door. In fact, I run it through a little adobe shed out back so we can clean up any time we like and have plenty of fresh water without walking more'n twenty feet out th' door. Jist help yourself anytime you're ready. No offense meant, but if'n you ride into San Antone dressed in them Injun duds and with that long hair, you're libel to get shot. And you sure won't get no banker to give you no money. Why don't you pick out some new duds from the stuff on them shelves over there? You can pay me when you get your money. Maria's purty good with the scissors. She can cut your hair."

"How about a swap?" said Buck. "I've got more brand new weapons tied to my pony than I need and from the looks of your gun rack, you look like a man that could use some new rifles. Of course, they're Henrys, not the new model Winchesters but they are spankin' new." Buck went out of the front door and was back in two minutes cradling three Henrys in his arms.

"Well, I'll be skinned for a cat and sent to glory!" exclaimed Cal. "Podner, you are one surprise on top of another. One of those Henrys will pay for your new duds and I'll buy the other two off'n you."

"I'll take the clothes," said Buck, "but give most of the money to Angry, when he gets here. He might need some before I can return. I won't need much money between here and San Antone and I'll have money when I come back. I'll leave my pack horse here, if that's alright with you?"

"Sure, " said Cal. "I'll put him in a little pasture that I got down on the river. Plenty of grass and water for him. He'll be fatter 'n a tick on a hound dog's ear by the time you get back."

Buck rode into San Antonio at mid-afternoon of the second day after leaving Cal and Maria. San Antonio was a bustling place, in a slow dusty way. He found a big bank near the old Mission where Travis and the boys had fought Santa Ana. The old mission was a tumble down mess abandoned by all but the rats. *You'd think they would have kept this place up*, thought Buck. *I guess history don't matter much to these folks.* The sign on the front of the bank said that it was closed for the day and would reopen at ten the next morning. He found the telegraph office and sent a message to Luke via Durant alerting him of the situation and that he would be drawing on funds from their bank.

Buck found a little cantina on Laredo Street just south of Market Street where he got a meal and a room for the night in a boarding house next door. He had left his horse at the livery a few streets away near a big Mexican market. After supper, he took a stroll through the streets of the old city. Music poured from a dozen doorways. The air was filled with the smells of a wide array of foods being prepared by street vendors and cafes alike. Young people strolled around the plaza arm in arm. *This seems a happy place*, thought Buck. *I had almost forgotten that people could be this happy.*

After a night of deep, refreshing sleep, Buck awoke to the sound of a thunderstorm. Rain pored off the tile roof above him in a solid sheet. He pulled the window shut, dressed and climbed down the stairs and out onto the front gallery. He went into the cantina next door and ordered some eggs and tortillas for breakfast. The man who ran the cantina was a burly German with a thick chest, massive arms, and fringe of red hair around his bald head. He wore mutton-chop side burns and a big wide grin.

"Jew vant some sausages mit die eggs?" he asked.

"No, just the eggs," replied Buck. "And some more coffee, please."

"Ja, hit's coming quick!" shouted the German.

After breakfast, the storm had passed and the hot morning sun had already begun to dry things out. Buck went to the telegraph office to see if he had a reply from Luke. The message came in just as he was asking the operator. Luke said that he had spoken with Fred Miller at the bank and that all was needed was for the San Antonio bank to wire for the transfer.

As Buck walked out into the plaza, he spied a small crowd of men milling around a short, thin man in a big hat who stood on a box saying something to the crowd. The man in the big hat had the same big drooping sort of mustache that Cal Watson had sported. Buck moseyed over to the edge of the group.

The man in the big hat shouted, "We're reconstituting the Rangers to deal with all the killing and butchery along the frontier! The Government up in Austin has authorized me to muster a battalion of six companies. Each company will have seventy-five men. Any of you boys got the sand to be a Texas Ranger? Any man who thinks he can measure up should report out to the racetrack Saturday at ten in the morning. Bring your horse and gun and we'll test your skills."

Buck drifted away from the crowd. Of the twenty odd men gathered, he'd bet there were no more than two worth the Ranger's time. Half of them looked too fat or too drunk, or both. The other half looked like they had just walked off the farm.

Buck settled onto a bench at the front of the bank and

watched the folks going and coming across the plaza. At ten o'clock, the door to the bank swung open and Buck joined a half dozen people lining up at the teller's window. The man with the Big Hat who had been trying to recruit volunteers for the Ranger troop walked over to Buck and stuck out his hand.

"I'm Major John Jones," said the man. "I saw you at the back of the crowd out there on the plaza this morning. You look like a man who can handle himself. You looking for work? I've already assigned a captain and lieutenants for each company but I'll be needing some steady men to serve as my sergeants."

"No sir, I've got important business of my own to attend to right now," replied Buck. "I just got into town from San Felipe del Rio and a met a former Ranger there, named Cal Watson. Maybe he's the man you need? Also, I'm sorta partnered up with a man named Angry who used to scout for the Rangers. He should be with Cal by now. He may want his old job back."

"Well, we're pretty much having to let that country down there take care of itself for now," said Major Jones. "I plan to stretch my battalion along the frontier from up in Stevens County down as far south as the Nueces River. Governor Coke has us charged with dealing with the Indian problems along that line and protecting the farmers to the east of it. Captain McNelly is working with a separate battalion along the Rio Grande but he's ordered to address the problems with bandits to the east of Laredo. Will you be going back to San Felipe del Rio any time soon?"

"Yes, just as soon as my business here is completed," replied Buck. "I hope to leave today, or tomorrow at the latest."

"I'll write a letter to Cal Watson," said Major Jones. "Will you carry it to him for me."

"Of course," answered Buck. "Do you know the banker here? I need to talk to someone a bit higher up than this teller."

"See that man in the bowler hat?" asked Maj. Jones. "He's the bank manager. I'd talk with him."

"Thanks," said Buck. "If you want to write out your letter to Cal while I'm talking to this banker, I can get it from you on my way out."

"Sure thing," said Major Jones.

Buck walked over to the bank manager and introduced himself. "I'm Buck McDougal from Durant in the Nations and I need to arrange to have some funds transferred down here from my bank."

"I'm Jed Wilkinson," said the man in the bowler. "How much do you need to have transferred and what is the name of the bank in Durant?"

"I need six hundred dollars and my bank is the Bank of Durant," replied Buck. "My given name is Caleb but the bank knows me by either name. I've already telegraphed my cousin up there and the bank is expecting to hear from us today."

"Well then, this should be a simple matter," said Mr. Wilkinson. He wrote out a message on a telegraph form and called to a young boy sweeping the lobby floor, "Jimmy, run this over to the telegraph office." Then he said to Buck, "This may take an hour or two. Why don't you come back between one and two o'clock and we'll see if they have sent the necessary verifications?"

"Okay, I'll see you then," said Buck as he shook Mr. Wilkinson's hand.

Buck walked over to the counter where Major Jones stood. "You got that letter for Cal?" asked Buck. "I'm done with the bank for now."

"Here it is," said Maj. Jones as he folded the letter and placed it into an envelope. "I'm asking Cal if he wants to re-join the Rangers. But, from what you told me, he seems pretty settled in as a store keeper."

"I'll deliver the letter for sure," said Buck. "I expect to leave later today."

"Thanks, and remember the offer of a job is open," said Major Jones.

"I'll keep it in mind," said Buck as he walked away.

XXI

Becky finished her meal of roasted chicken and vegetables. The food was excellent. As Blue Flower cleared away the dinner things, Quintana strode into the room. "How are you called?" he asked Becky.

Becky looked him square in the eye and said, "My name is Rebecca Griffin. Your Comanche friend murdered my husband and his family in a raid on our store. They took me, and later poor Mary, and brought us here to you. Let me go home to my family."

"Well, *Señora* Griffin," said Quintana, "You have been sold to me by White Elk and I have plans for you in Mexico. Life is sometimes harsh but you will come to see that a life in Mexico is better than a death at the hands of the Comanches or a life as a whore to my men. But, let's not talk of such unsavory matters now. Have you had enough to eat? Would you like some wine? My vineyards produce the finest Madeira in all of Northern Mexico."

Becky accepted a glass of wine. Her family never used alcoholic beverages but she thought that taking the wine might delay Quintana's plans for her. Also, she had read of wine in the Bible and thought it might be interesting to taste.

She sat in a large leather chair facing the huge window on the front of the room. The window looked out onto the veranda and across the canyon toward the Pecos far below. A fountain of spring water noisily splashed in the center of the room behind her. The mist it generated cooled the entire room. Quintana stood beside the window and sipped his wine. He said, "This is a harsh country but with sufficient resources one can live a pleasant life. Do you like my little hacienda?"

"It is the grandest house I have ever seen," said Becky. "It appears that your evil business has made you prosperous."

"My business here is but a small part of my affairs," said Quintana. "This small camp serves mainly to keep the Comanches and bandits from stealing the horses and cattle on my ranchos in Mexico."

Gordo entered the room and said, "*Patron*, forgive my interruption but a problem has occurred with one of the new men,

Tomas. He has been caught stealing a rifle from the storehouse."

Quintana's eyes flashed with anger. "Bring him to me and assemble all of the men in front of the hacienda," he said. He turned to Becky and said, "Enjoy your wine, I must attend to this matter."

Quintana lifted a gun belt from a peg beside the door. The belt had two holsters in which sat two bone-handled revolvers. He buckled on the gun belt as he stepped out onto the veranda. Gordo dragged a thin, dark young man to his feet on the broad stone ledge between the veranda and the cliff's edge. Seventy or so of Quintana's men had assembled off to one side.

"Have I not seen to your every need?" asked Quintana. "If you needed a rifle why did you not ask for one? Gordo, give him his pistol. Now Tomas, you thief, defend yourself or die."

Gordo stuck a pistol into Tomas' holster and stepped quickly away. Tomas straightened up and spit on the stone in front of him. "I am not afraid of you," he said. "I do not beg for what I need. I take it." His hand flew to his pistol but Quintana drew one of his own revolvers and shot Tomas through the forehead before Tomas had time to aim and fire.

"I will not tolerate any violation of my rules," said Quintana to the assembled men. He dropped his pistol back into its holster, pointed to Tomas' body and said, "Gordo, take this trash and dump it into the Pecos for the turtles to eat."

Becky had watched from the window. She was surprised by Quintana's quickness with the revolver. She was certain that the dark young man would kill Quintana, but suddenly a red spot appeared on the dark man's forehead almost before she heard the shot. Though startled, she had witnessed enough brutality in the last few weeks that nothing shocked her anymore.

Quintana walked back into the room and hung his gun belt on the peg in the wall. "Now where were we before this unpleasantness?" asked Quintana. "Oh, yes, we were discussing my businesses. Tomorrow, I will take you to my rancho in the mountains to the south. Would like some more wine?" He refilled their glasses without giving her time to reply. "Perhaps some music? Consuela! Have Pepe and Guillermo come and play for us."

Becky had not seen Consuela sitting in a dark corner of the

room. Consuela disappeared for a few minutes and then returned with two men who walked in playing their guitars. The musicians played and sang softly from the far corner of the room. Consuela reoccupied her large wing-back chair. After an hour or so, the music and wine had its effect on Becky. She was suddenly very sleepy. Her last recollection of the evening was of being carried down the hallway by Quintana.

Shouting from the front of the hacienda awakened Becky. She was alone in her room. She pulled a bed sheet around her and hurried to the window. Quintana, Gordo and several men stood in the sunlight at the edge of the canyon looking down at something below. Becky dressed quickly and walked into the hallway. She almost bumped into Blue Flower who was hurrying down the hallway with a bundle of dirty laundry in her arms.

"What has happened?" asked Becky.

"The woman who came with you cut the manhood from one of Quintana's men while he slept after abusing her," whispered Blue Flower. "Then she ran to the cliff and threw herself over the edge. I must go now or Consuela will have me beaten."

"I see that you are awake," said Quintana as he walked into the hallway. "We will leave soon for my rancho in the mountains. You will find that my hacienda there is not so primitive as this."

Quintana made no mention of Mary. He excused himself and went into the back rooms of the hacienda. Within an hour, an entourage had been assembled in front of the stables. Becky, Consuela, and two other women climbed into a carriage pulled by four horses. Quintana sat astride a magnificent black stallion at the head of a column of ten of his men. White Elk rode beside Quintana with his men directly behind. A supply wagon and another ten of Quintana's men formed a column behind the carriage. Gordo drove the carriage and another man sat next to him holding a double-barreled shotgun.

"*Vamos!*" shouted Quintana with a wave of his hat. They rode up a dusty narrow road to the top of the canyon wall and turned southeast.

"We will reach the river crossing before noon," said Consuela. "The crossing is sometimes difficult depending on the flow of the river."

The day was quickly hot and the wagons and horses raised a huge cloud of white choking dust. The landscape outside was a hodgepodge of rock and dust and brush. There were large areas completely covered in prickly pear cactus. Heat waves shimmered between them and the horizon. Consuela drew the canvas curtains closed and tied them in place. It provided some relief from the dust but increased the heat. The women were soon covered in sweat. Becky and the others moistened cloths with water from a canteen and mopped at their faces from time to time. It was small relief from the heat.

After several hours, the carriage stopped. Becky and Consuela opened the curtains and tied them back to allow the breeze to flow through the carriage. Ahead of them lay the Rio Bravo. The river was muddy and perhaps 300 yards wide. The road led down to it through an arroyo to a gravelly flood plain. Across the way, Becky could see where the road led up out of the river canyon.

One of the men had ridden out into the water until it was belly deep on his horse. The horse and rider were not quite half way across. He waved his hat back to the waiting column and soon, the carriage lurched forward. Gordo shouted down from his seat, "The river is only deep for a short distance. Do not move around in the carriage when we cross or you may cause the carriage to tip over."

Gordo stopped the carriage at the water's edge to allow two of the men to tie their lariats to the back corners of the wagon. Consuela explained, " The two men will keep the carriage from drifting and tilting in the current while the horses swim."

The river crossing was accomplished without mishap. Water rose a few inches inside the floor of the carriage but otherwise the women were high and dry. The gravel bar on the south side of the river gave way to a flat rock shelf. Quintana and his men dismounted and a large open tent was set up on the rock shelf. The *cocineros* soon had a fire going and lunch preparations underway. Several long tables were assembled in the shade of the tent.

"Come, walk with me," said Consuela as she set out along the water's edge. "We will reach the small village of Ojo Dulce tonight. Tomorrow we will enter the mountains and it will be much cooler. The main hacienda is in the valley of the Rio San Rodrigo. The sierras are very tall and *muy bonita*. I think you will like our rancho. Life can be pleasant if one does what is asked and does not complain."

"You will find that I speak freely," said Becky. "I am not afraid to die, if that is to be my fate. The Comanches and the Kiowa, who brought me, killed my husband, his family and two of our friends. If it is in my power, I will see them dead. You, Blue Flower and the other women have treated me well and I wish no ill toward you. Quintana has not been cruel to me so far. As of now, I wish him no ill either but I have been stolen from my people. One day, I will find a way to return home."

"Perhaps," said Consuela. "Or perhaps, you will find that your new life is not so unpleasant. But, let's eat now. I see that our lunch is ready and being carried to the tent."

By late afternoon, a large mountain range loomed on the horizon to the west and south of them. The men set up a camp just south of the village of Ojo Dulce. Becky felt tired and grimy after the dusty ride. The women washed as best they could but water was limited. After dinner, the men sat near a large fire and began to gamble. A few played their guitars and sang. White Elk and his men camped a short distance to the west. White Elk still did not completely trust Quintana and he did not want his men to drink any more liquor. They had been sick most of the day from the effects of their drunkenness of the night before.

"*Buenas dias*," said Quintana as Becky emerged from the tent that she shared with the other women. The sun had just begun to rise above the low hills to the east. "The travel today will be much better. We will soon leave the dust and begin climbing into the mountains. It will be cooler."

"When will we reach your ranch?" asked Becky.

"We have been traveling through it since mid-afternoon yesterday," replied Quintana. "My holdings are quite large. This rancho is four days ride from north to south and perhaps a bit more east to west. I have others farther south and also west. My family has been in Mexico for over a century. My great-great grandfather received these lands from the King in Spain when this was New Spain."

"With all of this wealth, why do you trade with the Comanches and keep bandits and murderers among your men?"

asked Becky.

"My ancestors fought with the Comanches and the Apaches, and also the bandits. My father and I learned that it was more profitable to make them partners instead of enemies. I lose fewer horses and cattle by trading generously with them than my grandfathers did by fighting them. My father and I have found that there are two great motivators of men, greed and fear. My men and, to a lesser extent, the Comanches, fear me but find me to be generous in trades. My men trade their time and sometimes their lives for a life of relative plenty. The Comanches bring me women and sometimes children to sell in return for horses. The Comanches have a great weakness for horses. You may consider my ways ruthless and cruel but I find them necessary. To have great power, one must present a powerful image. Now, it is time to leave. Board the carriage, *por favor*."

XXII

Angry rode into San Felipe del Rio from the west just before sundown. Three brown-skinned boys scattered at his approach. "*Indio! Indio!*" they shouted.

He rode slowly through town and tied his ponies to the hitching rail outside Cal's store. As he stepped down from his mount, Cal burst from the doorway.

"Well, I'll be hanged for a sinner! By gol, if you ain't a ghost from the past!" exclaimed Cal. "How long has it been? Twelve, maybe fifteen years? Come on in and meet Maria. I got married since I knowed you." Cal gave Angry a big bear hug and half dragged him to the door of the store. "Maria, come see what the cat drug in!"

"Welcome to our home," said Maria. "You must be Angry. Cal has talked of you often."

"I am honored to know the wife of my good friend," said Angry.

"I have made some tea from the berries of the Agarita bushes," said Maria. "Would you like a glass? It is cool and refreshing."

"Yes, thank you," replied Angry as Maria disappeared into the back of the store.

"Let's sit out back under the tree," said Cal. "It's cooler and Maria will bring us the Agarita tea."

Once they were seated Cal said, "I met your friend, Buck, a couple of days ago. He's gone off to San Antone to get some money. He pretty much explained the situation with his woman and Quintana. He said that the same bad patch of Comanches he's after also killed your wife and boys. I'm powerful sorry to hear of your misery. Buck said you were both itchin' to catch 'em and kill 'em for what they done to his people and yours."

Angry took a long sip of the lemony-tasting berry tea and said, "The ones that killed my family joined the ones who attacked Buck and his people. I was tracking them when I came upon Buck's camp while he tracked the other group. All but one of the Comanches who attacked my family have now been killed. I will hunt the last one when he leaves Quintana's camp. I need some bullets for this Henry rifle that Buck gave me. I have only ten left. Do you sell such bullets?"

"Yes, I do. The '66 Winchesters in .44-40 use the same ammunition. I have it in stock. How much do you need?" asked Cal.

"I have no money," replied Angry. "I will trade one of my ponies for one box and for some food to carry with me."

"Keep your dern pony," said Cal. "You take what you need and you keep your stuff. You saved my hide more'n once when we was Rangers up on the Nueces. 'Member that time I was holed up in that little shack when Beto Gonzales and his boys was shootin' at me. You came gallopin' in on that big tan horse Cap'n Shaw give you. You were screamin' your war yell and shootin' ever'thin' in sight. Dang near skeert me as much as you did them bandits. Them what you didn't shoot is probably still runnin'. I expect my hide's worth a box of bullets and a dab of grub. 'Sides, Buck sold me three Henry rifles and said to give most of the money to you."

"Thank you, you are a true friend," said Angry. "But, I will pay you for these things when I finish my business with the Comanches. Keep Buck's money safe for him. The rifles were his, not mine. The money is his."

"Will you stay the night and have dinner with us?" asked Cal.

"No, there are too many eyes that see for Quintana in this town," replied Angry. "I must leave now so that they think I only came here to get supplies. When this business is finished, I will return for a visit. I go now."

Angry gathered up a small bag of dried beans, some jerky and the box of rifle shells and stepped out onto the gallery at the front of the store. He waved to Maria and said to Cal, "Thank you again, my friend. *Hasta luego.*"

"*Adios, compadre,*" said Cal.

Angry tied his parcel onto one of his ponies and mounted the other. He rode slowly through the sleepy town to the west before turning south to cross the Rio Grande. He felt certain that Quintana and the Comanches would eventually head for Quintana's ranch in the mountains of Mexico and he planned to be waiting for them. He would shoot the Comanche that killed his sons from ambush. He knew an excellent place to hide above the road that led south from

Ojo Dulce. If Buck was unsuccessful in the purchase of the woman, perhaps Angry could rescue her as well as kill his enemy.

     Buck's trip to San Antonio had been successful. He had the money he would need to buy Becky and had purchased a suit of clothes before leaving town. His plan was to dress as a prosperous rancher and ride into Quintana's camp seeking to buy a young woman to help care for his children. With any luck, Quintana would sell Becky to him and they would just ride away. Once Becky was safe, he could rejoin Angry and extract his revenge by killing the remainder of the Comanches. At least, that was his plan.

     Late in the afternoon of the day after he left San Antonio, he stopped for water for himself and his horse at the Frio River. As he knelt to drink, he heard a horse nicker in the brush on the far bank. Instinctively, he rolled to his left, away from his horse. A bullet slammed into the mud where he had been kneeling. Buck scrambled away from the water and dived behind a pile of flood debris. Two more bullets hit the huge cypress tree that the debris was lodged around. Buck's horse bolted and ran back up the road to the east.

     "*Señor*, give us the money you got from the bank and we will let you live," said a voice from the brush.

     Buck said, "I'm wounded. Your shot broke my leg. Here is the money." Buck removed his cash from his money belt, stuffed the cash inside his shirt, and filled the money belt's pouch with grass and leaves. He closed the pouch and threw his money belt out into the road.

     "Throw out your pistol," said the bandit.

     Buck pulled off the belt and holster holding his old cap and ball Colt and set it on the ground next to him. He unfastened the gun belt with the .44 Smith & Wesson in the holster and flung it high in the air toward the road. He heard the bandits mount and start their horses across the Frio. When they reached the near side, one dismounted and knelt to pick up the money belt. Buck stood up from behind the pile of debris and shot the second bandit from his horse. An instant later, he shot the startled bandit holding his money belt. A third bandit had been waiting at the far side of the river. He had apparently seen enough and he galloped off down the road to the west before Buck could shoot him. Buck gathered his belongings and caught the horses of the bandits as well as his own. His horse had only run a short distance before it had stopped to graze. He tied the dead bandits onto their horses and mounted his own.

A few miles west, he entered the little dusty town of Uvalde. He stopped in front of the general store and asked a man seated in a rocking chair, "You got a sheriff in this town?"

"My name's Fisher and I'm more or less the town Marshal," said the man in the chair. "Let's see who you got across them horses."

He stepped down off the gallery and pulled each bandit's head up by the hair. He then exclaimed, "By dang, these are the Yemez boys! They been raisin' trouble all up and down this road. Where's the other one, the young one? There're three of 'em."

"The third one run off while I was shootin' these two," said Buck. "They tried to rob me at the river crossin' a few miles east. I saw one of them hangin' around the bank when I was in San Antonio. I guess that's how they knew I had some money."

"Well, you're lucky they didn't just back shoot you," said Marshal Fisher. "They don't usually face a man down."

"They thought that I was injured and unarmed," said Buck.

"That explains it,' said the Marshal.

"I have business at San Felipe del Rio," said Buck. "I need to be on my way. I don't like the look of that sky to the southwest and I'd like to get across the Nueces before the rain hits."

"Okay, pardner," said the Marshal. "I'll take these two off your hands. I don't think the young one will give you any trouble. My guess is that he lit out for the border and his mama's place. Just to be safe though, I'd watch my back, if I was you."

"Always," said Buck as he spurred his horse and rode west out of town.

Buck camped for the night in a grove of pecan trees along the west bank of the Nueces. He made a hasty supper and hobbled his horse just before the line of storms hit. As the lightning neared he moved himself and his horse well away from the trees. Rain hammered down in torrents and the thunder roared continually.

It stormed off and on all night. When he had crossed the Nueces, it was barely two feet deep. By daybreak, the river was a raging monster twenty feet deep or more. *I sure am glad I crossed yesterday mornin' before this flood,* thought Buck. *I coulda been stuck on the east bank for a day or more waitin' for this to run off.*

Buck wrung out his clothes and blanket as best he could, packed up, saddled his horse and remounted. By evening, he could see San Felipe del Rio just ahead. He rode to the shed behind Cal's store, unsaddled and put his horse in with his packhorse that was now in the shed. Cal came out of the back door of the store with a shotgun in his hands and shouted, "Who's that bangin' around in my shed?"

"Don't shoot!" shouted Buck. "It's just me."

"Welcome back," said Cal as Buck walked up to the back of the store. "I didn't figure you'd be back for at least another day or two. You have any luck in San Antone?"

"Yep," replied Buck. "Ever'thin' went slicker'n a baby's butt. I ran into a couple of desperados at the Frio crossing but they're roastin' with Satan right now. Oh, I got a letter for you from a Major Jones."

"Major Jones," said Cal. "Who's he?"

"He's raisin' up a battalion of Texas Rangers to fight the Comanches and Apaches," said Buck. " I think he wants you to join up. His letter probably explains it all. He asked me to join, but I told him I had other business. I also told him that you were pretty settled in out here. And I mentioned Angry to him. Has Angry showed up yet?"

"He was here a couple of days ago," answered Cal. "He got a few provisions and headed down into Mexico to try and catch or kill the Comanche what kilt his boys. Come on in, Mary's got a mess of beans and some chicken on the stove. You can fix yourself a plate."

Just after breakfast the next morning, Buck set out for Quintana's camp dressed in his 'Rich Rancher' outfit, as Cal called it. At mid-morning, he stopped at the head of the trail leading down into the camp. There was a little adobe hut at the trailhead with two of Quintana's men lounging in the shade of a large mesquite tree.

"Hello," said Buck as he dismounted. "I would like to see *Señor* Quintana Gomez. I am told that he sometimes can arrange for a rancher such as myself to acquire young women for work as servants."

"Quintana is not here," said one of the men. "He left almost a week ago to go to his rancho in the mountains to the south."

"Is there someone else that I can do business with?" asked Buck.

"Si, you can speak with Diego," said the guard. "He is *Jefe* when *El Patron* and Gordo are away. But you must leave your weapons here. No stranger is allowed in the camp with weapons."

Buck unfastened his gun belt and handed it to the guard. He pulled the Henry from its scabbard at handed it over as well. He had left his other weapons with Cal. "Nothin' left but my teeth," smiled Buck. His attempt at humor was lost on the two men.

"Follow this trail down into the canyon. Diego will be at the big hacienda. If he is not there, one of the women will get him for you," said the guard.

Buck remounted and rode slowly down into the canyon. His back itched between his shoulder blades. *About where they'll shoot me*, he thought. But no shot came. He dismounted at the large house and tied his horse to an iron ring hanging from the stone on the corner column of the veranda. He walked onto the veranda and called out, "Hello, I'm looking for Diego."

Blue Flower stepped out onto the gallery and approached slowly with downcast eyes, "I am sorry *Señor*, but *Señor* Diego has gone down to the river to attend to a matter. May I get you something to drink while you wait? I will send a boy to fetch *Señor* Diego."

"Some water will be fine, thanks," said Buck. "Are there other young Indian women here? I am looking for a young woman to care for my children. I was told that a young Choctaw woman was recently brought here and might be available."

"There are no more young women here now, but you must discuss that with *Señor* Diego. The young Choctaw woman was here for only one night. She was taken to Mexico with *Señor* Quintana. I must go. I will be punished if I am caught discussing such business. I will bring you water, but please ask me no more questions."

Dang it, thought Buck, *too late again*. He took a seat at a heavy oak table in the shade of the wide veranda. The woman brought a glass and a pitcher of cool water and set it down on the table in front of him.

"Do you know where *Señor* Quintana was goin' in Mexico?"

asked Buck.

"*Si*, they went to his rancho in the mountains. I was taken once. It is in the canyon of the Rio San Rodrigo," said Blue Flower. "Why do you ask?"

"Just curious," said Buck.

Blue Flower turned suddenly and looked down the trail to the river at the sound of approaching hoof beats. "I must go now," she said as she scurried back into the hacienda.

A small, dark man on a white gelding rode up to the front of the veranda and swung down from the saddle. "I am called Diego Garza," said the man. "I am told that you wish to do business?"

"Yes, my name is Sam Nixon," said Buck. "I've got a ranch on the South Llano River. I am on a cattle-buying trip through south Texas and northern Mexico. A man in Uvalde told me that servants could be bought here. I'm lookin' for a young woman to help care for my children."

Diego said, "I see that Blue Flower has brought you some water. Please, sit back down. May I have some food brought or perhaps something a bit stronger to drink?"

"No, thank you," replied Buck. He didn't like the look of this Diego. The man would not look him directly in the eye and had a nervousness about him. He wore heavy spurs with enormous rowels. *Brutal to his horses*, thought Buck. Buck knew he could not trust this man and, in fact, disliked him intensely even though they had only met.

"*Señor* Quintana often acquires young women for such work," said Diego. "In fact, he left only a few days ago with such a woman. But we have no one suitable just now. Perhaps, in a few weeks, one may come available."

"If one becomes available, please have *Señor* Gomez contact me. He can leave a message that 'help is available'. Have him use those words. Have him contact the bank in Fredericksburg," said Buck. "I must leave now to meet with my cattle buyer. *Adios*."

"*Adios, Señor*," said Diego.

Buck rode slowly back up the trail to the guard post and retrieved his weapons. He turned his horse east toward San Felipe del Rio.

XXIII

The Rancho San Rodrigo headquarters was huge to Becky's eyes. In addition to the massive hacienda and ranch buildings, there was a small chapel, a store and a cantina. In fact, it was a town not unlike her hometown of Durant except that he buildings here were of stone and adobe. Quintana's hacienda was like a castle to her. A high wall made of stone and adobe surrounded the entire compound. Two massive wooden gates stood open at the southeast side of the compound. The river roared past along the side of the north wall. Tall mountains rose from both sides of the canyon and off to the western horizon. Another set of gates opened at the back of the compound to the west.

Quintana's entourage streamed through the gate and into the compound, raising a cloud of brown dust. The Comanches, Gordo and Quintana rode across the plaza and up to the front of the hacienda. The carriage followed them. The guards broke ranks and dismounted at the cantina. Quintana dismounted and said to Gordo, "Here, take my horse and take White Elk and his men to the remuda so that he can select his horses. Except for my stallion, he may choose any twenty that he wishes."

"*Si*, Patron," said Gordo. He climbed down from the carriage and mounted Quintana's black stallion. He wheeled the stallion to the left. Then, he and the Comanches rode off northwest toward the gate at the rear of the compound.

The women stepped down from the carriage and followed Quintana across the flagstone plaza to the gallery on the front of the hacienda. The house was enormous, easily four or five times larger than the one at the Pecos. Two well-dressed men sat at a large polished table sipping glasses of dark red wine.

"Follow me," said Consuela as she crossed the wide gallery and walked through the massive front door and into the house. Becky complied. The room that they entered was even more magnificent than the one that had so impressed Becky at the Pecos. Consuela led her through the room and down a long hallway to a staircase. "Your room is the first door on the left at the top of the stairs," said Consuela. "You may rest until you are summoned."

Consuela disappeared back the way they had come as Becky climbed the stairs.

"Reynaldo, my old friend," said Quintana as he embraced the taller of the two men. "How are things in Chihuahua? Have they made you Governor yet?"

Reynaldo laughed, "You always know how to humiliate me before others. Please meet my good friend *Señor* Vincente Ortega."

"Welcome to my humble home," said Quintana as he shook the man's hand. "What brings the two of you across the mountains from Chihuahua City?"

Reynaldo replied, "I have brought Vincente to you as he seeks to find a *niñera* to care for his granddaughter."

"*Si*," said *Señor* Ortega. "My daughter has been ill since the baby was born and is too weak to care for her child. I have a local woman now who is nursing the baby. Her own baby died. But, I do not find this woman to be suitable for the long-term care of my granddaughter. Reynaldo has told me that you sometimes have suitable persons for such work."

"You are in luck, my new friend," said Quintana. "The young woman in the yellow dress who just entered the hacienda is available for such duties, provided that we can arrive at a mutually agreeable price."

Vincente said, "Name your price and I will pay it. Money is of no concern, if you guarantee that this woman will provide suitable care for my granddaughter."

"She is young and intelligent," said Quintana. "She has a strong will but I feel that, if you apply proper attention that she is not mistreated, she will serve you well. More wine?" Quintana picked up a small silver bell from the table and gave it a shake. A servant dressed in white appeared almost instantly. "*Niño*, bring me a glass and more wine for my guests."

The three men seated themselves at the table. Quintana asked, "How is business in Chihuahua? I have heard that there is growing unrest among the cattlemen over the bandits in the area."

"The bandits only prey on the weak," replied *Señor* Ortega. "Leave a few of them hanging from trees on your rancho and the problem disappears."

The servant reappeared with the wine and asked, "Should I

have Juanna serve the dinner here or inside?"

"Here, in about an hour," replied Quintana. He turned back to his guests and asked, "Reynaldo and Vincente, how long can you stay?"

"We must return to Chihuahua City and can only stay here a day or so more," replied Reynaldo. "Vincente is worried about his daughter and I have urgent business that cannot wait. If you accept our pardons, we will allow the young woman to rest for a day after your journey while we prepare for the trip back to Chihuahua. If you are not offended we will leave the day after tomorrow."

"*Si*," replied *Señor* Ortega, "I worry for my daughter and her child. Can the young woman in the yellow dress ride? The way across the mountains is no good for a carriage."

"She rode across all of Texas on horseback with her hands and feet bound," replied Quintana. "I think she probably can ride as well as any of us. I will instruct Consuela to have her ready in proper attire for a hard ride whenever your preparations are complete."

White Elk selected his horses with care. Like most Comanches, he had a quick eye when it came to evaluating horses. Gordo and two vaqueros helped White Elk and his warriors split the selected horses away from the main remuda and drive them back down the canyon toward the hacienda compound. As they neared the back gate, White Elk rode on ahead. He dismounted at the edge of the gallery and walked up to the table.

"*Señor Ortega*, this is my business associate, White Elk," said Quintana. "Reynaldo and White Elk know each other."

"I have selected my ponies," said White Elk. "As you said, they are of good quality. My men and I will leave now."

"Won't you and your men remain for the night and have some food before you leave?" asked Quintana.

"We are far from our home and must return," said White Elk. He did not trust Quintana and could see that the other two men had only looks of disgust for him and his warriors.

"Until we meet again, then," said Quintana. "*Adios*."

White Elk strode proudly to his pony and swung onto its back. His warriors were moving the horses up to the front gate as he mounted. He dug his heels into the flanks of his pony and rode to join his men.

"That one does not trust us," said Gordo as he dismounted. "*Buenas tardes, Señor* Jimenez."

"Gordo, I see that you are still getting enough to eat," laughed Reynaldo. "This is my good friend, *Señor* Ortega. He has been doing some business with your *Patron*."

"It is good to meet you *Señor*," said Gordo. "Excuse me, *por favor*, but I have duties which cannot wait."

"One moment, Gordo," said Quintana, "our guests will be leaving us in two days. See that they have anything that they need for their journey."

"*Si, Patron*," replied Gordo as he left.

Señor Ortega turned to Quintana and said, "We will leave with the woman as soon as we are prepared, with your permission. And thank you for providing us with provisions for our trip."

"*De nada*. It is nothing and of course, I understand your need to return to your daughter and grandchild promptly," said Quintana.

White Elk and his men pushed the herd of horses back up the road toward the Rio Bravo until they were well out of sight of the guards of Quintana's compound. Instead of continuing on to Ojo Dulce, they turned east across the desert, trailing alongside the bed of the Rio San Rodrigo. They camped for the night about twenty miles downriver from Quintana's compound. The river was dry for long distances but occasionally there was enough water to supply their needs. They found a little grove of cottonwoods growing on the riverbank near a small pool of muddy water.

As they sat around their campfire eating the food that Gordo had given them, White Elk said, "We will camp tomorrow along this river and then proceed to Piedras Negras. We will likely find some of our band at Piedras Negras. If not, we will raid alone. You two can guard our ponies while I visit Piedras Negras to see what is the situation there and across the Rio Bravo in Eagle Pass. When I was last in Eagle Pass, the soldiers at Fort Duncan were few in number and the town was unprotected. We should be able to steal guns from the store in Eagle Pass. Also, there are many small farms and ranches between there and the Rio Nueces where we can find more ponies."

White Elk's plan was to raid the area between the Nueces and the Rio Grande as far to the east as Laredo before turning back toward the north and northwest and home on the Llano Estacado. To the east of Laredo, the ranches became larger and more heavily defended. The smaller operations to the west and northwest were weaker. Attacking them came with fewer risks. A month or so of raiding should allow his group to amass a sizeable herd of horses to drive north. White Elk thought that one hundred to one hundred fifty was about the maximum that the three of them could manage. If he could bring such a large herd to the Comancheria, he would gain much honor among the elders.

They slowly pushed their small herd along the river. It was early in the afternoon of the third day when they made camp five miles southwest of Piedras Negras. White Elk rose from the pool after a long drink and said, " I will ride to Piedras Negras to see if any of our people are there. You two guard our ponies until I return. I should be back by sunrise tomorrow, if not sooner."

White Elk grabbed a handful of his pony's mane and swung onto its back. He rode up out of the riverbed and across the scrubby desert toward town. After a couple of miles, he turned due north so that he could follow the Rio Bravo into town. He did not want anyone to know the direction of their camp and ponies.

An hour later, he stopped on a little hill overlooking the town. He tied his pony to a bush and sat on a large flat rock on the edge of the hill. His sharp eyes soon picked out four paint ponies that most certainly were Comanche ponies. The ponies were hobbled and grazing on the brush and sparse grass one-half mile south of the town. At last, he spied their owners sitting in the shade of a juniper tree. It looked like they were playing dice on a blanket. He mounted his pony and rode in a wide arc to a spot near where the Comanches sat.

White Elk called out, "*Haa ma rɯawe.*"

"Hello to you," replied one of the men. "Who comes to our camp?"

"Broken Nose, is that you?" asked White Elk. "And, who else is with you?"

Broken Nose replied, " I am here with Little Hawk, Gray Buffalo and Bear Claw. White Elk, what brings you to our camp?"

White Elk slid from his pony and walked into the shade of

the juniper. He said, "Black Hand, our Kiowa brother, and your cousin, Running Bird, are camped on the Rio Escondido to the southwest. We have twenty good ponies and plan to get more before returning to the Comancheria. What are you four doing playing dice in the dirt?"

Broken Nose replied, "We are waiting for dark so that we can ride into town and get our friend, One Eye, out of jail. The Mexicans captured him while we were in town last night to buy some bullets. The Mexicans were upset because One Eye stuck his knife in the storekeeper. The man was rude to us and deserved to die. The fat pig screamed so much about his wound that the Mexicans began to chase us. The rest of us escaped but One Eye's pony was shot from under him during our escape. They will probably shoot him or hang him soon. I don't think these Mexicans like us."

They all laughed heartily at his joke. In fact, most Mexicans were terrified of Comanches and killed them whenever they could.

"I will help you rescue One Eye," said White Elk. "Do you want to join me, Running Bird and Black Hand? We plan to steal more ponies from the Mexicans and Texans before we return home."

"Yes, we will join you," said Broken Nose as the others nodded in agreement. "But, first we must get One Eye, and maybe make the Mexicans pay for our trouble."

"What is your plan?" asked White Elk.

Broken Nose answered, "We will wait until the moon is midway across the sky. Most of the men in town are bandits and do not care what we do. And by that time of night, most of rest of the men in town will be drunk or asleep. Bear Claw and Little Hawk will set the store and stable at the far end of town on fire. While the sheriff and townspeople who are awake rush to the fire, the rest of us will kill the jail guard and free One Eye. There are always some ponies tied outside the cantina. One Eye can take one of them. We will kill anyone we meet on the way out of town. I do not think that they will chase us far at night. They are too afraid of us."

"It is a good plan," said White Elk. "When we leave town, we should ride north across the Rio Bravo for a few miles in case anyone follows. That way they will not look for us where Black Hand and Running Bird are waiting. You can then circle to the east and back across the Rio Bravo to the south. I will ride west in the

Rio Bravo to hide my tracks and get our friends and our herd of ponies. We will meet you at the place where the rocks look like a buffalo, to the south twenty miles. Do you know the place?"

"Of course," said Broken Nose. "You and I once fought the Mexican soldiers there."

"Yes, that is the place," said White Elk.

The five of them passed the evening in darkness. They did not want to build a fire which might alert the town of their presence. As the moon passed overhead, they mounted and split up according to Broken Nose's plan.

Bear Claw eased through the back door of the livery and set fire to a haystack in one of the stalls. As he slipped out the back door, Little Hawk, who had tipped over a can of coal oil on the back porch of the general store and lit it, met him. Both buildings roared with fire in minutes.

Men poured from the cantina and ran shouting toward the inferno. While chaos reigned along the dusty street, Broken Nose and his men broke down the back door of the jailhouse. Gray Buffalo killed the guard with an arrow to the heart. It took only seconds to locate the keys to the makeshift jail cell and free One Eye. They were out of the back door and mounted before anyone detected them. Then they were off at a gallop. They made a big loop to the northwest and crossed the Rio Bravo before turning east. White Elk waved goodbye as he splashed northwest in the river's edge. After three miles he turned south and rode hard back to where Black Hand and Running Bird waited.

Broken Nose and his band rode up over the north bank of the river. They roared through Eagle Pass to the astonishment of a few drunks standing outside the saloons. After a few miles on the road to Laredo, they swung south across the river again to make their rendezvous with White Elk and his group.

XXIV

Angry had picked up the trail of Quintana's entourage and the accompanying Comanches at the river crossing. The tracks led south to the outskirts of Ojo Dulce. He avoided the village and circled it to the east. It was likely that Quintana had 'eyes' in this village since it was near the ranch headquarters. Angry's circular route struck the road two miles south of the village and soon came to the spot where the road passed through a section of tall rocks. He made camp in the rocks and decided to wait for the Comanches to return north. He was certain that they would have traded the women for horses and that they would probably drive them directly back to the Comancheria. It was the most logical thing for them to do. He would patiently wait and then kill his man when the Comanches passed below the rocks. He would kill the other two as well if he got the chance but the killer of his sons was his primary target.

After four days of waiting, Angry became impatient. He waited until night and then rode slowly south along the road. After several miles, he came to the place where the Comanches had turned their herd of horses east. *Behind them again*, thought Angry. It was difficult to tell in the moonlight, and the Comanches had tried to disguise them by dragging brush, but the tracks looked at least several days old. He dug his heels into his pony's flanks and trotted east along the trail left by the Comanches.

A few days later, he found the spot where they had camped along the Rio Escondido southwest of Piedras Negras and was surprised that they had stayed for at least two days. He could see that one rider had ridden off toward the north and then returned from the southeast. The Comanche that rode Angry's stolen horse had remained at this camp with the herd of horses. *I should not have waited at the rocks so long*, he thought. *If I had come directly here rather than waiting, I would have caught my enemy with only one companion.* He cursed himself quietly.

The trail left by the horse herd led south-southeast. Angry rested for a few hours in the shade of the cottonwood trees along the river before setting off in pursuit. That night he found the spot where five other riders had joined the Comanches before heading southeast across the desert. The horse droppings were no more than one day old so he was gaining on his quarry. But now he had a larger force of enemy to face.

Angry knew this country well. Fifteen years earlier, he had served as a scout for Captain Owen Shaw of the Texas Rangers out of Laredo. He had tracked bandits and hostile Indians all over this area of Mexico and across the Rio Bravo in Texas. The Comanches traveled in an arc to the southeast. If they maintained this direction, they should reach the Rio Bravo near Laredo. The country was sparsely settled. There were a few cattle here and there browsing in the sparse brush. *The Comanches will probably attack some of the ranches to steal their remudas*, thought Angry. *Good, that should slow them down even more. The more ponies they are herding, the more difficult it will be for them to move quickly.*

Just after sunset, Angry spotted a tall plume of black smoke rising from the eastern horizon. He urged his pony forward. An hour later, he stopped on a ridge top and looked down on the glowing coals of the burned out farm. There had been a small house and a barn and a couple of sheds. The house and barn had been burned to the ground but the sheds remained intact.

The big yellow moon was halfway above the horizon as he rode down to the farm. A spotted dog limped up to him, whimpering. It was dragging an arrow, which was stuck just beneath the skin of its right hip. Angry jumped from his pony and called softly to the dog. The dog slinked belly to the ground over to where Angry squatted.

"Come here, fella," cooed Angry. "Let's get that arrow out of your backside." Angry snatched the arrow out of the dog with one quick movement. The dog squealed in pain and ran off, fifty feet away, before plopping down to lick its wound.

"Sorry," said Angry, "but you'll feel better for it."

The dog whined its appreciation and returned to its licking. Angry stood up and walked in a big circle around the smoldering ruins. *Comanche arrow*, he thought. He tossed the arrow aside and examined the ground outside the corral. There among the confusion of tracks were those of his stolen pony. *Ha*, thought Angry, *I'm gaining on you.*

In a little shed off to the side of what had been the barn, Angry found the Mexican family. All had been shot dead, even the baby. *These Comanches need to die. I will have to kill them all,* thought Angry.

He spent most of the night digging graves in the hard ground with a shovel he had found. The moon had set by the time he finally lay down for a few hours sleep. He awoke to find the dog sitting patiently beside him. It wagged its tail when Angry sat up. Angry pulled a piece of jerky from his pack and held it out to the dog. The dog eased forward and gently took the dried meat from Angry's hand.

"You will have to hunt for yourself," he said. "Your family has been killed. You are like me, I guess."

The dog whined its approval.

Angry loaded his gear and mounted. He rode off to the east in the direction that the Comanches had taken. The dog followed him to the edge of the clearing and then stopped. It looked over its shoulder toward where the house had been and barked twice. Then it took off behind Angry at a steady lope. It had a bit of a limp but seemed no real worse for wear. The arrow had apparently glanced off of something and barely penetrated its hide.

"I will call you Arrow," said Angry. "Let's see if you can hunt Comanches."

As though the dog understood, it bounded ahead of Angry's ponies, nose to the ground along the path of the Comanches. Angry laughed out loud. "Maybe so," he said.

Buck followed the carriage tracks down to the crossing of the Rio Grande. He debated whether to head across the river or to head back to Cal's place. Quintana's trail south was days old and he had only brought his S&W revolver and Henry rifle with him. If he rode hard, he could pick up the rest of his gear and his spare horse from Cal and be back here at the river crossing before nightfall. *Better to have it and not need it than to need it and not have it,* thought Buck. He spurred his horse and raced the few miles east to San Felipe del Rio.

"Where's the woman?" asked Cal as Buck reined up to the front of the store.

"I can't seem to quite catch up to her," replied Buck. "Quintana has taken her to his ranch down in Mexico. I got to the Pecos camp too late. I'm just here to collect my traps and my spare horse."

"I'll get Mary to pack up some travellin' grub while you gather your stuff," said Cal as he turned and walked back into the store.

Buck had changed out of his fancy clothes and packed them in an oilskin pouch that he tied onto his spare horse along with extra ammunition and the food that Mary gave him. "Much obliged for all y'all have done for me," said Buck. "I'll try to find Angry while I'm in Mexico but if I miss him, tell him that I'll help hunt the Comanches as soon as I can get Becky safe."

"Sure thing," said Cal. "Watch your back, this border country is crawlin' with bandits and hostiles."

Buck gave a wave to Maria and spurred his mount west. Quintana's trail was easy to follow. Once across the Rio Grande, there was only one road south that could accommodate the carriage. He stopped for a few hours rest at midnight but was back on the trail before sunup. He found one of Angry's campsites at midmorning but the tracks were old. *With this big crowd of Quintana's, Angry will wait until the Comanches leave Quintana,* thought Buck. *That's what I'd do.*

In Ojo Dulce, Buck talked with a Texas cowhand at the bar of the cantina. "How long you been in this town?" asked Buck.

"I been here a couple of weeks. Why?" asked the cowman.

"Did you see a bunch of riders with a carriage heading south?" asked Buck.

"You mean Quintana?" asked the cowman. "Yeah, I seen the skunk and his little army. I lay low whenever he's near. He's *muy malo*. Three years ago, I was workin' for Joe Chesterly up on the Nueces. Quintana and his men hit the ranch house while we was roundin' up steers in the canyons. He killed my *compadre* and our camp cook and stole Joe's wife and daughter. We took off after him. Quintana's crowd came bilin' out of the Pecos canyon and kilt ever dern one of us except me. I was shot to pieces but got away by hidin' three days in a coyote den. Like I say, I don't want no more of Quintana. By the way, my name's Sam…Sam Spavins."

"It's good to know you," said Buck. "My name's Sam too. I'm Sam Nixon. I'm planning to do a little business with *Señor* Gomez."

"Well," said Spavins as he spit a stream of dark brown

tobacco juice onto the floor, "Quintana passed through about a few days ago. I expect he's headin' for his ranch on the Rio San Rodrigo a ways south of here. If'n you're a friend of Quintana's, I bid good day."

"I'm no friend of Quintana," said Buck. "In fact, I've never met the man. But he has something that I want. I aim to buy it or take it from him."

"Good luck," said Sam Spavins. "You'll need it. I expect they'll be shovelin' dirt over you soon. Or, more 'n likely □lettin' the buzzards pick your bones."

Buck finished his drink and walked out into the blazing sunshine. *Lordy, it's hot,* he thought. He put his foot into the left stirrup and swung aboard his horse. Dust devils danced across the road before him. He took a drink of water from his canteen and rode south out of Ojo Dulce.

That night, Buck unloaded both pistols, cleaned them thoroughly and reloaded them. He ate the last of the food that Mary and Cal had given him and then slept until dawn. After coffee, he dressed in his 'Rich Rancher' rig but strapped on both pistols. He wore the S&W .44 cal on his right hip and his old favorite, the Colt cap and ball, in a holster across his belly to his left. Over the years, he had maintained his speed in drawing the Colt as he had done in his youth. He had no doubt he could match any single adversary. *But now, I'm ridin' into a hornets' nest and they all got stingers,* he thought. *Best I stick to the original plan to buy her back and calmly ride away.*

At mid-afternoon, he cut across the trail of the Comanches and the twenty horses they drove. Though the signs were old, he could see where they left the road and swung to the east. *Lord, but I want to go get them sumbucks,* he thought. *But I figure I'd better go after Becky first.*

Most men would have been tricked by the Comanches' attempt to cover their tracks but Buck knew the trick of tying brush to the horses' tails. Besides, he recognized the tracks of Angry's pony on top of the scratches in the dirt. *It looks like Angry's a few days or so behind 'em,* he thought. *I best get a move on. I don't want them gettin' too far ahead while I'm off after Becky.*

Buck continued on the road south. He rode up of the front

gates to Quintana's ranch compound just as the sun touched the mountaintop to the west. A fat, dark Mexican stood under the arch of the entrance. He cradled a double-barreled ten-gauge shotgun casually in his left arm with the barrels across the front of his body.

Buck said, "My name is Sam Nixon. I would like to speak to *Señor* Quintana Gomez about buying a servant woman to care for my children."

"We have none to sell," said Gordo. "We had a little Choctaw but she was sold and taken away by her new *Patron*."

"Do you know where she was taken?" asked Buck, his eyes flashing.

"It is not for me to say," answered Gordo.

Just then, Quintana strolled out of the shade of an arbor to the right of the gate. He was dressed in riding clothes and wore two bone-handled revolvers facing butt forward, one on each hip.

"I am Quintana," said the man. "Gordo is correct. We do not have any women for sale at the present time. Why are you so interested in the Choctaw woman?"

The man's got a swagger to him, thought Buck as he swung down from the saddle, then he said, "My business."

Quintana asked, "Do you seek the charms of young Choctaw women? This one could warm a man's bed."

Buck tensed and his eyes flared with blue fire. The look was not unnoticed by Quintana. Quintana then said, "Ah, perhaps you are the man from whom she was taken? My Comanche friend White Elk told me of a big man like you with blue eyes who haunts his dreams. I have learned to trust White Elk's dreams. I have found that his dreams often foretell events yet to come."

At that instant, all three men made critical mistakes. Gordo began to reach for the shotgun's hammers with his right hand. Simultaneously, Quintana's hands crossed his belly to draw his pistols. Like lightning, Buck drew his big Colt and like thunder, it boomed three times before Gordo could fully cock and raise the shotgun. Quintana managed to pull his pistols but took two shots to his chest before he could raise them and aim. Gordo took one of the heavy .44 caliber balls through the brain. Before Quintana had hit the ground, Buck realized that Becky's location had possibly just died with Quintana.

Dang it! Thought Buck. Before he could worry too much

about what he had just done, a bullet whined past his right ear and another kicked up the dust at his feet. Quintana's men poured out of one of the buildings and started to shoot in Buck's direction. Buck shot two of them with the Colt before switching to the S&W. He grabbed the reins of his horse and pulled it and the packhorse back outside and behind the wall to the right of the gate.

He quickly looped the reins through an iron ring hanging from the adobe wall, grabbed the Henry rifle from its scabbard, and peeked around the edge of the gate. Three men were crouched over the bodies of Quintana and Gordo having an animated discussion. At least a dozen, maybe more, crept along the walkways leading toward the gate. Buck fired two shots from the rifle in the general direction of the larger group of creeping men. The three men near Quintana's body dived to the ground while the men at whom Buck had shot, scattered like quail. Buck ran back to his horse, untied him and leapt into the saddle. He was away and out of rifle range before Quintana's men had a chance to shoot. *They'll probably decide to discuss their options without Quintana before they come after me*, thought Buck.

Buck turned out of the road into a thicket and looked back toward the compound. Quintana's men were busy sacking the compound for anything of value. They had no more interest in Buck. Quintana was dead and all his riches were unprotected. They behaved like the thieves and riffraff that they were. Buck eased back through the woods and circled around to follow the river back to the north wall of the compound. He hid his horses in a thick stand of trees and ran to the wall just as darkness fell. Many of Quintana's men rode out of the gate and headed back toward Ojo Dulce. Buck slipped through the gate and eased his way toward the big hacienda.

Buck poked his head into the kitchen door of the little building just behind the hacienda. Two women stood next to a large wooden table having an animated discussion in Spanish. Buck cleared his throat and said, "Do either of you speak English?"

Both women appeared to be terrified of Buck but one said, "*Si*, yes, a little bit. Please do not harm us, we are mere servants."

"I intend no harm," said Buck. "Do you know where the Choctaw woman, that was here a few days ago, was taken?"

"Yes *Señor*, she was taken on the trail to the west through the mountains to Chihuahua City."

"When and how far is this Chihuahua City?"

"Two days ago and Chihuahua is many days to the west, but I do not know for certain."

"Much obliged," said Buck. He slipped back out of the kitchen and made his way back to his horses.

Becky had never seen such mountains. The trail that they were on followed the river ever upwards until it led up and over a mountain pass. There were six of them in their little traveling party. *Señores* Ortega and Jimenez, Becky, a cook named Paco, and two servants named Chama and Mano. Paco served also as the trail guide and often ranged ahead of the others. The trail was very steep in places and they stopped many times to rest the horses. Becky was now certain that she could never find her way home. Even if anyone had tried to find her, how could they possibly know where she was now? She had no concept of Mexican geography and knew only that she was far south and west of home. As they topped the pass, she could see nothing but mountains ahead. In two days of hard travel, they had not gotten very far west of Quintana's ranch. Mostly they had switched back and forth up and down the sides of steep slopes.

That night as they camped, *Señor* Ortega approached Becky and said, "I have thought about what you have said about your past and how you came to your present circumstances. I assure you that you will not be harmed by me or by my workers as long as you do not cause trouble. The past is done, for good or ill. You will live in pleasant surroundings and should decide that you have a new life and a new family. Our journey ahead will be difficult once we leave these mountains. We must cross a hot and dry desert, another mountain range, and an even drier desert. The way will be difficult for us all. Any attempt to escape will be fatal, as no one can survive alone in these deserts. Even the Apaches and Comanches avoid them. This is why we take this difficult route. The risk of attack by bandits and savages is low."

Becky nodded that she understood but in her heart she knew that one day she would find a way to return to her own people. For now, she would comply with reasonable demands and bide her time. In a way, she was dependent on Señor Ortega since he had the horses and knew the geography. If she were to be able to escape, she did not want to return to Quintana's ranch and had only a general notion of the direction toward home. She vowed to herself to pay attention to any descriptions of roads or trails to the north and to study maps if they were available at her final destination.

XXV

Buck rode hard until he was certain that no one had followed him. It was dangerous along the narrow river trail in the dark, especially leading a packhorse. After an hour, he decided to stop rather than risk injury to himself and his mounts. *Here I go in the wrong dang direction to help Angry catch the Comanches,* he thought. *Well, Angry can take care of himself. He did long before he met me, and Becky is too close to pass up the chance to find her. Besides, this Grandee she's with has no reason to suspect he's bein' followed. That gives me an edge.*

He was in the saddle as soon as there was enough light for him and, more importantly, the horses to see the trail. He pushed as hard as his mounts could go and switched horses every hour. At mid afternoon, he found the signs of their first camp. Becky's footprints were obvious in the soil next to the stream. She wore boots now and hers were easy to pick out from the larger tracks of what seemed to be four or five men. The shod horses that they rode left much easier tracks to follow than the unshod Comanche ponies that Buck and Angry had trailed across Texas.

That night, Buck settled into his blankets next to a small spring that poured out of the rock wall next to the trail. It was cold up here but a bit of a relief after all the weeks in oppressive heat. He thought back to the time when he and his cousin, James, were in competition for Becky's hand. How silly those times now seemed after the horrors since the attack at the store. These people, who had Becky now, were not the Comanches who killed Grandfather and James. In fact, they might be fairly nice people if one overlooked the fact that that bought others for servants. What should he do when he overtook them? The fact that they did business with Quintana did not necessary mean that they were cruel or even criminals. Since they had bought Becky as a servant, they would not likely sell her to him. If the remainder of their journey was anything like the trail from Quintana's compound, they would not give her up for mere money. He would have to take her, either by stealth or by force. Circumstances would dictate. He drifted off to sleep as these thoughts raced through his mind.

Becky decided that she had had enough of just sitting at their nightly camps. They had crossed the first mountain range, a bone-dry desert, and were well into the second range. She pitched in to assist Paco with cooking the evening meal. Paco had driven two metal rods into the ground on either side of a small campfire. A third rod was run through loops that had been formed on the upper ends of the two vertical rods. An iron stew pot hung from a hook on the horizontal rod. Becky bent over the pot to give the stewing meat and peppers a stir while adding some herbs that Paco had given her. Meanwhile Paco made tortillas from masa and water. Chama and Mano had been sent off hunting to find venison to supplement their meat supply. Reynaldo and Vincente sat on a big flat rock smoking their cigars and drinking coffee. The sounds of a series of rifle shots echoed from the mountainsides around them. It was impossible for her to tell the number of shots or even the direction of their source.

"Chama and Mano must have found an entire herd of deer," said Reynaldo.

Vincente snorted, "Ay! They are my men and they are terrible marksmen. We will be lucky if they hit anything. And, after all that shooting, I counted four or five shots; there will be no game within miles. Everything will have run away."

The two continued laughing as Reynaldo tipped a little more brandy into their coffee cups. Becky stood up from stirring the steaming pot and looked toward the path leading into the boulders north of the campsite. With a clattering of loose rocks, Chama bolted from behind one of the boulders in a half run, half stagger and fell at the feet of Reynaldo and Vincente. He had been shot several times and was gasping to catch his breath. From the amount of blood on his clothing, it was evident that he was mortally wounded.

"What has happened? Who shot you?" exclaimed Vincente.

Vincente, Reynaldo and Paco quickly armed themselves as Chama rasped out, "Bandits. They come."

"Quick, Paco, douse the fire and help me pull Chama to safety. EVERYONE, GET BEHIND THE BOULDERS NEXT TO THE WALL OF THE CLIFF!" shouted Vincente.

Benito Mendoza and his men had tired of the poor candelilla harvesters who scratched out a meager living by boiling down the plants and extracting wax in the little village of Boquillas del Carmen. The only cantina in town served only poor quality *pulque* and there was little of value in Boquillas other than the wax. Carrying enough of it the long distances necessary to sell the wax was not worth their effort. Let the peons do that. Benito decided to strike southeast through the mountains. There were rumors along the border that miners now found gold and silver in the mountains to the south and southeast. Perhaps they could find some gold or silver that one of the mines might be moving toward Chihuahua City.

Benito stood up from the small table in the cantina and spoke to his two men, "*Vamos*, let's go. I have had enough of the fat women and poor drink in this town. We ride to find riches!"

They rode south, skirting the western edge of the Sierra del Carmen for two days before taking the old mining trail east and up into the mountains. Just before dark on the third day, they stumbled upon two men with rifles walking up the trail toward them. As one of the men raised his rifle to take aim, Benito shot him with his revolver. Benito and his men rode in among some large boulders and dismounted. He and his men managed to shoot the second man several times as he ran back down the trail but they lost sight of him in the failing light.

"I know that we hit him," said Benito. "I could see him stagger each time we shot but is he dead? Julio, go see if he is dead."

"Are you loco?" replied Julio. "I'm not going down there in the dark and get shot by some *pendejo* of a peon."

"You are both worthless cowards," said Benito. "I'll go myself. Be careful that some coyote doesn't get the both of you while I am gone."

From the glow behind the ridge to the east, Benito knew that a fat yellow moon would soon provide plenty of light. He moved carefully to the spot where he had last seen the man running. There was a pretty good trail of blood splotches that he could see even in the poor light. He quietly eased around a bend in the trail and heard voices and horses snorting just below him near the base of the cliff that this trail descended.

"Did you find him?" asked Julio far to loudly as he and Chuy scrambled to join their leader.

"Shh!" hissed Benito as he jabbed Julio in the ribs with his elbow. "Be quiet you fool," he whispered. "There are more of them down below."

All sounds from below had abruptly ceased. Then they saw a gun flare an instant before a bullet whined just inches over their heads. Benito, Julio and Chuy dropped to the ground. Chuy fired a few wild shots in the general direction of the gun flare.

A sliver of the big yellow moon eased above the rim of a tall mountain to the east. Benito could see the hobbled horses of the people below him but he could not pick out any of the travelers. Then, he heard a moan from behind the rocks next to the cliff.

"Chuy, you move to that spot on the cliff above them," whispered Benito. "Julio and I will ease down the trail. They will not be able to see us until we are almost on them. If you see anyone, shoot him."

Buck knew that he was getting close. At most, he was only a few hours behind Becky and the others. The sun set early in the mountains but there was a long period of twilight, and tonight there would be a bright moon. Near dark, he thought that he heard the sound of gunfire somewhere up ahead. The distance was difficult to judge due to the reverberations from the cliff sides around him. He thought that the party could be hunting for meat. He had seen the signs that they had killed some game at several of their previous camps. He was glad that he had decided to keep moving slowly onward rather than stopping to camp for the night. He topped a little ridge just as the moon popped over the mountain behind him. Down below, he could see the horses of the party he was tracking and something reflecting in the moonlight atop the cliff above the travelers. Just then, an orange muzzle burst spit from the spot of the reflection atop the cliff. Someone was shooting at the traveling party!

Lordy, ain't this a complicated mess, thought Buck. He moved down a few yards below the ridgeline and tied his horses to a small tree. He grabbed his rifle and a box of cartridges and eased down the trail to get a better vantage point. He was still confused as to who was shooting at the travelers and why. *Well, I don't have all the facts but sure as sunrise, that peckerwood atop the cliff is shootin' towards where Becky may be. If I can spot him, I'll remove him from the puzzle*, he said to himself.

As Buck moved to a better position, Benito and Julio made their way down the trail and stopped just around a bend from the little meadow where the traveling party had stopped for the night. Julio darted toward the horses in an attempt to lead them off. Vincente popped up from his hiding spot and shot, hitting Julio in the hip. Benito fired and hit Vincente in the chest. Chuy began firing again from atop the cliff and the traveling party returned fire both toward Chuy and toward Benito.

During a lull in the firing, Benito shouted, "Give yourselves up and we will not harm you further. You are surrounded and I have many men. We only want your money and your horses. Give us those and you can leave alive."

Paco whispered to Reynaldo, "*Señor*, I think there are only two plus the one that *Señor* Ortega shot."

"*Si*," whispered Reynaldo, "but Vincente is dead and so is Mano. Chama is so badly wounded that he is taking his last breaths as we sit here. We do not know how badly the one that Vincente wounded is injured and we are only two. I cannot be certain that this bandit does not have more men nearby. We are in a desperate situation."

Reynaldo then shouted in Benito's direction. "We have nothing of value. You have killed three of our party. We are throwing out our only weapons. Do not harm us."

Reynaldo threw Chama's old hunting rifle and Vincente's carbine high into the air toward where Benito hid. He kept his pistol and repeater and Paco still had his rifle, plus a shotgun that they used for bird hunting.

"Ok, that's smart," said Benito. "Now come out where I can see you."

Reynaldo whispered to Becky, "Hide yourself and keep quiet." To Paco, he said, "Put your rifle and the shotgun in easy reach but stand up empty handed. I will do likewise."

As the two men stood up and raised their hands into the air, Chuy fired from the cliff top. Paco fell forward. An instant later, a rifle boomed from the trail to the east and Chuy pitched to his death from the cliff top.

Buck levered another cartridge into the Henry's breech and

ran in a zigzag pattern down the trail. Reynaldo dropped to the ground and grabbed his guns. Paco moaned. He was alive and obviously only slightly injured. Both Reynaldo and Benito shared the same thought, *Who is this firing from that direction?*

Benito edged toward where Julio lay moaning. "Can you fight?" he asked.

"My leg is broken up high near the hip," replied Julio. "I am bleeding badly and I cannot take the pain."

"Then, *Vaya con Dios*," said Benito as he crawled into the shadows toward the trail to the west. When he got to the bend in the trail where he knew he was out of sight, he jumped to his feet and ran back to where his horses were tied. *Maybe life with the candelilleros back in Boquillas wasn't that bad after all*, he thought as he galloped back up the trail leading both of his companions' horses.

Buck stopped behind a house-sized, red boulder fifty yards east of the campsite. "Hello, the camp," he shouted. "I'm am a friend."

Becky's heart leapt in her chest. She barely managed to yelp, "Buck, can that really be you?'

"It's me, alright. Are you okay?" answered Buck.

"Yes," she replied before she burst into tears of joy and relief.

"You men," called Buck. "Where's the rest of them what's shooting at you? Don't shoot me, I'm coming in."

Reynaldo stepped back toward the cliff from his hiding spot. He said, "Come Stranger. We will not shoot our rescuer."

Paco sat up and put his fingers to a small gash where the bullet had grazed his temple. Reynaldo saw that his wound was slight and said, "Paco, see if you can't determine whether the bandits have left, but be careful."

As Buck stepped into the camp, Becky lunged into his arms. He held her with his left arm but kept the rifle in his right hand where he could swing it up and fire, if necessary.

"Oh, Buck," cried Becky. "I thought you had been killed at the store. How did you find me?"

"Wounded but not killed," he said. "Time enough to tell the

tales of our travels later but first, let's deal with the issue at hand." To Reynaldo, he said, "I'm Buck McDougal and I've come to fetch Becky back home to her folks. What's your stake in this?"

Just then, Paco returned. He eyed Buck suspiciously as he wiped his knife blade on his trouser leg and said, "*Señor* Jimenez, the bandits have left. I heard their horses running up the trail to the west. I finished off the one we wounded with my knife. He was dying anyway and killing him was just a mercy."

Reynaldo nodded and said, "Relight the campfire, Paco." To Buck, he said, "I am called Reynaldo Jimenez. The two dead men here are my dear friend Vincente Ortega and his servant, Chama. I assume that Vincente's other servant, Mano, is dead somewhere up the trail. My friend had purchased Rebecca to serve as a *niñera*, how you say a nanny, from a man named Quintana Gomez. But you must have spoken to Quintana or else you would not be here?"

"I spoke to him right before I had to kill him," said Buck. "I found out about your group from one of Quintana's servants. Here's the straight of it. I'll help you tidy up your dead and then you can be on your way. Come mornin', I'm takin' Becky with me. I intend you no harm but I'll not tolerate any interference. I've had to kill quite a few to get to here and I won't lose any sleep over anyone who gets in my way. Oh, yeah, Becky's goin' to need that horse she's been ridin'. I'll pay you for it."

"The horse is yours, *Señor*. Consider it a small gift for saving us from the bandits," said Reynaldo.

Paco and Buck dug five graves by moonlight for the two bandits and the three members of Reynaldo's party. Buck retrieved his horses from where he had left them tied. He unsaddled his mount and removed the pack from the packhorse. Once they were hobbled and set loose to browse, he moved Becky's horse near his and placed her tack next to his. He took her blankets and made her a bed near a little campfire that he had built a few yards from Reynaldo's campsite. He wrapped his blanket around his shoulders and sat down across the campfire from where Becky lay.

"Buck, I..." began Becky.

"Shh, sleep now," interrupted Buck. "We'll have a lot of time to talk on our way back. There's been more'n enough excitement for one day. Talk can wait. It's enough that you are alive. You are safe now. I'll be right here all night."

Becky could hardly believe that Buck was here and alive and had saved her. How could she sleep? She had a thousand questions. It was true that she was physically and emotionally exhausted. As she relaxed for the first time in many weeks, she dropped into deep sleep.

Buck could tell by her regular breathing that Becky was asleep. He eased over to her and adjusted her blanket to cover her better against the night's chill. He knew that she had wanted to talk and for him to comfort her but somehow he felt distant. He was having difficulty sorting through his emotions. Somehow, his hatred for the Comanches had gradually taken control of him. He still had strong feelings for Becky, or at least he thought he did, but he felt that he had a job undone. He needed to get her to safety, of course. But, he absolutely had to find the Comanches and kill them. Nothing would get in the way of that except his own death.

He eased over to Reynaldo and Paco's campsite and whispered to Paco, "No sense us both standing guard. Get some sleep. I'll wake you in a few hours and you can stand watch while I get a little sleep."

"*Si, gracias,*" said Paco as he settled into his blanket.

An hour before daylight, Paco shook Buck's shoulder. Buck jerked awake and drew his Colt. He relaxed and said to the startled Paco, "Thanks pardner, I guess I'm still kinda jumpy." Paco wandered back to his camp while Buck busied himself with saddling the horses and loading his packhorse. Becky assisted with the loading. They shared a quick breakfast of leftover stew and tortillas with Reynaldo and Paco. Becky and Buck swung up into their saddles and started back toward the east, Reynaldo called out, "*Vaya con Dios*, you have a long and difficult trip ahead, as do we."

Buck replied, "So long."

XXVI

"Gray Buffalo, the great bow hunter of our band!" chided One Eye. "Not everyone can shoot at a running Mexican and hit a dog! I will call you Dog Shooter from now on."

"My arrow hit that fence post when the Mexican ran behind it," said Gray Buffalo. "It only glanced off into the dog's backside."

They all laughed at One Eye's joke. The raid on the little farm had only netted them one new horse.

"We should ride to Laredo," said Broken Nose. "These Mexicans around here are too poor to have many horses. At the rate of one pony per raid, it will take us six moons to have enough. And, besides look at what a sorry pony this one is. I will be surprised if he doesn't die on us."

"There is a large ranch one half sun to the east," said White Elk. "There are many vaqueros there, so there will be many ponies. We will attack them at night and drive the ponies away while the vaqueros sleep. There will only be a few guards to kill. We will use the bows on them."

"Their dogs had better beware if Dog Shooter is to attack the guards," laughed One Eye.

"We will see who can shoot the bow," said Gray Buffalo. "One Eye has used his rifle too long. I don't think he remembers the bow."

One Eye and Gray Buffalo were brothers and they constantly chided one another. Both were excellent shots with bow or rifle, and everyone in the group knew it.

The Comanches moved their horse herd through a little draw as the sun began to set behind them. White Elk rode to the head of the herd and raised his hand. "We should stop the ponies here and make camp," he said. "Black Hand and Running Bird will stay with the ponies while the rest of us will ride over that ridge to the east. The ranch that I told you about is just beyond the ridge. Let us rest for a bit to allow the vaqueros time to go to sleep before we attack."

They pushed the herd of horses into a little box canyon to the west side of the draw and blocked them in with a big pile of thorny Whitebrush. Then, they dug a hole to hide the light from a small fire that they made to roast a deer and two turkeys they had killed earlier in the day. After eating, they rested for a few hours. At midnight, White Elk arose and said, "Let's go."

From the ridge top, they saw that two vaqueros were driving a herd of seventy-five to eighty horses slowly south toward the ranch house. "They have taken them to the river for water," said White Elk. "And now they are returning them. If we hurry, we can drive them back north before they reach the ranch. Those two vaqueros will be easy to kill if we rush them now. Little Hawk, ride back to where our ponies are hidden. You and Black Hand and Running Bird should drive them north to meet us at the river."

Little Hawk rode back as the others galloped east toward the unsuspecting vaqueros. They hit the herd of horses at a full run and had them turned almost before the vaqueros could react. One Eye shot one of the vaqueros with his bow but the other started shooting with his pistol. Discretion ruled over valor, though, when the vaquero saw that he was alone and badly outnumbered. He wheeled his horse back to the south and raced for the ranch.

"He will alert the other vaqueros!" shouted Broken Nose. "Can you catch him, Gray Buffalo?"

Gray Buffalo always rode the swiftest of mounts. He was legendary in the tribe for winning at horse races, so much so that no one would challenge him anymore. He raced away after the fleeing Mexican almost as Broken Nose spoke. His big paint stallion ate up the ground between him and the racing Mexican. But they were almost to the ranch before Gray Buffalo was within range to shoot with his bow. The vaquero screamed, "Indios! Indios!" at the top of his lungs. His pistol was empty and the guards at the gate were either drunk or asleep. Gray Buffalo's first arrow hit him in the lower back just as he raced through the gate. The second arrow knocked him from his horse. Finally, the ranch was aroused by the vaquero's dying screams. Gray Buffalo spun his pony around and galloped off into the darkness. The guards closed the heavy wooden gate and prepared for an attack as he disappeared into the night.

"Did you get him?" asked White Elk as Gray Buffalo caught up to his companions.

"Yes, but only as he reached the ranch," answered Gray

Buffalo. "They think we are about to attack the ranch. I think they may not follow for a little while. The vaquero that I chased will not tell them anything. He is dead."

"Quickly, to the river!" shouted White Elk.

They began shouting and snapping their short whips at the horses to the rear of the herd. In less than a minute, the entire herd was at a dead run to the north. The herd hit the river at a gallop but the Comanches had run them into a section that was a little over belly deep. That was enough to stop them. They held the herd in the water until Black Hand, Running Bird and Little Hawk arrived with the other horses. They waited for the newcomers to drink before pushing the herd across the river into Texas.

They drove the herd due north through the dense brush for two hours. The trail through the brush was narrow and the brush was covered in spines. It was slow work but there was no danger of the horses straying away from the trail due to the denseness of the brush. They stopped at a small clearing. Their spot was easily defended should the Mexican decide to follow. No more than two or three riders could pass up the trail abreast into the clearing. The Mexicans would know this and certainly abandon the chase at the river.

Angry had followed the Comanches' trail from the small ranch where they had slaughtered the Mexican family, to the ridge above the large ranch. The big ranch seemed deserted. *Strange*, thought Angry. He rode slowly down the ridge to the road leading north from the ranch. The dust of the road was a huge confusion of tracks and difficult to read in the first light of dawn. Arrow sniffed about in a large circle and then set off at a lope to the north baying as he went.

My read, too, thought Angry. *The Comanches have stolen more horses here and the men from the ranch are after them.* Angry kicked his mount in the flanks with his heels and trotted off after Arrow. He had lost sight of the dog as it had raced ahead and around a curve in the road. He kicked his mount up to a gallop. As he rounded the curve he met Arrow racing back toward him with his tail tucked between his legs.

Before Angry could stop and turn back, rough-looking vaqueros surrounded him with their pistols drawn. He dropped his reins and raised his hands. Arrow disappeared into the brush and was nowhere to be seen.

An older man on a big gray mare rode up to the front of the group where Angry waited. "*¿Habla español?*" he asked.

"*Un poco. Ingles es major*," answered Angry.

"Ok, in English, then," said the man. "Where are your horse thief friends? How many are they?"

Angry replied, "They are Comanche. I am Lipan Apache. They are my enemies. I seek to kill them to avenge my wife and sons."

"Maybe yes and maybe no." said the man. "Alberto, bind him," he said to one of the vaqueros. He turned to Angry and said, "We will take you back to my rancho and determine if you tell the truth."

The vaquero tossed a loop from his riata over Angry and bound his arms to his sides. They took his bow and his rifle and led him and his packhorse back to the ranch. Angry was roughly pulled from his pony and dragged to a small shed where his feet were tied. A braided rawhide riata was looped around his neck and snubbed to a rafter above Angry's head. He had to stand up straight or the noose around his neck would tighten. "You will talk by morning," said the vaquero as he walked out of the shed.

Angry stood half asleep in the darkness with the riata digging into his neck when he detected the smell of a dog. "Is that you, Arrow?" he whispered. The dog whimpered in recognition.

Angry began struggling with the rawhide throngs that bound his wrists. His hands were numb from the tight thongs and his back and legs ached from standing all night. The noose around his neck choked him as he struggled to free himself. Arrow seemed to understand and started chewing on the leather thongs that bound Angry's feet. "Good boy," whispered Angry as he worked at a knot at his wrists with his own teeth. Just barely, he felt the throng loosen a bit. At least, his hands were in front of him so that he could get at the leather with his teeth. He gnawed in earnest at the knot and finally bit through the thong. Once his wrists were free he pulled himself up by grabbing the rafter and slipped the riata off over his head. He dropped to the ground and finished Arrow's job of untying his feet. A quick peek outside confirmed that the vaquero guarding the front gate was asleep and the way was clear for his escape. "Come on boy," he said to Arrow. They both raced through the front gate and into the darkness.

Angry loped up the road for two hours before he reached the river. The rain during the night had washed out the Comanches' tracks but a herd that size wouldn't be too hard to find again. But first, he would need to find a horse of his own and a weapon. The brush around here and mesquites would not serve for bow and arrow making and he didn't have the time to search this country in hopes of lucking upon better wood. *I will just have to go down river to Laredo and see if I can find one of my old Ranger outfit compadres or someone in the Lipan village nearby who will advance me a horse and rifle*, he thought.

He waded across the river. Arrow was reluctant to swim across. The dog had never seen that much water in one place in his life. He ran back and forth on the south side of the river barking and whining. Angry trotted up the sandbar and over the north riverbank and out of sight. Ten minutes later a sopping Arrow came running up along side Angry wagging his tail. Angry could swear that the dog grinned. They both set off down the narrow dusty trail toward distant Laredo.

After several days of walking, Angry and Arrow both stopped and sniffed a new smell in the air. They were both getting close enough to town to smell it on the gentle southeast breeze. Towns had a smell about them that was different than that of the countryside.

XXVII

Buck had drawn a crude map based on directions that Paco had provided. If Paco's directions were correct, and if Buck could locate the passes and trails that Paco described, he and Becky should cut several days off of the trip back to the Rio Grande. They would ultimately follow La Parida Canyon and strike the Rio Grande nearly across from where the Pecos entered from the north. There were many dry and dangerous miles yet to cross.

As they headed east through the first of the mountain ranges they would cross, they rode side-by-side whenever possible. Becky first asked about the results of the raid on the store. Buck confirmed her fears that both James and Grandfather had been killed. They talked about their respective journeys from the store to Palo Duro and then south across Texas.

Becky asked, "Was that you who attacked the Comanche hunting party at the soldier fort on the Pecos? If so, you weren't alone?"

"Yes, that was us," replied Buck. He then told her about meeting Angry Who Runs Far and how they had been just a day or two behind her all the way to Quintana's Pecos camp. He told her of his trip to San Antonio and his plan to buy her from Quintana, his trip to Quintana's compound, and the killing of Quintana and Gordo.

Becky told her story and assured Buck that, all things considered, she had been treated well by her captors. She also told him of White Elk's dreams that Buck followed them, were now confirmed.

Buck explained that he intended to see Becky to safety but that he was determined to find White Elk and the other raiders and kill them all. Following that pronouncement, they rode in silence for the remainder of the day, each deep in his or her thoughts.

The next day was a brutal trek to the northwest across an arid desert. They camped for the night just inside what Paco's map called Canyon El Cibolo. *That's if I'm on the right trail*, thought Buck. An intermittent stream trickled, in places, along the floor of the canyon. After a meager dinner of beef jerky and coffee, they went for a walk up the canyon. The coolness of the twilight was welcome after the blistering heat of the day.

"Becky, I don't know what to say to you," said Buck. "We were happy as in-laws while you and James were married but now, I don't know how to say what needs to be said."

"Me too," said Becky. "I think that too much has happened to us in too short of a time for us to sort through it. Our lives before the attack on the store seem years ago to me instead of only a few months. I feel that we were still children then or at least somehow innocent. Perhaps, we just need time. For now, let's just be good friends. We can let other things wait."

"I expect you're right," said Buck. "Back before the attack on the store, I thought that I had put horror behind me in Tennessee. The Yankees killed my family and tried to kill me. Then, I found Grandpaw, James and Luke, and then you. I had a family again only to lose it to those murderin' Comanches. I'm just havin' trouble gettin' my mind straight. I just can't see past killin' those Comanches. Until I do, I don't think I can plan any kind of future for me or anyone else. I sure hope you can understand."

As they waded through the shallow stream and rounded a bend, they suddenly heard the tinkling of a bell. Suddenly, a small boy darted from behind a bush and ran downstream shouting, "*Abuelo, Abuelo, Mira! Mira!*"

The boy's grandfather stepped out of the shade and did indeed 'look!' a bit wide-eyed at first. "Hola! Hello!" He called as he saw that Buck and Becky intended no harm. Between Buck's limited Spanish and the old man's limited English they were able to communicate, after a fashion.

The old man explained that he and his grandson were herding their goats back out of the canyon to their small village a few miles to the north of the canyon entrance. Buck explained that they were returning home after many troubles. He bought a young goat from the old man who was more than pleased to receive the silver dollar. Buck confirmed that they were where he thought they were and got additional information about the trail ahead. The old man assured Buck that after they left the east end of the canyon, they would cross another flat desert with much sand. They should keep due east and they would, after a day or two, reach the streambed that led into La Parida Canyon. The stream would likely be dry, so the old man's advice was to pack as much water as they could carry because they might not find more until they reached the Rio Grande.

Buck and Becky led the goat back to their campsite. While Becky built up their campfire, Buck killed and cleaned the goat. It soon roasted on a spit. Coyotes sang off to the west and a pair of screech owls called from the brush along the canyon to the east. Nighthawks made their bull roars as they swooped after insects above the trickling stream. Becky turned to Buck and said," In its own way, it is beautiful here. Thank you for rescuing me. I now feel very safe."

"We're not clear of danger yet," said Buck. "But, I guess we can relax a bit. It can't be too dangerous here or else that old man and boy wouldn't be herdin' their goats without a guard or, at least, a gun of some sort. I reckon that we so far off the beaten path that even the bad Indians and bandits can't find us. Let's see if that goat is done. You hungry?"

Their trip across the next stretch of desert and through La Parida Canyon was dry and exhausting to them and their horses but uneventful. They sat resting in their saddles and looked across the Rio Grande at a big cave on the Texas side. Off to their left they could see where the Pecos flowed into the Rio Grande. Buck said, "Let's splash our way downstream along the shallows on this side and see if we can find a spot to cross and climb up out of the canyon. It can't be too far north of the river to the road between Quintana's Pecos camp and the road to San Felipe del Rio. I know someone in San Felipe del Rio who can help us."

About four miles downstream and around a big bend, Buck spotted a little canyon coming down from the north where he thought they could lead the horses up out of the river canyon. They swam their horses across without incident and camped for the night at the mouth of the little canyon. They were plenty of deer and javalena tracks leading back and forth from the river up a game trail in the little canyon. Buck had no doubt that they could get to the top of the canyon here.

The next morning, they followed the trail up and out of the Rio Grande's canyon. They had to dismount and scramble a bit here and there but, all in all, it was a relatively easy climb. Late that afternoon they dismounted in front of Cal Watson's store in San Felipe del Rio. As they stepped up to the door, Cal burst out grinning like a mule eating briars. "By gol, looks like you done found your gal," he said. "We'd about given you up for dead. Did you get them Comanches, you was huntin'?"

"I ain't half dead yet," exclaimed Buck as he grasped Cal's hand. "This here's Becky that I told you about and no, I didn't get the Comanches yet. Angry's still after them the best I can tell. It sure is good to see you."

"Y'all come on in," said Cal. "Maria, look what the cat's drug in."

Maria came from behind the store counter and clasped Buck's hands. "We were so worried about you. And, this must be your young *senorita*, no?"

Buck put his arm around Becky and ushered her forward. "Becky, this here's Maria and the ugly one's Cal. These are the nice folks I told you about who helped me."

"I am most happy to meet you both," said Becky. "Your help was certainly part of my rescue. And, I am no longer *senorita* but am now Widow Gibson. How do you say it in Spanish? I do not know the correct word."

"*Viuda*," said Maria, "forgive my poor memory. Buck had told us of your husband. I am so sorry for your loss, but come, you must be exhausted. I will show you where you can take a relaxing bath as soon as I heat some water. Also, I'll show you where you can rest."

The two women walked out the back of the store as Cal and Buck went out front to tend to Buck's horses. Cal asked, "How'd you find her? Did you buy her back or what?"

Buck told a short version of Becky's rescue and their trek back to San Felipe del Rio as they disencumbered the horses and turned them out into Cal's horse trap.

"I've got a big favor to ask," said Buck. "I know you've got this store to run and I hate to ask you to leave Maria alone but I'd like for you to take Becky to San Antone and put her on the stage north so's she can get home. I'll pay you one hundred dollars for your time and trouble. I need to catch up with Angry and finish my business with the Comanches. What do you think? Will you do it?"

"Lordy," said Cal, "that's more money than I make in two months. It's way too much for a few days ride to San Antone and back. And, of course I'll do it but I won't take your money. I owe my life to Angry and I'm worried near to sick about him chasin' them cutthroats alone. Maria's kin to near half the folks in town here. She'll be fine for the few days it takes me to take Becky to San Antone. "Sides, I need to pick up a load of goods I ordered that're waitin' in San Antone. Now's as good a time to make the trip as any."

"Thanks, I haven't directly told Becky about this though I've made it clear to her that once she was safe I was goin' after the Comanches. Give me the night to tell her in my own way before you break the news. You can take her to San Antone whenever it suits you. She could use a few days rest and she knows how to run a store. Maybe she can be of some help while she rests up. And, the money is yours. It is a small price compared to the size of the favor."

That evening, after supper, Buck and Becky took a stroll to San Felipe Springs. "You've changed, Buck," she said. "You're not the same boy I knew back in the Nations. Can it be only a couple of months ago? You seem distant and too serious. You've got a far off look in your eyes. I don't feel that I know you anymore."

"I've done some hard things since you were taken from the store. I've killed men without hesitation or remorse. At times, I have felt overcome with hatred for the Comanches. Had it been in my power, I would have killed every Comanche and Kiowa in Palo Duro Canyon, man, woman and child. I don't really like the person I've become but I can never get back to the person I was until this is done. I've asked Cal to take you to San Antone and put you on the stage for home. He's agreed. Here's three hundred dollars for travel money and any clothes and female gear that you need. Whatever money you have left over you can deposit in my account at the bank when you get home. I know it seems hard for me to send you off but I've got to catch the ones who killed Grandpa and James and make them pay. Until then, I won't never have a chance to be the old Buck again."

Buck reached over and wiped a few tears from Becky's cheeks. She caught her breath and said, "I want to see the old Buck again. I can wait. How do I know that they won't kill you?"

Buck kissed her lightly on the forehead and said, "Remember White Elk's dreams you told me about? His spirits told him straight.

I'll get him and his bunch. You'll see. Ol' Buck found you, didn't I? I'll get this job done too."

PART III

South Texas – Spring, 1874

XXVIII

After tearful goodbyes and promises, Buck rode out of San Felipe del Rio and splashed across the Rio Grande. He rode hard and switched mounts often until he reached the spot where he had last seen Angry's tracks. Wind and rain had wiped out any sign of the tracks. He decided to keep in an easterly direction to see if he could either pick up the trail again or find some sign that the Comanches had passed. He spurred his horse and rode hard through the cactus and scrub brush of the Mexican desert in the light of a rising moon.

A few days later, just after midnight, Buck arrived at the small ranch of the slaughtered Mexican family. The fresh graves told most of the story. He found a Comanche arrow lying on the ground. It was the same one that Angry had discarded after removing it from the dog. Buck made camp for the night in a little shed and allowed his horses to rest. He had covered at more than one thousand miles since leaving his family's store and home in the Nations. The horses that he had now had covered much of that distance. He and his horses had rested a bit in San Antonio and at Cal's place in San Felipe del Rio, but not much. He had been able to get them some grain to restore their strength and he had packed some for use along the way. All of them, he and his mounts, were pretty much exhausted.

At three in the morning, a line of strong thunderstorms moved over the area. Buck awoke to the sound of rain pounding on the shed roof. He was up at first light. After a quick breakfast of hot coffee and bacon, he mounted and thought, *I'm goin' to have to guess where they are headed from here. Taggin' along after them, I'll likely never catch up. Sooner or later, they'll have to swing north across the Rio Grande and west back to Palo Duro Canyon. If I cut north after good daylight, I should hit the river pretty soon. If the water's not up, I'll cross the river and follow it to Laredo. Maybe I can find Angry there, or at least word of him. And, just maybe I can get ahead of the Comanches for once.*

The night's storms had cleared the air and cooled the desert.

The brush and cactus spines glistened with lingering raindrops. The ground was muddy but drying fast. Buck set out in a north by northeast line following a little road of sorts. He was tempted to follow the large trail to the east but he made up his mind to ride into Texas before turning east. He hit the river at mid-morning and was at the outskirts of Laredo by noon the next day.

Cal Watson had told Buck to look up an old Ranger friend named Jessie Boseman if he made it to Laredo. Cal said that the last he had heard, Jessie was the town Marshal in Laredo and that Jesse could be trusted.

Buck rode down the dusty main street, dismounted and tied his horses up to the hitching rail outside a clapboard building with a sign over the door that said 'Marshal'. He knocked most of the dust off of himself with his hat and walked into the Marshal's office. There was no one inside except for three drunks sleeping in one of the jail cells. He walked back out into the street. Laredo was a busy and rowdy town. Wagons were being loaded in the front of several stores and a fair number of disreputable types leaned on the fronts of buildings here and there or wandered back and forth across the street.

Buck angled across the street to a cantina, pushed through the swinging doors and walked up to the bar.

"What'll it be, *Compadre*?" asked the bartender.

"Cold beer, if you got it," answered Buck. "I've got half the dust in Mexico in my throat."

The bartender returned in a few minutes with a glass of beer and set it down on the bar in front of Buck. "That'll be five cents."

Buck slapped a coin onto the bar and took a long drink from the glass. It wasn't exactly cold but it was wet and slid down his throat like honey. He let out a big sigh and set the glass back on the bar. He turned back to the bartender and asked, "Where's your Marshal? There's nobody in the office but three drunks locked in the cell."

"The Marshal's gone off to meet Cap'n McNelly downriver in Rio Grande City," answered the bartender. "McNelly's forming up another company of Rangers and called for Jessie. Jessie rode with him before the war. I expect the Cap'n wants Jessie to rejoin the Rangers. You need a lawman? Willie, our blacksmith, is Acting Deputy when Jessie's out of town."

Buck replied, "No, a Ranger friend of mine told me to look up Jessie if I made it to Laredo. Thanks for the beer and the information."

Buck finished his beer and wandered back out into the street. He nosed around in a couple of stores and bought a couple of 'air tights' of peaches. He had a weakness for canned peaches. By late afternoon, there was still no sign of the Marshall. He ambled back down the street to where his horses were tied and remounted. He rode out to the end of town and stopped at the livery. After he had made arrangements for his horses, he strolled and next door to the smithy.

A big, burley man with a bald head and a full, blue-black beard heated a horseshoe on the end of a long pair of tongs in a bed of coals. He was bare-chested behind his heavy leather apron. Sweat poured off of him in rivers that dripped onto the dirt floor. He gave the bellows a pump or two before picking up the shoe with the pair of tongs and moving the shoe to a well-worn anvil where he gave it a couple of whacks with a hammer. After a brief inspection, he plunged the hot shoe into a barrel of water. Steam roared up from around the tongs.

"That'll do!" he exclaimed in a loud voice. "How's about you, feller? What can I do you for?"

"I'm lookin' for a feller named Willie," said Buck.

"Well, you done found him," said the big man. "You need some smithin'?"

"No, I need some information," answered Buck. "Cal Watson over in San Felipe del Rio suggested that I see Jessie Boseman, if I was ever in Laredo. I'm on the trail of a bunch of murderin' Comanches and Kiowas. I lost their trail after that rain last night. I was wonderin' if anybody had seen them. They're drivin' a herd of horses up out of Mexico."

"Nope, I ain't heared a thing about no Comanches," said Willie. "I'll guarantee that if anybody 'round here abouts had seen 'em, ever'body in town would know it. When the Comanches is raidin', ever'body gets spooky. Jessie rode over to Rio Grande City a couple of days ago. He should be back tomorrow. It's already near to quittin' time and I'm fixin' to close up for th' night. Why don't you go have supper with me at the cantina and then you can bunk at my place for the night?"

"Sounds good to me," said Buck. "Is that big roan stallion outside in the corral for sale? One of the Comanche ponies that I've been ridin' is favorin' his right foreleg and I need another mount."

"Yep, he's for sale," said Willie. "His name's Thunder."

After inspecting the paint pony and determining that he merely had a bruised foot, Willard said, "I'll take the paint pony and twenty dollars for the roan."

"Deal," said Buck. "Now, how about supper? I'm buyin'."

Jessie rode into town at mid-morning. He dismounted outside the Marshal's Office and stepped up on the boardwalk. Buck sat on a bench to the right of the front door whittling a piece of cedar into the shape of a bird. An empty peach can sat on the bench next to him.

"You waitin' for me or just whittlin' and eatin' peaches?" asked Jessie.

"Depends on who you are," answered Buck. "I'm lookin' for a feller by the name of Jessie Boseman."

"Well podner, you found 'im. I'm Jessie. What can I do for you?"

Buck put away his pocketknife and stuck out his hand. "I'm Buck McDougal. Cal Watson said to look you up in I ever made it to Laredo."

"Pleased to meet you," said Jessie. "How's Ol' Cal doin'? Is he still store keepin' over there near the Pecos? I ain't seen him in nigh on ten years."

Buck replied, "He's doin' just fine. He's married and happy as a puppy with two tails. He's got a pretty wife who can cook like nobody's business. He seems to be happy with his store. I met a Ranger Major named Jones in San Antonio and carried a letter from him to Cal. I think Jones wants Cal to join the frontier battalion of the Rangers. In fact, Major Jones tried to get me to join while I was in San Antonio."

"I just come from downriver at a meetin' with Cap'n McNelly who's addin' another company to his Special Force of Rangers to clean up the bandits along the border from here to Brownsville. I signed on as a lieutenant and will head down river as soon as I can get someone to take over as Marshal here. Lookin' for a job?"

"No, I don't want to be tied to a town," said Buck. "I've been trailin' a bad patch of Comanches and a Kiowa or two for months. They killed some of my friends and kin up in the Nations. I trailed them to Palo Duro Canyon and then down into Mexico. They took a woman who was married to my cousin. They killed my cousin and Grandpaw. I teamed up along the way with an Apache named Angry. Some of the Comanches killed his wife and boys. Anyhow, we caught some of them along the Pecos and sent them off to Hades but we never caught the main batch. I was trailin' them up through Mexico and lost the trail after a big rain. As far as I know Angry's still on their trail. I came here hopin' that Angry would be here or somebody might have news of Comanche raids here about."

Jessie said, "By gum, ever' tenth Lipan is named Angry somethin' or another. You mean 'Angry Who Runs Far'?"

"That's the one," said Buck.

"Why shoot," said Jessie, "I know the scamp. Best derned scout I ever saw. Back in the ol' days me and Cal and Angry tore up this country trackin' Meskin bandits and Injuns. 'Course, I been gone two-three days but I ain't heard of no Comanche raids lately. And, I ain't seen Angry in maybe ten or twelve years. We can check with Willie, my deputy, to see if anythin' got reported while I was gone."

"I've already asked Willie and he hasn't heard a thing," said Buck.

"Tell you what," said Jessie. "How's about I enlist you in the Rangers? My commission allows me to muster as many good men as I can. If you made it here the long way 'round from the Nations, like you say, and you ain't been scalped, then you sound like Ranger material to me. And, any friend of Cal Watson's good enough recommendation for me."

"I don't want to go chase no bandits in Brownsville," said Buck. "I got some Comanches to kill. They're either still down south or already headed back to their stronghold in the Palo Duro. I won't sign on for nothin' 'til I get them."

"I can see that. Don't get your dander up. Here's what we can do," said Jessie. "I'll sign you up as a sergeant in the Rangers and detail you to join up with Major Jones' Frontier Battalion. You can slaughter all the Comanches you want on your way up to Kerrville to report to Major Jones. And you don't have to be in no rush to get there. As a Ranger, you can help us plus we'll keep an eye out for your Comanches and we'll let you know if'n they wander down toward the coast. Ain't likely if'n they're movin' a horse herd. They'll likely wander more or less back towards the Llano and Palo Duro. I expect you'll run into them between here and the Nueces. As a Ranger, you're less likely to be hanged as a rustler 'sides, you'll earn a dollar and two bits a day. Of course, once you get to Kerrville, the captain there might reduce your rank. What do you say?"

"Let me think on it," said Buck. "I'll let you know by mornin'."

XXIX

Sergeant Buck McDougal, newly enlisted in the Texas Rangers, rode north out of Laredo right after breakfast. Buck wore a shiny badge over his heart. Willard, the blacksmith, had fashioned a pair of crude badges out of silver coins by cutting them to a star within a circle. He pinned them to Buck and Jesse's shirts. "Them old Rangers never had badges. Us honest folks never could tell the Rangers from the outlaws 'til the fight was over. Now you two look more like lawmen," he said with a laugh.

During the night, Bob Lemmons, a black man who was locally famous as a mustanger, rode into town and reported that a series of Comanche raids had occurred on ranches out in the brush country just to the north and east of town. People had been killed and horses taken. "Sounds like your bunch," Jessie had said to Buck. "Your first orders is to go get that bunch. I wish I had some men to send with you but you and I are the only Rangers here. The men in town will want to stay to protect their families and livestock."

"That's okay, I knew I was on my own when I left the Nations months ago. I'll be careful," said Buck.

On further questioning, the mustanger said that the reports were that the Comanches drove a large herd of horses toward the north. Buck now knew for certain that this was his bunch.

When Buck reached the fork where the river road headed west, who should come loping up but Angry and a flea bitten dog. Angry looked like he had been beaten up a bit. One eye was still a little puffy and black and he had signs of rope burns around his neck and wrists.

"Well, you look a sight," said Buck. "Where's your horses and gear?"

"Did you find the woman?" asked Angry.

"Yes, I surely did," exclaimed Buck. "She got sold before I could buy her back from Quintana. I trailed you and that Quintana bunch down into Mexico. Where you split off after the Comanches, I went on south to Quintana's ranch. I lost my derned temper and killed Quintana and his fat sidekick before I could find out where they sold Becky. A servant gal at Quintana's ranch put onto the trail of the men who bought Becky. I tracked her down and got her back. She's at Cal's place in San Felipe del Rio or on her way back home by now. Cal promised to take her to San Antone to catch the stage north. Oh yeah, Quintana let slip that the head of that bunch of Comanches is named 'White Elk'. I think he's the one what shot me and stole Becky.

"And, by the way, I met an ol' friend of yours named Jessie Boseman in Laredo. He talked me into joinin' th' Rangers." Buck turned so that Angry could see the badge pinned to Buck's leather shirt. "I'm headin' up to Carrizo Springs to check on some Comanche raids. I expect it's our bunch doin' it. But, what happened to you?"

"I had almost caught up to the Comanches," said Angry, "when a group of Mexicans captured me. They thought I was part of the Comanche raiding party. The Comanches had killed two of their men and stolen most of their ponies. They tied me up and left me necked up to a rafter in a shed over night. I managed to escape and thought that I might be able to get a horse and gun in Laredo. I've been walking for the last week and, here I am."

"Let's split up the load of stuff on my pack horse. You can ride him," said Buck. "You want to keep after the Comanches?"

"Absolutely," said Angry.

They redistributed the things that Buck had tied on the horse. Angry took the spare Henry rifle and said, "I lost the last one you gave me. Sure you want to trust me with another one?"

"I reckon you're good for it," said Buck. "Where you get th' dog?"

"I found him at a little farm where the Comanches killed a little family of Mexicans," said Angry.

"I saw the graves," said Buck. "Is he as worthless as he looks?"

"He's tracking these Comanches just like we are," said Angry. "I think he has a score to settle, too."

Bear Claw and Running Bird cleared the brush away from the entrance to the little box canyon. Then, Black Hand and Little Hawk herded the horses out onto the narrow trail. White Elk and

Broken Nose trotted up the trail to the north while the rest blocked the way south and pressed the horse herd to follow White Elk and Broken Nose.

"We cannot push these ponies too hard," said White Elk. It will be two sleeps before we can reach the little place called Ancaster where there will be enough water for them."

"I know the place," said Broken Nose. "There are only a few families there. We can take a few more ponies and run the Mexicans off or kill them. There may also be a white family or two. They may try to fight us."

"I think that tomorrow we should leave two or three of our men to move the herd north while the rest of us raid the village," said White Elk. "The horse herd will make it difficult for us to attack the whites and Mexicans without scattering the herd."

Broken Nose said, "Yes, I think that is a good plan. If we are lucky, we can surprise the settlers. This herd makes so much dust that they will see us coming unless some of us ride ahead."

They plodded north all day and made camp near a little thicket of mesquites. There was a bit of grass for the herd to browse in a three-acre meadow. Running Bird, One Eye and Gray Buffalo rode off to hunt meat. The others busied themselves by either gathering mesquite sticks for the fire or keeping watch over the herd.

"Do you smell smoke?" asked Running Bird.

"Yes, there must be a camp or a house to the west from where the wind is blowing," said One Eye.

The three of them eased off of their ponies and tied their reins to bushes. One Eye led the way as they slipped quietly through the brush.

"I smell goats," said Gray Buffalo. "I bet there is a Mexican goatherd camped just ahead."

"Quiet, brother," said One Eye. "They will hear you."

The three spread one hundred yards apart as they crept west. The thickness of the brush prevented them from seeing one another but they were practiced in this tactic. They broke into the open meadow of the shepherd's camp almost simultaneously. An old Mexican man and a young boy sat by a little fire outside of a three-walled jacal. There were two dozen goats nibbling on the brush at the far edge of the meadow. The lead nanny had a collar around her neck from which a small bell tinkled. The old Mexican stood up suddenly at the sight of the three Comanches who silently appeared from the brush.

"Ay! Ay!" shouted the old man. "*Escapado*! Run away!" he shouted to the open-mouthed boy.

The old man raised an ancient shotgun, aimed toward Gray Buffalo who was the closest attacker to him, and pulled both triggers. Nothing happened. In his panic, he had failed to cock the hammers of the old weapon. One Eye sent an arrow through the old man's throat before he could correct his mistake. Gray Buffalo's arrow and a bullet from Running Bird's rifle struck the old man's body an instant later as he was falling to the ground. The boy had vanished into the brush.

"I will catch the boy," said Running Bird. "He cannot be far."

"Forget him," said One Eye. "We came for the goats. The boy is of no use to us. It will be dark soon and we could spend half the night looking for him."

They killed four of the goats and dragged them back to where their ponies were tied. They were back in camp skinning the goats in minutes.

"Our great hunters!" exclaimed Bear Claw. "All they have found is four stinking goats. Are there no deer or buffalo in this country? I do not like the smell or the taste of goat. It is not fit meat for a Comanche. Even the white farmers won't eat them!"

"Good," said One Eye. "There will be more meat for the rest of us who are not so refined in their tastes. Although, I do remember one time on the Washita when I came to your camp and you were cooking three skunks for your dinner, Bear Claw. I'll admit that skunk has a special flavor if roasted with wild onions but I don't think it rates high as a meal for a noble warrior."

They all laughed at One Eye's joke. Most of them also knew that a roasted fat goat was superior in flavor to the meat of deer or rabbit. The smells from the fire even brought Bear Claw close to check on the progress of the cooking from time to time.

After they all, including Bear Claw, had eaten their fill of the tasty roasted goats, White Elk stood and said, "Broken Nose and I have talked and decided that it is difficult to raid in this dusty country while herding these ponies. The dust cloud they make can be seen for miles. I think that we should have three of us continue to move the ponies slowly northwest toward the Llano. The other five can raid the Mexicans and whites along the way to add more ponies to the herd. We can change who herds and who raids every few sleeps. If we are lucky, we may need more herders and fewer raiders. That is my plan."

In Comanche culture, each warrior was free to decide his own path. There were no strict leadership rules. However, warriors would often follow an individual whose deeds had gained respect. White Elk was known by all to be fearless and to have strong medicine. He plans were not discarded lightly.

They discussed the plan for a while and finally Little Hawk stood and said, "It is a good plan. Look at all the ponies we have now. White Elk's *puha* has been strong and his plans sound. To show my approval, I will take first turn as herder." He sat back down.

In turn each man stood and spoke in agreement with the plan. By mutual agreement, Little Hawk, Black Hand and Bear Claw would take the first rotation as herdsmen. The others would be free to raid.

"Follow our trail in the morning," said White Elk to the herdsmen. "There is water enough for the pony herd at the little village that we will attack."

That night, White Elk's dream about the big white man returned. He woke himself with a shout.

"What is it?" asked One Eye. "Did you hear something?"

"Just a dream," said White Elk.

"Tell me about this dream," said One Eye. "Sometimes dreams tell us what we should do."

"It is just an old dream about a big white man," said White Elk. "I have had this dream before when I felt that the white man was near. I have not felt his nearness for many sleeps. But now this dream is back. Go back to sleep. It is just a dream."

But neither White Elk nor One Eye believed that it was just a dream. White Elk was known among the people to have prophetic visions in his dreams. One Eye knew that White Elk had dreamed of Carson's raid at Adobe Walls every night for a week before the actual attack. Since that time, everyone paid attention to White

Elk's dreams. *I will have to learn more about this dream. I think that the spirits are trying to tell White Elk something*, thought One Eye as he drifted back to sleep.

White Elk and his men hit the little village of Ancaster just as the sun was fully up. The village consisted of a few cabins and five nearby farmhouses. The residents who survived the initial attack fled to one of the farmhouses. The house was made of adobe and stone and easier to defend than the mud-chinked jacals made of sticks woven between mesquite posts. At least, a dozen men, women and children made it to the 'fortress'. The Comanches rounded up another twenty horses to add to their herd. They burned all of the jacals and farmhouses except for the one being defended by the settlers.

White Elk and One Eye rode their ponies defiantly back and forth just out of the range of accuracy of the farmers. After an hour, the farmers quit shooting and decided to save their ammunition for the inevitable charge.

"When do we attack the house?" asked Broken Nose. "These farmers might get lucky with their shooting, if we just stay here in sight. Perhaps we should ride on. We have their ponies and they will be too afraid to follow us."

"Our pony herd needs water and we must get it here. Let's wait for the others to arrive with the pony herd," said White Elk. "Then you will see my plan."

The main herd of horses arrived in mid-afternoon. After the horses had had all of the water that they wanted, White Elk called the group together, and said, "We can drive the herd toward the house. We can hide among the ponies and ride up to the house and kill all of the whites and Mexicans."

Everyone nodded in agreement. They pushed the herd toward the farmhouse and rode low along the side of their ponies' necks. The horse herd soon swarmed around the adobe walls of the house. The men inside began shouting back and forth to one another: "Do you see them?" They must be out there." "I can't see nothin' but horses and dust." "I can't see nothin' over here."

Black Hand jumped from his pony's back onto the low roof of the kitchen on the back of the house. He scrambled up onto the main roof of the house and began to dig into the roof with his knife. Little Hawk joined him. The others began making their war cries from all sides of the house. The settlers began shooting randomly from the windows. The Comanches waited until a clear target appeared at a window and then shot him. The women and children began to scream and cry as more of their men fell.

In less than an hour, it was over. Black Hand and Little Hawk had dropped through their hole in the roof into the middle of the main room of the house. Simultaneously, Bear Claw and Gray Buffalo had burst in through front and back windows. The slaughter was quick and brutal. The last two surviving women had shot each other to prevent capture by the Comanches.

"Burn it, said Broken Nose. "Let's go."

"The next good water is the Nueces River," said White Elk. "With this herd, it is at least two sleeps north."

That night they feasted on the livestock that they had taken from one of the farms and sang of their victory against these settlers who dared resist them. In the deep hours of the dark night, White Elk's dream returned. Each time the dream was a little different, as though the spirits were revealing a bit more of the mystery. Tonight the big man spoke to White Elk for the first time. He said only, "Horse blood! Now, you're mine," over and over as White Elk looked up at his face. What on earth could the big man's words mean? As in the dreams before, White had a feeling of helplessness, as he lay unprotected at the big man's feet.

He awoke suddenly in the darkness. He shivered twice even though it was a warm night. He was covered in sweat even though the night air was pleasantly cool. He was unable, or unwilling, to go back to sleep. Finally, he got up and went for a walk. He thought, *This must be the man that Little Wolf and the others fought at the Old Soldier fort on the Pecos. He comes again. I will be ready. The spirits are warning me to be alert to his presenc*e. He smiled at his interpretation and watched the light of dawn begin to grow in the east.

Buck and Angry picked up the trail of the horse herd on the second day. As they trotted along, Angry said, "Look, buzzards circle low over there." He pointed to a spot just west of their line of travel.

Buck stood up in his stirrups to get a better look over the top of the brush and said, "Better go see, I guess."

They rode into the little clearing of the goat herder's camp. Arrow bristled along his backbone and growled. He faced a clump of Whitebrush twenty feet away. Someone had been digging a shallow grave at the edge of the meadow. Nearby lay the decomposing body of an old man. Buzzards roosted in a mesquite tree next to the little three-walled shed. It was obvious that they had already been at work on the body.

"Hello!" called Buck. "Who's that hidin' over yonder behind them bushes? We ain't gonna hurt you." He turned to Angry and said, "Call off your dog. Who's ever back there ain't gonna come out to get chewed."

Angry called to Arrow. The dog obediently backed off and sat down.

"Dang," said Buck. "I didn't know you could speak dog so good." He then rode over to the clump of Whitebrush and said, "Come on out of there. Who killed the old man? We're Texas Rangers and were after a patch of murderin' Comanches." He turned to Angry and whispered, "I know you ain't joined up yet, but I expect you will."

A ten-year-old boy stepped from behind the brush. His dark eyes were wide with fear. He said, "My name is Manolo. The Indios killed my *Abuelo* and took some of our goats. I ran away and hid in the brush. The Indios did not follow me. Later, I saw their camp over there." He pointed toward the northeast. "They had many horses."

"Well, let's finish buryin' your Grandpaw," said Buck. "Where's the rest of your family?"

Buck and Angry dug a deeper grave and slid the old man's remains into the hole. After he was covered, the boy planted a little wooden cross that he had made into the soft mound of dirt. He knelt and said a prayer and then stood up.

"I must tend to the goats," said the boy, wiping tears from the corners of his eyes. "Otherwise the coyotes will get them. My father will come in a few days to check on us, I mean me. We have eight small herds of goats spread across the country. My older brothers tend the other herds. My father makes a circuit from group to group. I am not afraid. See, I have my *Abuelo*'s gun and I know how to shoot it."

Buck looked at the old muzzle-loading shotgun propped against the wall of the shed and shook his head. "I expect you can Manolo," he said. "I sure do hate leavin' you here alone, but you seem to have done alright so far by yourself."

"My father says that I am sufficient," said Manolo proudly.

"I guess you are," laughed Buck. "Well, we need to be gettin' after the Comanches who killed your Grandpaw. They've killed lots of other folks, too. They're a bad bunch." He turned to Angry and said, "Let's ride, *Compadre*."

"Thank you for your help with my *Abuelo*," said Manolo as he waved goodbye.

"*De nada*," said Angry as he spurred his horse into a trot.

As they rode off to the north, Buck said, "Tough little feller, wasn't he? Kinda reminds me of me when I was that age."

Angry laughed, "I bet you were meaner."

"Maybe so," said Buck.

They rode into the devastated village of Ancaster just at sundown. A few coals smoldered at what had been the larger houses. Buzzards and flies rose in clouds at their approach. There were pockets dead farm animals and clusters of dead people scattered over several square miles. The dead livestock reminded Buck of the day his mother died. *Just like them Yankee renegade soldiers*, he thought. *I never got them Yankees to pay for what they done but, by gol, these Comanches'll pay*.

"Must of been twenty or thirty killed here," said Buck. "Can't tell how many were in that burned out big house over yonder on that ridge. But it looks like they fought 'em for a while. See how the tracks of the horse herd go round and round what was the house? And from the direction of their wounds, those two dead horses look like they were shot from the people in the house."

"Yes," replied Angry. "We must catch these Comanches and punish them for all these people as well as for our own. The next water is the Rio Nueces north of here. The Comanches will go there next. The herd will slow them. The little town of Carrizo Springs is northwest of us. If we ride hard, we can get ahead of the Comanches. They will take their herd due north for the river before following it west. It is what I would do."

They buried all of the bodies that they could find in a mass grave. Then, Buck said, "It is gettin' cloudy. We will have a dark night, no moon or even stars. Let's move upwind of this stench and camp 'til mornin'. We can water the horses good before we leave and then push as hard as we can tomorrow without cripplin' our mounts."

XXX

Little Hawk and Bear Claw had ridden ahead of the herd to scout for a place where the brush would not be too thick along the bank of the Nueces. As they sat on their ponies looking down on the river below them, they saw a huge herd of cattle. Fifteen riders popped their whips, shouted, and whistled as they urged at least two thousand cattle across the swift water. Another three men were north of the river near a covered wagon, watching over a remuda of thirty horses. The Comanches quickly rode back south before being spotted by the drovers.

"We must tell Broken Nose and White Elk that there are many ponies that we can take," said Little Hawk. "Hurry!"

As they approached the Comanche horse herd, Little Hawk raised his right hand and shouted, "Stop the ponies!"

"What is it?" asked White Elk. "Why are you so excited? Why should we stop here? These ponies need water and so do we."

Little Hawk and Bear Claw both began to talk at once. "There are many cattle just ahead crossing the river. They are being driven by a group of whites and Mexicans. They also have many ponies with them."

"How many men?" asked Broken Nose.

"Maybe twenty. No more," answered Little Hawk.

"How are they armed?" asked White Elk.

"We were not near enough to see and the cattle raised so much dust," said Bear Claw.

"Come," said White Elk to Broken Nose. "We must see for ourselves. The rest of you keep these ponies here. If they get nearer to the river and smell the water, we will not be able to hold them."

White Elk and Broken Nose rode away to the north following the trail of Little Hawk and Bear Claw. They stopped short of the hilltop and tied their ponies to a small mesquite tree. After creeping through the brush to the crest of the hill, they stopped to peer down on the cattle herd. Half the herd had made the crossing and grazed in the grass along the north bank of the river. Most of the drovers popped their whips and swung their riatas at the rear of the half of the herd still south of the Nueces.

"I only see five or six who look like grown men," said Broken Nose. "The rest look like they have only passed twelve to sixteen winters."

"Yes," said White Elk, "but they all wear pistols and a few have rifles in scabbards on their ponies. Our own youth can shoot well at that age. I think that some of these can shoot too."

"Where do you think they go with all those cattle?" asked Broken Nose.

"I saw this last year at the Red River just west of where the Washita joins the Red," said White Elk. "The whites gather these cattle from the brush country and drive them all the way across Texas and the Nations. I was told that they sell them for money in Kansas. It seems strange to me. Why don't they just eat them here? The whites do many strange things that I do not understand."

He continued, "I think we should wait until it is dark. These clouds will keep it dark tonight. We can get close to the herd, frighten them, and make them run to the north. The men will all chase the cattle to stop them. They will leave their pony herd lightly protected and probably by their least experienced boy. We can then take the ponies and add them to ours. We should return to our herd and move them to the northwest. If we drive them to the river west of here, they will not be seen by the cattlemen. Our ponies will remain near the river for they are tired and thirsty. We can leave Black Hand and Bear Claw to guard our herd. Once we take the cattlemen's pony herd, we can drive it west along the river until we reach our herd."

When they returned to their companions and horse herd, White Elk explained his plan to the others. He turned to One Eye and Gray Buffalo and said, "You two are our best hunters. We need the scent of a panther to frighten the cattle. See if you can find one and kill it. I saw some fresh tracks at the little creek we crossed two hours ago."

"I saw the tracks as well," said Gray Buffalo, "but they appeared small for a panther unless it is a young one or maybe a big bobcat. But we will go."

John Patterson had pulled together a herd of twenty-five hundred brush country cattle. There were somewhere between three million and six million wild cattle roaming the south Texas brush country at the end of the Civil War. They were there for the taking if you could catch them. The problem was that nobody in south Texas would pay a Yankee nickel for one of them. If you needed beef for the table, you went out and shot one. You hunted them like deer, except that they were meaner and wilier than deer. Over nearer to the coast, hide and tallow outfits had made a meager living for years but out in the brush country nobody but a fool considered these cattle to be more than a nuisance.

Recently though, a number of outfits had shown that there was good money to be made by driving a herd up to the railheads in Kansas along the old trail that the Indian trader, Jesse Chisholm, had laid out. John had hired on a group of men, boys really, who could ride and rope and were dumb enough to agree to drive these wild cattle nearly a thousand miles.

It took the better part of a month to gather the cattle into a big pen that they had built. Two days without water took the fight out of most of the cattle. They drove the thirsty cattle to water and then northwest to skirt around San Antonio. San Antonio was known to be full of rough men who would steal a herd if it happened by at a convenient distance. Most of the cattle rustlers did their work closer to Kansas so that they would only need to herd the cattle for a few days and the cattle would be good and 'trail broke'.

After a week on the trail, most of the cattle had adapted to the idea of being driven by these men. Reaching the Nueces was a big milestone because it meant that dependable water would be available for the next several hundred miles and they would be leaving the worst of the dense brush behind. Most of the cattle and quite a few of the crew had never seen as much water at one time as flowed down the Nueces. In reality, the Nueces is only sixty feet wide and a few feet deep in most places, but to south Texas boys and cattle that was a lot of water. Getting the cattle to cross the river was no simple task. First of all, they were thirsty and preferred drinking to wading or swimming.

"Let 'em spread out there and have a drink," Patterson shouted to his crew. "Luis, bring the remuda and the chuck wagon on across. Travis, get the herd started across once they've had a drink."

Luis Cardenas had worked cattle and horses most of his long

life. He was in his seventies though he looked and acted a good twenty years younger. He was now the *cocinero*, cook, for the outfit. He was also John Patterson's partner in this drive. They had worked together for over forty years.

Luis said, "We will camp here for the night. There is plenty of grass for the cattle and horses and the boys need a rest."

John nodded his agreement. He handed the reins of his mount to Willie Johnson who was assigned to the remuda. He said to Willie, "Turn him out with the rest. Luis says we stop here for the night."

Three hours after dark Gray Buffalo and One Eye soaked pieces of buckskin in the urine and blood of the big tom bobcat that they had killed. They tied the buckskin strips to the brush just upwind of the cattle herd. They tied the carcass of the dead cat to the tail of one of the ponies from their herd and chased the frightened pony into the cattle herd. At the same time, Little Hawk screamed like a panther from the brush at the river's edge. That was all it took to put the twenty-five hundred cattle up on their feet and into flight. The two boys riding night herd did not have a warning or a chance to stop the fleeing cattle. Luis came out of his bedroll shouting, "Mount up, boys! Stampede! Stampede!"

The entire crew was up, horses saddled and away within minutes. Even as dark as the night was, the dust of the stampeding cattle was easy enough to follow.

"Race for the front and try to turn them back onto themselves!" shouted John Patterson. "If we can get them into a mill, they'll quit runnin'. Willie, you stay here with Luis and watch the remuda."

Away the crew galloped, north into the dim light of the night. The Patterson crew got the cattle stopped after a six mile run through the brush. Fatigue and the dense brush had more to do with stopping the stampede than did the cowboys. John Patterson said, "Boys, y'all keep 'em bunched up here while Travis and I go fetch Luis and Willie. It'll be daylight in a few hours. We'll be back before mid-mornin'."

Willie never heard a sound from the man who cut his throat. He just felt a sudden surprise at the warm blood gushing down the front of his shirt. Luis stood up from his blanket when he heard the boy moan and fall. He only had time to fire one shot into the darkness in the direction from which he thought that the bullets had come. One of the bullets had hit him in the right chest and the other through his left shoulder. He slumped to the ground, dying.

The Comanches had the remuda running west along the river before Luis was dead. In twenty minutes, they had blended these horses in with their larger herd and had the whole group moving upriver to the west.

"Our trail will be easy to follow," said Broken Nose to White Elk, "and they are better armed and in greater numbers than our band."

"I know," said White Elk, "but I think that they will stay with the cattle. They have far more cattle to watch after than they had ponies. I think the cattle will be more important to them. But we should not stop until we are well away from this place."

They trotted the herd west along the river for ten miles before stopping. They let the horses drink and graze along the north riverbank while they themselves slept for the few remaining hours of the night. Just before dawn, White Elk's dream returned. This time he, Black Hand and Little Hawk charged on horseback toward the big man through the thick brush. He could feel the thorns scratching his legs and smell the sweat of his pony. Then, he awoke with a start. *Perhaps, this is the end of the dream where I kill the big man*, he thought. He smiled as he looked to the east along the fog-enshrouded river. *Killing him will be good*, he thought.

John and Travis rode up to last night's campsite to find Luis and Willie dead and the horse remuda gone. Travis said, "Look over here, Mr. Patterson. It looks like they drove our horses west along the river. Who do you think it was?"

"Meskin bandits, I expect," said Mr. Patterson. "Dang it! I sure do want to go after them sumbucks but I can't 'cuz of the cattle."

Then he said, "Travis, you ride back to the herd and bring three of the hands back with you. We'll need your mount and three more to make up a team for th' chuck wagon. You boys can take turns herdin' and ridin' in th' wagon 'til I can git over to Uvalde where I can buy more horses. While you're gone, I'll bury Luis and Willie and pack up the gear scattered about into the wagon."

"Yessir," said Travis as he remounted and rode off.

John buried the boy and his dear friend and knelt at the head of Luis's grave. "You're the best friend I ever had," he said. "I'm powerful sorry you got kilt, Ol' Pard." He said a little prayer to himself.

A noise from the south brought him quickly to his feet. He drew his pistol and stood to see who splashed across the river towards him. A big man on a roan stallion and an Apache on a paint mare rode straight for him. The big man wore a silver badge on his buckskin shirt.

"Looks like you've had some trouble," said Buck as he dismounted. "I'm Ranger Buck McDougal and this here's my friend Angry."

"Yes," said John, "I'm John Patterson. We had a stampede of our cattle last night and while we was off chasin' the herd, some Meskin bandits killed my partner and a boy and stole our remuda."

"It was Comanches not Mexicans," said Buck. "Angry and I are on their trail and aim to make them pay for all the havoc they've been raisin'. We been chasin' 'em all across Texas and Mexico. We've narrowed the distance from over a week, to now, a few hours. I expect we'll catch 'em today. We'll make 'em pay for killin' your people and lots of other folks, too, includin' some of my kin and Angry's wife and youngin's."

"You boys hungry?" asked John. "There's a pot of bean on the tripod over last night's fire and I got plenty of beef already cut. I can burn you a couple of steaks in a few minutes. I'm just waitin' for some of my crew to come back so's we kin use their horses as a wagon team."

"Well, we'll take you up on that," said Buck. "We've been mostly living on rabbit and such for months. While you're rustlin' up the grub, Angry and I'll scout around a bit for tracks, though it seems pretty clear the whole bunch rode west."

After they had eaten and thanked Mr. Patterson for the food, Angry and Buck returned to their chase of the Comanches. The trail was plain and fresh. A herd of over two hundred horses left fairly plowed-up ground in their wake.

XXXI

Broken Nose arose from his blanket and walked over to where White Elk stood. "I think we have enough ponies," said Broken Nose. "Any more and we will not be able to manage them and we are still many suns from home."

"Yes," said White Elk, "I agree. You and the others can continue home to the Comancheria with all of these ponies. Running Bird will go with you and speak for my part if decisions are to be made about the distribution of the ponies to our people. As you know, the Nueces soon will turn north into its canyons. Beyond, lie the Llano and Concho Rivers. From the Concho, it is not many suns ride to our home. I would like to raid a little more. I think I know a place where I can get more guns for our people. Besides, herding horses is boring to me. I will take Black Hand and Little Hawk with me. I have had a dream in which the three of us kill an enemy of mine. I think he follows us now."

"Yes," said Broken Nose, "I, too, have felt that we are being followed. I feel that you should do as the spirits tell you. I will take the others and these ponies to our people."

Broken Nose and White Elk explained their plan to the other men. They broke camp and White Elk, Black Hand and Little Hawk split away from the others and the herd. They rode northeast through the dense brush. The trail was narrow and winding. White Elk turned and said, "It is two sleeps ride to Waggoner's Well. It is a place that will have travelers moving from Frio City to Pleasanton. The men of both towns and the nearby ranches are busy this time of year moving cattle herds north. If we hide near the road, we can catch a wagon alone and perhaps steal many guns. The whites are careless along this road because they believe that we are not brave enough to strike them there. Also, the ranches nearby will be poorly defended. We may be able to steal some more women for sale to Quintana."

Two hours before sunset, Angry turned to Buck and said, "I can taste dust and smell the pony herd. The pony droppings are fresh. I think we are getting close."

"I smell 'em, too," said Buck. "You want to hit 'em now or wait until dark?"

"I think now," said Angry. "The dust and noise of their herd will cover our approach. If we wait until dark, they will more easily hear us coming and they will likely be in a group. Managing a herd this large will require that they spread around the ponies."

"Exactly what I was thinkin'," said Buck. "If we do this right, we can take 'em out one or two at a time startin' with the ones ridin' drag. There's eight of 'em and I sure would like to whittle down the odds a bit. The leaders'll be ridin' up front out of the dust. I want to catch White Elk alive so's he can know who caught him and why. Try not to kill him, if you shoot him. Let's see if we can sidle up to whoever's ridin' drag and take them out kinda quiet."

As they rode over the crest of a low hill, they could now see the dust cloud from the horse herd two miles ahead. They dismounted and checked their weapons. They cached Buck's pack up in a big mesquite tree. Angry looped a rawhide riata over his dog's head and tied him to the mesquite. "I'll be back for you, Arrow," he said. To Buck, he said, "That'll keep him out of our way or at least slow him down gnawing through the riata." They both knew that the dog might spoil their chances of surprising the Comanches.

"Okay, we'll come back for my pack and your dog when we're done," said Buck. "Let's go, *Compadre*."

They galloped ahead until they had entered the dust cloud before matching their pace to that of the herd. Angry angled off to the left a bit. Ahead of him, Angry could just barely see one of the Comanches. It was Bear Claw with a big bandana tied across his nose and mouth to protect him from the dust. He snapped a short whip at the rumps of the horses at the rear of the herd.

Angry rode up on his right side and jerked him from his pony by his hair. Bear Claw hit the ground flat of his back. In the same moment, Angry jumped from his horse and onto Bear Claw. The fall had knocked the breath out of Bear Claw. He struggled to regain his breath as Angry leapt onto him and slashed his throat. Angry jumped up and ran ahead to catch his pony and remount.

Meanwhile, Buck had eased up behind One Eye and looped

his rawhide riata over One Eye's head. Buck whirled his mount and spurred hard. He intended to merely jerk One Eye from his pony but the jerk was strong enough to also break One Eye's neck. Buck dismounted and finished the job with his knife. Angry appeared from the swirling dust. His face and chest were covered in dust as sweat ran down his torso leaving little trails on his skin. Buck was so dusty that he looked grey all over.

"Two down," said Buck as he remounted. "Those were the easy two. The others'll be out in the open. We ain't likely to slip up on them so easy. You want the right or the left?"

"Left," said Angry as he rode back into the dust cloud.

Buck angled toward the right side of the dust cloud. He stayed in the dust just enough to conceal himself a bit as he peered ahead to see where the rest of the Comanches were. The herd swirled along at a lope in front of him. He could only see two of the Comanches. Gray Buffalo rode along the right flank of the herd popping his whip and shouting at the horses. Broken Nose was out in front, leading the way. *Where's the rest of 'em?* thought Buck. *Surely there ain't four of 'em ridin' the left flank?*

In their haste to catch up to the herd and, to some extent, due to carelessness, Buck and Angry had missed the tracks of White Elk, Black Hand and Little Hawk that led away from the herd. That mistake had been made two hours earlier.

Well, thought Buck, *seems to me that I best worry about the quarry at hand and hope that Angry ain't runnin' into a nest of 'em on his side.* The herd loped up a hillside before him and he could now see that there was only one Comanche riding left flank. *Look's like there's only the three of 'em,* thought Buck. *I'll worry about the other three later.*

Out of the corner of his eye, he could see that Angry galloped his horse along the left of the herd toward the Comanche ahead of him. Buck pulled his Henry from its scabbard and took aim on the Comanche directly ahead of him. His first shot missed but the second shot brought down the Comanche's pony. Gray Buffalo was instantly on his feet. He ran away from the herd to keep from being trampled while looking left and right for his attacker. He looked back toward the rear of the rushing herd and saw Buck charging toward him. He raised his rifle to aim just as a bullet from Buck's rifle hit him in his right thigh, breaking his femur.

Gray Buffalo's own shot went wild as he fell. He jacked another round into the chamber and swung up his rifle from a sitting position but he was too late. He could see Buck's stallion still running toward him but there was no rider. *Did I hit him?* he thought. *Where is he?* Too late, he spotted Buck standing two hundred yards away aiming the Henry. As Gray Buffalo swung his own rifle to the left to align Buck in his sights, he saw the puff of smoke from Buck's rifle. He never heard the shot. The bullet smashed through his left eye and tore out the back of his skull.

Broken Nose had heard the shots and wheeled his pony to the right of the oncoming herd. He saw Gray Buffalo fall with his pony and the big man charging along the right rear flank of the herd. *It is White Elk's big man*, he thought. *Is he alone? Surely, he is not that foolish.*

The horse herd had grown accustomed to following one or more of the Comanches. The lead horse veered toward Broken Nose and stopped. The herd began to stop as it bunched up on itself. Broken Nose had seen the big man jump from his saddle and take aim toward where Gray Buffalo had fallen, but now the horse herd surrounded him in great confusion. The big man had fired his rifle again but had now disappeared from sight. He had been six hundred yards back or more, too far for an accurate shot. Broken Nose then heard a shot from the riverbank and looked toward where Running Bird rode. *Where are One Eye and Bear Claw?* he thought.

Angry spotted Running Bird ahead of him through the last of the dust from which Angry emerged. He instantly recognized Running Bird as the man who had killed his sons. In fact, Running Bird still rode Angry's horse.

Rage overtook reason as Angry charged forward toward Running Bird. A rifle shot banged from off to Angry's right. *Buck*, he thought. Running Bird heard the shot as well, reined his mount to a stop and wheeled to the left. The horse herd thundered past him. He looked over his shoulder across the backs of the running horses. He saw a big man on horseback across the herd from him jump from his saddle. He raised his own rifle to shoot the man just as Angry's horse collided with him and his horse at full gallop. Both horses and both men went down.

At the last instant before the collision, Angry had flung himself through the air toward Running Bird. His timing was off just a bit and he landed beyond the jumble of Running Bird and the two kicking, squealing horses. Running Bird's shot went wild as he lost his grip on his rifle but he had his long bone-handled knife in his right hand as he regained his feet. Angry was up on his feet with his knife in hand as well.

The two men circled each other as the horse herd swarmed around them. Running Bird made a thrust with his knife toward Angry's midsection. Angry sidestepped to the right and slashed down with his blade across Running Bird's forearm. Blood poured from the wound. Running Bird gave a yell and threw himself onto Angry. Angry buried his knife into Running Bird's belly while Running Bird's knife stabbed through Angry's upper left chest.

The two men rolled in the dust among the legs of the horses. The horses nearby screamed in fright and pushed away from the fighting men. Angry ripped upwards with his knife as Running Bird tried to pull his own knife out of Angry's chest. Running Bird's grip on the hilt of his knife loosened as Angry's knife tip found its way into Running Bird's heart. A few gasps and it was over. Angry stood over his fallen enemy and howled his war cry. Running Bird's knife still protruded from Angry's chest.

Angry staggered down the riverbank and into the cool, clear water of the Nueces. He was unable to pull Running Bird's knife from his chest. The knife was wedged between his collarbone and his upper ribs. Angry sat down in the river and let the cold water rush over the burning in his chest.

The dust had begun to settle and drift off downwind now that the herd had stopped. Buck started running forward looking for his horse, Thunder. *There he is*, said Buck to himself. "Thunder! Here, boy!" he called. The big roan stallion looked at him like he had lost his mind. Buck laughed at himself. "You ain't no dog, are you," he said as he picked up the reins and swung into the saddle.

As he turned west toward the front of the herd, he heard the whine of a bullet overhead immediately followed by the report of a rifle. Broken Nose was shooting at him. Buck sank his spurs into Thunder's flanks and rode into a thicket of small mesquites to his right. He took a quick peek across the herd but no one was in sight.

Angry and his man must have rode over the riverbank, he thought, *and that one shootin' at me ain't White Elk. White Elk musta either rode on ahead or split off back behind us somewheres.* He urged Thunder around the thicket and farther to the right. He stood up in his stirrups quickly and looked for Broken Nose. He just caught a glimpse of Broken Nose, as the Comanche rode into the brush five hundred yards to the west. *It's gonna be cat and mouse from here*, Buck thought. He wheeled Thunder to his left and spurred him out into the open again, then charged west toward where he had last seen Broken Nose.

Broken Nose heard the galloping horse approaching from the east and turned to shoot the rider as he passed by. The big roan galloped past riderless. Broken Nose turned on his pony as the big man came running almost silently up behind him. He swung his rifle toward Buck but before he could swing it fully around it flew from his hands. Buck had drawn his big Colt revolver and shot through Broken Nose's left forearm, hitting the rifle and knocking it out of Broken Nose's grasp.

Broken Nose jerked his reins to the left and ran his pony directly at Buck. Buck shot the horse twice through the heart and jumped out of the way of the falling horse. Broken Nose leapt clear of his dying mount and landed on his feet. He crouched ten feet from Buck. His broken left arm hung limply at his side. He held his knife in his right hand.

Buck leveled the Colt at him and said, "Where is White Elk? Tell me and I'll make this quick."

Broken Nose whipped his right arm back to throw the knife but Buck shattered his elbow with a shot. The knife flew into the brush behind Broken Nose, who screamed in pain. He began chanting his death song as Buck repeated, "Where is White Elk?"

Broken Nose stood and charged toward Buck. Buck sidestepped and whacked him along the side of the head with his pistol barrel as he ran past. Broken Nose was out cold in the dust. Buck walked over to Broken Nose's dead horse and cut the reins. He tied Broken Nose's feet together and bound his wrists the leather reins. "You'll keep. I'll tend to you later," he said to the unconscious Comanche.

Buck ran to where Thunder stood and leapt into the saddle. He rode in a looping path west of the horse herd and confirmed that White Elk and the other two had not ridden ahead. *Musta split off back down the trail somewheres*, he thought. *Now, where's Angry?*

Buck rode over to the riverbank and looked back to the east. There sat Angry, four hundred yards down river in water up to his neck. He seemed to be struggling with something under the water.

Buck shouted, "What'n the heck're you doin'?"

He touched his spurs to Thunder's flanks and galloped to a spot next to Angry. He jumped off of his horse, climbed down the riverbank, and splashed into the water.

"This knife is stuck," said Angry. "I killed the one who murdered my family but he put this knife in me."

"Let's get you up here on the bank and see what I can do," said Buck. "Lay back on the gravel, I'm gonna put my foot on your shoulder and give the knife a yank. I expect it's gonna hurt some and you're likely to bleed like a stuck hog. Be ready to slap your hand over the wound when I yank the knife out."

Buck yanked the knife out and threw it aside. The wound did not bleed as much as they had expected. It bled enough, but a manageable amount. Buck helped his friend back into the water and they washed out the wound. Buck climbed the riverbank and led Thunder down to the water's edge. He took his fancy "Rich Rancher' shirt out of his saddle bag and made a bandage from it.

Buck helped Angry onto Thunder's back and led them back downriver to fetch Angry's pony. Just then, they heard riders approaching from the east. They ducked down behind the riverbank as the riders reined up at the edge of the horse herd.

"There's some of our brands," said John Patterson. He then shouted, "Ranger Buck! Ranger Buck!"

Buck raised up from behind the riverbank and said, "Why, hello, Mr. Patterson. I thought you was goin' to stay with your herd."

"Well, I was fixin' to," said John, "but while I was settin' there waitin' on my boys to come back, I got madder and madder about poor Luis and little Willie. I figured that me and Travis and these three other boys could come see if'n we could lend a hand with killin' them what killed our own. Look's like we got here too late for the party."

"We didn't git 'em all," said Buck. "Three of 'em split off from this group herdin' the horses and I got one of this crowd trussed up over yonder in the brush. I broke both of his arms but he was still feisty when I whacked him upside his noggin' with my Colt."

"Where's th' murderin' sumbitch?" said John. "I'll send 'im to th' Spirit Land quick enough."

"Not just yet," said Buck. "I want to see if I can git a little information out of him first. Then you can have him." He turned to Angry, who now sat on the gravel bar at the water's edge, and said, "Angry, how're you doin' Pard? At least, you got your man."

Angry sat up straight with a bit of a groan and said, "I killed my enemy but his knife has cut me deep. I am not sure I can help catch the others unless we wait a few days."

"Mr. Patterson, I got a couple of favors to ask," said Buck.

"Name it," said John. "If'n it's in my power, you got it."

Buck said, "I aim to find the other three Comanches. At least two of them are the ones that killed my cousin and Grandpaw. The trail's hot and I don't want to lose them. Angry needs some mendin'. How about you let him and his dog ride in your chuck wagon as far as Uvalde? There's a town Marshal there by the name of Fisher who seems to be a steady man. You can leave Angry with him." He turned back to Angry and said, "Ol' Pard, once you heal up sufficient, light out for Cal's place. I'll either meet you there or send word where to find me."

Angry grunted his agreement as Travis and one of the cowhands helped him up the riverbank.

John Patterson said, "That's one favor, you said there was two?"

"Cut your stock out of this herd," said Buck, "but drive the rest to Uvalde. Tell Marshall Fisher that they belong to the Rangers and he should git a message up to Major Jones in Kerrville. Major Jones'll decide what to do with them."

"You got yourself a deal," said John. "Let's take a look at the sumbitch you got hog tied."

Arrow came trotting up with a proud look on his face. John laughed and said, "I see your dog managed to finish chewing through that rope you had him on. We saw where you had cinched him to that mesquite. He was none too happy when we rode by."

Broken Nose was just coming to when Buck and John rode up to where he lay in the brown dust. Arrow trailed along growling deeply in his chest. Buck dismounted and rolled Broken Nose onto his back. Buck asked in Kiowa, "Do you speak English?"

Broken Nose replied in English, "I have nothing to say. Kill me and be done with it."

"Where is White Elk and the Kiowa?" asked Buck.

"Ask the spirits," said Broken Nose. "I know only that you will never kill White Elk. His medicine is too powerful. My spirit will dance when White Elk carries your scalp to our people. Go find him if you have enough courage to chase him."

Buck turned to John and said, "He's of no use to me. He's all yours. I've got to be goin' if I'm gonna catch the other three. I need to back trail a bit to find where they split off from this group. Take good care of my compadre. Adios."

John said, "You want some help? I can send Travis with you. He's a good man and a crack shot."

"Thanks, but this is somethin' I need to do alone," said Buck, as he swung up onto Thunder's back and rode off downriver. He looked back over his shoulder and saw Travis swinging a rope over a limb of a big mesquite as John dragged Broken Nose up onto a paint pony.

Hangin's too good for 'im, thought Buck, *but it'll keep his spirit wanderin' down here forever. He'll never be able to meet up with his ancestors.*

XXXII

White Elk, Black Hand and Little Hawk made their camp in the dense brush country just southeast of Waggoner's Well. The south Texas brush country consists of approximately twenty-eight thousand square miles of extremely dense thorny brush. Except along the streams where pecan, sycamore, and cypress trees flourish, the land is covered in seven to eight foot tall brush, interspersed with game trails, large areas of prickly pear cactus and mesquite and huisache trees. It is said that every living thing sticks, stings or stinks. While not exactly true, the country is tough and was filled with wild Longhorn cattle and just about every kind of wildlife, from alligators to cougars and even jaguars.

Waggoner's Well was located in the middle of this sea of tough country. It was a watering spot for travelers moving east and west between Frio City and Pleasanton as well as those moving north and south between San Antonio and Laredo. White Elk knew that traders often passed through the area with their wagons loaded with goods. He especially hoped to capture one filled with rifles and ammunition.

Little Hawk had killed a Longhorn calf with his bow and was busy cooking a huge veal roast over their campfire.

Black Hand said, "I do not like this kind of meat. It is too mild tasting. I prefer buffalo or, at least venison. They are more fit for a Kiowa warrior."

"You want buffalo, kill one," said Little Hawk. "Buffalo do not like this brush. They like open country better. I do not like this brush either. I feel closed in all the time. I prefer the Llano where a man can see to where the sky meets the grass."

White Elk said, "We will return to our home country soon, my old friend. Do not let Black Hand bother you. He just likes to complain. While you two argue and cook our food, I will go to the white man's road and look for sign. I will not be gone long. Try not to kill each other or burn the meat!"

Just after mid afternoon, Buck found the spot where White Elk's little raiding party had left the herd. The tracks wandered through the brush in a northeasterly direction. He stopped just before sunset to camp for the night. Traveling through all of these thorns was difficult enough in daylight. In dark, it was madness. In addition to the danger to himself and his horse from the thorns on the brush and cactus, huge rattlesnakes roamed the darkness looking for the millions of rodents that lived on the seeds and roots of the brush.

Buck had found a little open meadow about one-half acre in size. There was grass for his horse and enough open ground on which he could bed down without sleeping in the thorns or on a snake den. The gentle southeast breeze wafted the sweet scent of huisache and mesquite blossoms. Inca doves and cardinals made their last calls of the day. Bands of coyotes began singing from every direction. Somewhere off in the brush to the east, he could hear a herd of javelinas grunting. *Lot's of critters in this brush*, thought Buck, *just too thick to see 'em*. In fact, the ground was covered in tracks. Although, Buck didn't spot too many of the local resident critters, he knew that they were all around him and could be easily hunted if he had the time and the inclination.

Buck unsaddled and hobbled Thunder and spread his blanket for the night. He dug a little fire pit and built a small fire to heat his coffee, to warm up the beans John Patterson had given him, and for its company. As he lay back on his blanket, he looked up at the millions of stars that shone brightly. *I wonder if Becky's lookin' at this sky tonight? I expect she's on her way north from San Antone by now. She should be back home to her folks in a week or so. I'm sure she'll be okay. After all, she lived through bein' a Comanche captive. And, I hope ol' Angry's mendin'. John Patterson seemed a good man, he'll look to Angry*. He drifted off to a fitful sleep while these questions ran through his mind. Little did he realize that twenty miles away, White Elk's dreams of the 'big man' had him tossing restlessly on his blanket all night.

Buck was mounted and moving at first light. The trail left by the Comanches was easy to follow in the dusty ground. Though it wound back and forth, dodging this clump of brush or that, the course was steadily to the northeast. By midmorning, the tracks were fresh as were the last horse droppings that he had seen. The Comanches couldn't be more than a mile or two ahead.

Buck nearly fell off Thunder's back when a big flock of turkeys burst from the brush to the right of the trail almost under

Thunder's feet. Thunder had reared in surprise.

"We're both kinda jumpy," said Buck. "I feel we're awful close to our man. And you sense it, too, don't you, boy?"

Thunder shook his head and blew dust from his nose. A second later, an arrow flew just over Buck's left shoulder. Buck whipped out his pistol and fired in the direction of the fleeing Comanche. Buck had surprised Little Hawk who was on foot following the flock of turkeys when he heard the turkeys fly and Buck's horse blow.

Buck charged after Little Hawk but hadn't gone more than two hundred yards when he was met by White Elk, Black Hand and the now-mounted Little Hawk riding at full gallop toward him. He leaned low on Thunder's neck and ran right through them, firing as he went.

And then he was down and scrambling into a little arroyo to fort up behind his fallen horse. Thunder had taken three arrows in the throat and wheezed his last breaths. The front of Buck's shirt was covered in Thunder's blood.

He crouched behind the dead horse and surveyed his surroundings. His back was to a wall of dense brush and the arroyo in which he lay was clogged with brush to his left and right. *They'll have to come at me from the front or nothin'*, thought Buck. He peeked up over Thunder and saw nothing but dust.

He quickly sat up and grabbed his rifle from the scabbard. Bullets and arrows flew from the brush and struck the saddle and Thunder's belly. Buck couldn't see them and they couldn't see him as long as he lay behind Thunder. *Surely, I musta nicked at least one of 'em when I busted through 'em*, thought Buck. *Heck, I coulda touched that one on my right. I could even smell him. He was that dang Kiowa who killed Grandpaw.* Buck could taste the bitterness of hatred on his tongue.

Minutes stretched. Buck could smell the mesquite and huisache flowers mingled with the smell of his own sweat and the horse he was pressed against. Grasshoppers ratcheted in the brush and flies buzzed around the pool of blood in the dirt in front of Thunder's neck. Inca doves made their strange calls and a mockingbird ran through his song routine. The Comanches started screaming their war cries. *Tryin' to spook me*, thought Buck. He took in a deep breath and roared like an angry bear. It was something that he had taught himself to do as a boy. He did it one night while separated in the woods from his cousins, James and Luke, while they were all coon hunting in the woods near Durant. It had frightened his cousins so badly that they had run home. The Comanches didn't run for home but they did stop their war cries. *Give 'em something to think on*, thought Buck.

Buck heard a horse nicker in the brush fifty yards in front of him. He popped up and fired the Henry in the direction of the sound. He heard a man shout in pain. A shower of arrows and bullets slammed into Thunder's hide. After a few minutes, an arrow came down from almost straight up and hit the ground just behind him. *Tryin' to lob one into me*, thought Buck. He crawled to his right and popped up from behind Thunder's rump and fired two quick shots at a little movement he saw in the brush. He popped back down and scooted to his left just as a volley hit Thunder's rump where he had been.

I'd better be a little more choosy with my shots, thought Buck. *Poor Thunder's layin' atop the saddlebag with ammunition for the Colt and the Henry. The Colt's empty and I've got seven left in the Henry. The S&W Model Three's got five in it and there's another dozen or so for it in the belt.*

White Elk and Black Hand had been breaking up their camp and preparing to leave while Little Hawk had gone into the brush where they had heard a turkey hen yelp. Suddenly Little Hawk came running toward them. There was a boom as a pistol shot whined overhead.

All three leapt onto the backs of their ponies and charged in the direction from which Little Hawk had just run. They broke out of the brush into a clearing at full gallop just as the big man from the Choctaw store came charging out of the brush on the far side of the clearing. Black Hand and Little Hawk fired arrows at the horse of the charging man while White Elk tried to clear a jammed cartridge from the breech of his rifle. The big man charged right through them and shot Black Hand in the belly as he rode past. The man also shot Little Hawk's pony twice in the side, just missing Little Hawk, who had swung off to the side of his pony's neck just as the man fired. White Elk and his group wheeled about as they entered the brush on the far side of the clearing and prepared for another charge.

"Wait," said White Elk, "his pony is down. Do you see him?"

Just then, White Elk saw Buck pop up from behind the fallen horse and grab his rifle. White Elk fired quickly as did Little Hawk and Black Hand. Little Hawk and White Elk began shouting their war cries. Black Hand's wound was bleeding heavily and he was moaning as the pain hit him in waves. He did not shout with the others. The big man roared like an angry bear.

"Is he a man or a spirit?" asked Little Hawk. "I thought that you said you had killed him when you took the woman. How could he ride within a hand's width of us and not have our arrows or your bullets find him? And, now he makes the war cry of the bear."

"Do not be foolish," said White Elk. "If he were a spirit, could we have killed his pony? Surely, a spirit would ride a spirit pony. He is only a man and I shall kill him."

Black Hand's horse nickered and an instant later, a rifle shot shattered Black Hand's right knee. Black Hand cried out in pain and slid from his pony. Blood spurted from a severed artery in his leg. Immediately, White Elk and Little Hawk returned fire. White Elk jumped down from his pony and picked up Black Hand's bow and quiver. Black Hand lay moaning in the dust.

"Watch what I do and do the same," said White Elk to Little Hawk. White Elk aimed his arrow nearly vertically and fired. "Perhaps we can drop an arrow over the big man's pony," he said. Little Hawk and White Elk repeated the high shots a few times before two rifle bullets came zinging through the brush between them.

"Black Hand will die from his wounds," said White Elk to Little Hawk. "He is no longer of help to us. If we wait here, the big man may get lucky with his shots. I do not want to let him escape, as he surely will tonight. I think we should attack him. Your pony is bleeding badly. He may not be able to run. Take Black Hand's pony. I do not think that the big man can kill us. I did not see it in my dreams."

Lordy, why is it always so derned hot? thought Buck. He took off his hat and swabbed his face with his bandana. Another pair of arrows dropped down from the sky. One buried itself into Thunder's rump and the other just nicked Buck's left calf, pinning his pants leg to the ground.

Buck snapped the arrow shaft and lifted his leg off of the shaft of the arrow. *Good shooters*, he thought. *I best figure out somethin' before they plunk me with a lucky shot.* He popped up and fired three shots into the brush where he thought the Comanches hid. Then he shouted, "What's wrong, White Elk? I thought you Comanches were not afraid of white men."

The sound of brush popping and hoof beats came from the direction he had just fired. White Elk and Little Hawk came charging from the brush barely fifty yards away. Buck quickly stood up to face them and shouldered the Henry. He could see Little Hawk's arrow coming toward him as he fired the Henry. The rifle bullet hit Little Hawk in the center of his chest and knocked him backwards off of his pony. Little Hawk's arrow went through Buck's left side just below the ribcage and rattled on through the brush behind him. Buck jacked another round into the Henry and shot White Elk's pony through the heart. The pony continued forward for three bounds before falling forward in a heap. White Elk's left leg was trapped beneath the dead horse. His rifle was just out of reach and the bow he carried had been broken in the fall.

Buck walked over to where White Elk lay penned beneath the pony. Buck's blue eyes blazed as he looked down on his enemy. White Elk looked up at him and said, "How do you live? I killed you once at the store and now you are covered in blood, yet you stand over me."

"Horse blood," said Buck with a smile.

EPILOGUE

Buck sat astride Black Hand's pony looking down on the town of Kerrville. The Guadalupe River wound past the town that sat nestled in a valley ringed by steep tree covered hills.

Now he sat contemplating how far he had come, both geographically and mentally, from the little Tennessee farm boy he once was. The job he had set out to accomplish when he left the store was done. He had avenged James and his Grandfather by killing their murderers and reclaimed Becky, but what now? Angry was down in Uvalde. Becky was surely home with her folks. Buck was now committed to a year in the Rangers. He'd have to write Becky and try to explain it. He'd need to get word to Angry as well.

He adjusted his hat and dug a heel into the pony's flank. As he rode down from the hill toward the little town, he remembered his boyhood wish for adventure. *If I'd only known what I was wishin' for*, he thought.

www.ingramcontent.com/pod-product-compliance
Lightning Source LLC
Chambersburg PA
CBHW070821120626
46556CB00002B/603